Velvet
Angel

Also available in Large Print by
Jude Deveraux:

The Velvet Promise
Highland Velvet
Velvet Song

Velvet
Angel

Jude
Deveraux

G.K.HALL &CO.
Boston, Massachusetts
1985

Published in Large Print by arrangement with
Pocket Books, a division of Simon & Schuster, Inc.

British Commonwealth rights courtesy of
Carole Blake Literary Agency.

G.K. Hall Large Print Book Series.

Set in 16 pt English Times

Library of Congress Cataloging in Publication Data

Deveraux, Jude.
  Velvet angel.

  Published in large print.
  1. Large type books. I. Title.
[PS3554.E9273V38 1985]   813'.54   85-818
ISBN 0-8161-3793-5

To Joan Schulhafer, who started as my publicist and became my friend. Thank you for all the love and laughter, and most of all, for all you taught me.

Velvet
Angel

Chapter 1

The South of England

August 1502

ELIZABETH CHATWORTH stood on the very edge of the steep cliff, gazing toward the sea of tall barley grasses. Below her, seemingly tiny men walked with scythes on their shoulders, a few rode horses and one drove a team of oxen.

But Elizabeth didn't really see the men because her chin was held too high and it was locked into place so rigidly that nothing was going to bring it down. A warm gust of wind tried to force her away from the edge but she braced her legs and refused to move. If what had already happened to her today and now what she faced did not sway her, no mere wind was going to break her stance.

Her green eyes were dry but her throat was swollen shut with a lump of anger and unshed tears. A muscle in her jaw flexed and unflexed as she breathed deeply, trying to control her pounding heart.

Another gust of wind blew her tangled mass of honey blonde hair away from her back and, unbeknownst to Elizabeth, one last pearl disentangled itself and slid down the torn, dirty red silk of her dress. The finery she'd worn to her friend's wedding was now shredded beyond repair, her hair loose and flowing, her cheek smudged—and her hands were crudely tied behind her back.

Elizabeth lifted her eyes toward heaven, unblinking at the bright daylight. All her life, she'd had her looks referred to as angelic and never had she looked so delicate, so serene, so much like a celestial being as she did now with her heavy hair swirling about her like some silken cloak, her ragged gown giving her the look of a Christian martyr.

But the farthest thoughts from Elizabeth's mind were ones of sweetness—or of forgiving.

"I will fight to the death," she murmured skyward, her eyes darkening to the color of an emerald on a moonlit night. "No man will best me. No man will make me submit to his will."

"Pleadin' with the Lord, are you?" came the voice of her captor from beside her.

Slowly, as if she had all the time in the world, Elizabeth turned to the man, and the coldness in her eyes made him take a step backward. He was a braggart like the hideous man he served, Pagnell of Waldenham, but this underling was a coward when his master wasn't present.

John gave a nervous cough, then boldly stepped forward and grabbed Elizabeth's upper arm. "You may think you're the great lady but for now

I'm your master.''

She looked him squarely in the eyes, showing none of the pain he was causing her—after all she'd had more than enough physical and mental pain in her life. "You will never be anyone's master," she said calmly.

For a moment John's hand released its pressure on her arm, but the next second he pulled her forward and pushed her roughly.

Elizabeth nearly lost balance, but by a supreme concentration she managed to stay upright and began to walk forward.

"Every man is any woman's master," John was saying from behind her. "Women like you just haven't realized it yet. All it'll take is one good man slamming away on top of you and you'll learn who's your master. And from what I hear this Miles Montgomery is the man to give you what you need."

At the name of Montgomery Elizabeth tripped, falling to her knees.

John's laugh was disproportionately loud as he acted as if he'd succeeded in some great feat. He stood by, watching insolently as Elizabeth struggled to stand, her feet tangled in her skirt, her bound hands making her awkward.

"Excited about Montgomery, are you?" he taunted as he jerked her to her feet. For a moment he touched her cheek, the soft ivory skin, running a dirty fingertip over her delicate lips. "How can a woman as lovely as you be such a termagant? You and I could be nice to each other

3

and Lord Pagnell would never know. What would it matter who's first? Montgomery will take your virginity anyway, so what difference does a day or so make?''

Elizabeth gathered the saliva in her mouth and spit it all into his face. It cost her a great deal of pain in her sore body as his hand came out to strike her face, but she ducked expertly and began to run. Her tied hands made speed impossible and John caught her easily, grabbing what was left of her skirt and causing her to fall, face down, on the ground.

''You vicious little slut!'' he gasped, turning her over, straddling her. ''You'll pay for that. I've tried to be fair with you but you deserve to be beaten.''

Elizabeth's hands and arms were pinned under her and in spite of all she could do, the pain was causing tears to gather in her eyes. ''But you won't beat me, will you?'' she said confidently. ''Pagnell would find out what you'd done and he would beat you. Men like you never risk harm to their own precious selves.''

John put his hands on her breasts and his lips on hers, grinding his mouth against hers, but Elizabeth showed no emotion whatsoever. In disgust, he moved away from her and angrily walked back toward the horses.

Elizabeth sat up and tried to regain her calm. She was quite good at not showing her inner emotions and now she wanted to save all her strength for the ordeal to come.

Montgomery! The name rang in her head. Of all her fears, of all her terrors in life, the name Montgomery seemed to be the cause of them all. A Montgomery had caused her sister-in-law to lose her beauty and most of her sanity. A Montgomery had caused her older brother's disgrace and her brother Brian's disappearance. And indirectly, a Montgomery had caused her own capture.

Elizabeth had been an attendant at a friend's wedding and by accident she'd overheard an odious man she'd known all her life, Pagnell, planning to turn a pretty little singer over to his corrupt relatives to be tried as a witch. When Elizabeth tried to rescue the girl, Pagnell had caught them and, as a joke, had decided to have Elizabeth delivered to her enemy, a Montgomery. Perhaps things wouldn't have been so bad if the singer, in a generous but not wholly intelligent gesture, had not given the information that she was somehow connected with a Montgomery.

Pagnell had bound and gagged Elizabeth, rolled her in a filthy piece of canvas and ordered his man, John, to deliver her to the notoriously lecherous, satyric, hot-blooded Miles Montgomery. Of all the four Montgomery men, Elizabeth knew that the youngest, a boy of only twenty years, just two years older than Elizabeth, was the worst. Even in the convent where she'd spent the last several years, she'd heard stories of Miles Montgomery.

She'd been told that he'd sold his soul to the

devil when he was sixteen and as a result he had an unholy power over women. Elizabeth had laughed at the story but she'd not told the reason for her laughter. She thought it much more likely that Miles Montgomery was like her dead brother Edmund and had ordered women to his bed. It was a pity that this Montgomery's seed seemed to be so fertile, for it was rumored that he had a hundred bastards.

Three years ago a young girl, Bridget, had left the convent where Elizabeth often lived to go and work at the ancient Montgomery fortress. She was a pretty girl with big dark eyes and swaying hips. To Elizabeth's disgust, the other residents alternately acted as if the girl were going to her wedding or to be a human sacrifice. The day before Bridget left, the prioress spent two hours with her and at vespers the girl's eyes were red from crying.

Eleven months later, a traveling musician brought them the news that Bridget had been delivered of a large, healthy boy who she named James Montgomery. It was freely admitted that Miles was the father.

Elizabeth joined in the many prayers offered for the girl's sins. Privately she cursed all men like her brother Edmund and Miles Montgomery—evil men who believed women had no souls, who thought nothing of beating and raping women, of forcing them to do all manner of hideous acts.

She had no time for more thoughts as John

grabbed a handful of her hair and pulled her to her feet.

"Your time for prayers is over," he said into her face. "Montgomery has made camp and it's time he got a look at his next . . ."—he smiled—"mother of his next bastard."

He laughed aloud when Elizabeth struggled against him, and when she realized he enjoyed her struggles, she stopped and gave him her coldest look.

"Witch!" he flung at her. "We'll see if this devil Montgomery can capture the angel you look like—or will he find your heart as black as his own?"

Smiling, his hand twisted in her hair, he brought a sharp little dagger to rest against her throat. When she didn't flinch at the feel of the cold steel against her skin, his smile changed to a smirk.

"Sometimes the Montgomery men make the mistake of talking to women instead of using them as God meant them to be used. I plan to see that this Montgomery has no such ideas."

Slowly, he trailed the tip of the blade down her throat to the high square neck of what was left of her gown.

Her breath held, her eyes on his, her anger held under rigid control, she stood very still. She would not goad him to use the knife on her.

John did not cut her skin, but the blade easily parted the front of her dress and her tight corset under it. When he'd exposed the full curve of her breasts, he looked back into her face. "You've been hiding a great deal, Elizabeth," he whispered.

She stiffened and looked away from his face. It was true that she dressed conservatively, flattening her breasts, thickening her waist. Her face attracted more men than she wanted, but aside from covering her hair she could do nothing about her face.

John was no longer interested in her face as he concentrated on slicing away the rest of her gown. He'd seen very few women nude and never one of Elizabeth Chatworth's station—or her beauty.

Elizabeth's spine was so stiff it could have been made of steel and when her clothes fell away and her bare skin felt the warm August sun, she knew that this was more painful than what had heretofore been done to her.

An ugly expletive from John, uttered from deep within him, made her blink.

"Damn Pagnell!" he cursed and reached for her.

Elizabeth stepped backward and tried to muster her dignity as she glared at John, saw he was practically foaming at the mouth. "You touch me and you're a dead man," she said loudly. "If you kill me, Pagnell will have your head—and if you do not, I will see that he finds out what you have done. And have you forgotten my brother's rage? Is your life worth one coupling with *any* woman?"

It took a moment for John to sober and bring

his eyes to her face. "I hope Montgomery causes you endless misery," he said with great feeling and stalked away to the carpet slung across his horse's rump. Without a glance at her, he unrolled it on the ground.

"Lie down," he commanded, his eyes on the carpet. "And let me warn you, woman, that if you disobey me I will forget Pagnell and Montgomery and your brother's wrath."

Obediently, Elizabeth lay down on the carpet, the short woolen nap pricking her skin, and when John knelt over her, she held her breath.

Roughly, he pushed her to her stomach, cut the bindings on her wrists, and before Elizabeth could even blink, he tossed the edge of the carpet over her and began rolling her in it. There were no more thoughts. Her only concern was a primitive instinct to continue breathing.

It seemed an eternity that she lay still, her head tilted back as she sought the air coming from the top of the carpet roll. When she was at last moved, lifted, she had to struggle to find air, and when she was tossed across the back of the horse, she thought her lungs would collapse.

John's muffled words came through the layers of carpet. "The next man you see will be Miles Montgomery. Think on that while we ride. He won't be as kind to you as I have been."

In a way, the words were good for Elizabeth because the idea of Miles Montgomery, of his evil ways, gave her some incentive to work hard at breathing. And when the horse jolted her, she cursed the Montgomery family, their house, their retainers—and she prayed for the innocent Montgomery children who were part of this immoral clan.

The tent of Miles Montgomery was a splendid affair: deep green sendal trimmed in gold, the gold Montgomery leopards painted along the scalloped roof border, pennants flying from the crown. Inside, the walls were lined with pale green silk. There were several collapsible stools, cushioned with blue and gold brocade, a large table carved with the Montgomery leopards and, against opposite walls, two cots, one abnormally long, both draped with pelts of long-haired red fox.

Four men stood around the table, two dressed in the rich uniform of the Montgomery knights. The attention of the other two men was given to one of the retainers.

"He says he has a gift for you, my lord," the knight was saying to the quiet man before him. "It could be a trick. What could Lord Pagnell have that you would want?"

Miles Montgomery raised one dark eyebrow and it was enough to make his man back down. Sometimes men newly in his service thought that since their master was so young, they could take liberties.

"Could there be a man rolled in the carpet?" asked the man beside Miles.

The subdued retainer craned his neck to look

up at Sir Guy. "A very small one, perhaps."

Sir Guy looked down at Miles and there passed a silent communication between them. "Send him and his gift in," Sir Guy said. "We will meet them with drawn swords."

The knight left and within seconds he returned, his sword pointed at the small of the back of the man carrying the carpet. Insolently, smirking, John half tossed his bundle to the carpeted ground and with his foot pushed it very hard, sending it, unrolling, toward Miles Montgomery's feet.

When at last the carpet stopped, there were four stunned faces as they gaped at what lay before them: a nude woman, her eyes closed, long thick lashes soft on delicately colored cheeks, great massive torrents of honey blonde hair wrapped and twisted about her, curls tickling her waist and the tops of her thighs. She was outrageously curved with large firm breasts, a tiny waist, long, long legs. And her face was something men expected to see only in heaven—delicate, ethereal, not quite of this world.

Smiling triumphantly, John slipped out of the tent unnoticed.

Elizabeth, half dazed from the lack of air, opened her eyes slowly and looked up to see four men standing over her, their swords drawn but aimed toward the ground. Two of the men were obviously retainers and she dismissed them. The third man was a giant, several inches over six feet,

11

steel gray hair, a scar running diagonally across his entire face. Although the man was indeed frightening, she somehow sensed he was not the leader of this group.

Beside the giant was another man dressed resplendently in deep blue satin. Elizabeth was accustomed to seeing strong, handsome men, but something about this one with his leashed power held in check so easily made her stare. The other men's eyes were fastened on Elizabeth's body, but this man turned and she looked for the first time into the face of Miles Montgomery, and their eyes locked.

He was a handsome man, very very handsome, with dark gray eyes under heavy, arched brows, a thin nose with slightly flaring nostrils and a full sensual mouth.

Danger! was Elizabeth's first thought. This man was dangerous to women as well as men.

She broke eye contact with him and in seconds she stood, grabbing a pelt from one of the cots near her and a war ax from the top of the table. "I will kill the first man who comes near me," she said, holding the ax with one hand while she tossed the pelt over one shoulder, leaving the other bare, one leg exposed from waist to bare foot.

The giant took a step toward her and she raised the ax, both hands on the handle.

"I know how to use this," she warned, looking up at the man with absolutely no fear.

The two knights took a step closer toward her

and Elizabeth backed away, looking from one to the other. The back of her knees hit the edge of the cot and she could go no farther. One of the knights smiled at her and she snarled at him in return.

"Leave us."

The words were quiet, uttered in a low voice, but it held command and all of them looked at Montgomery.

The giant of a man gave Elizabeth one last look, then nodded at the two knights and the three of them left the tent.

Elizabeth tightened her grip on the ax, her knuckles already white, as she glared across the space toward Miles Montgomery. "I will kill you," she said through her teeth. "Do not think that because I'm a woman I won't enjoy hacking a man to pieces. I would love to see the blood of a Montgomery spilled upon the earth."

Miles didn't move from his place by the table, but kept watching. After a moment he lifted his sword and Elizabeth drew in her breath, preparing for the battle to come. Very slowly, he placed his sword on the table and turned away from her, presenting his profile. Again slowly, he removed the jeweled dagger he wore at his side and placed it on the table beside the sword.

He turned back to her, his face expressionless, his eyes giving nothing away, and took a step toward her.

Elizabeth lifted the heavy ax and held it in readiness. She would fight to the death, for death was preferable to the beating and rape she knew this devil-man planned.

Miles sat down on a stool, several feet in front of her; he did not speak, but only watched her.

So! he did not think a woman a worthy opponent, but disarmed himself and sat down while she held a weapon of death over his head. With one lunge, she leaped forward and swung the ax at his neck.

Effortlessly, he caught the handle in his right hand, easily held it and looked into her eyes as she stood close to him. For a moment she was paralyzed, hypnotized by his eyes. He seemed to be searching her face for something, as if he asked silent questions of her.

She jerked the ax away from his grip and nearly fell when she found he released it freely. She caught herself at the edge of the table. "Damn you!" she said under her breath. "May the Lord and all His angels curse the day a Montgomery was born. May you and all your descendants writhe in the fires of hell forever."

Her voice had risen almost to a shout and outside she could hear movement.

Miles still sat there, watching her silently, and Elizabeth could feel her blood beginning to boil. When she saw her hands starting to shake, she knew she must calm herself. Where was the cool detachment she'd cultivated over the years?

If this man could remain calm, so could she. She listened and if her guess were correct, the sounds she heard outside were the men moving away. Perhaps if she could get past this one man, she could escape and get home to her brother.

With her eyes on Miles, she began to walk backward, circling him as she made her way toward the tent flap. Slowly, he turned on the stool and watched her. Outside she heard the whinny of a horse and she prayed that if she could just make it outside she'd be free.

Even though her eyes never left Miles's, she still never saw him move. One moment he was sitting, relaxed, on the stool and the next, just as her hand touched the tent flap, he was beside her, his hand around her wrist. She brought the ax straight down toward his shoulder but he caught her other wrist and held her.

She stood still, imprisoned lightly, painlessly, by his grip, and glared up at him. He was so close she could feel his breath on her forehead. As he looked down at her, he seemed to be waiting for something and then he looked puzzled.

With eyes as hard as the emeralds they resembled, she glared up at him. "And now what comes next?" she asked, hatred in her voice. "Do you beat me first or rape me? Or perhaps you like them both at the same time. I am a virgin and I've heard it hurts most the first time. No doubt my added pain will give you much pleasure."

For just a second, his eyes widened as if in astonishment and it was the first unguarded expression Elizabeth had seen on his face. His gray eyes locked into hers so hard that she looked away.

"I can endure what you deal out," she said quietly, "and if your wish is to see me beg, you will fail."

His hand released her wrist holding the tent flap and he cupped the left side of her cheek, gently turning her back to look at him.

She stiffened at his touch, hating his hands on her.

"Who are you?" he half whispered.

She straightened her spine even more and hatred flamed in her eyes. "I am your enemy. I am Elizabeth Chatworth."

Something passed quickly across his face and then was gone. After a long moment, he removed his hand from her cheek and, after a backward step, he released her other wrist. "You may keep the ax if it makes you feel safer but I cannot let you leave."

As if dismissing her, he turned his back and walked toward the center of the tent.

Immediately, Elizabeth was through the tent flap and out of the tent and, just as quickly, Miles was beside her, his hand once again encircling her wrist.

"I cannot let you leave," he repeated, this time more firmly. His eyes traveled downward to her bare legs and up again. "You aren't dressed for running away. Come inside and I'll send my man to purchase clothes."

She jerked away from him. The sun was setting and in the twilight he looked even darker. "I want no clothes from you. I want nothing from any

Montgomery. My brother will—"

She broke off at his look.

"Do not mention the name of your brother to me. He killed my sister."

Miles recaptured her wrist and gave a light tug. "Now I must insist that you come inside. My men will be returning soon and I don't think they should see you dressed like this."

She held her ground. "What does it matter? Isn't it the custom of men like you to throw female captives to their knights when they've finished with them?"

She wasn't sure but she thought she saw just a flicker of a smile on Miles's lips. "Elizabeth," he began, then paused. "Come inside and we'll talk there." He turned toward the dark trees near them. "Guy!" he bellowed, making Elizabeth jump.

Immediately, the giant stepped into the clearing. After only a cursory glance at Elizabeth, he looked at Miles.

"Send someone into the village and find some suitable women's clothes. Spend what you need." The voice Miles used to his man was quite different from the one he used with her.

"Send me with him," Elizabeth said quickly. "I will talk to my brother and he will be so grateful that you've released me unharmed that it will end this feud between the Chatworths and Montgomerys."

Miles turned back to her and his eyes were hard. "Don't beg, Elizabeth."

Without thought but with a cry of rage, she lifted the ax again and aimed for his head. In one seemingly practiced motion, he pulled the ax from her hand, flung it away and swung her into his arms.

She wasn't about to give him the pleasure of struggling against him and instead she stiffened, hating the feel of his clothes against her skin. The fox pelt hung to one side, baring the leg against his body.

He carried her inside the tent and gently laid her on one of the cots.

"Why do you bother with clothes for me?" she hissed. "Perhaps you should do your coupling in the fields like the animal you are."

He walked away, his back to her, and poured two goblets of wine from a silver vessel on the table. "Elizabeth," he said, "if you keep asking me to make love to you, I will eventually succumb to your temptations." He turned, walked toward her and sat on a stool a few feet away. "You've had a long day and you must be tired and hungry." He held out a full wine goblet to her.

Elizabeth swept it away, the wine spilling, staining one of the luxurious carpets that comprised the floor of the tent.

Miles glanced at it, unconcerned, and drank his wine. "And now, Elizabeth, what am I to do with you?"

Chapter 2

ELIZABETH SAT upon the cot, her legs well covered, only her head and one shoulder bare, and refused to look at Miles Montgomery. She would not lower herself to try and reason with him as he seemed to consider her ideas begging.

After a time of silence, Miles rose and stepped outside the tent, his hand holding the flap doorway open. She heard him order a basin of hot water.

Elizabeth didn't respond to his momentary absence but thought that he had to sleep sometime and when he did, she would escape. Perhaps it would be better to wait until she had some proper clothes.

Miles didn't let his man enter with the water, but carried it in himself and set it at the side of the cot. "The water is for you, Elizabeth. I thought perhaps you'd like to wash."

She kept her arms folded across her chest and her head turned away from him. "I want

19

nothing from you."

"Elizabeth," he said and there was exasperation in his voice. He sat down beside her, took her hands in his. He waited patiently until she turned her angry glare toward him. "I am not going to hurt you," he said gently. "I have never beat a woman in my life and I don't plan to start now. I cannot allow you to jump on a horse wearing practically nothing and ride across the countryside. You wouldn't last an hour before you'd be attacked by hordes of highwaymen."

"Am I to believe you're any better?" Her hands clasped his for a moment and her eyes softened. "Will you return me to my brother?"

Miles's eyes looked into hers with an almost frightening intensity. "I . . . will consider it."

She thrust his hands from hers and looked away. "What could I expect from a Montgomery? Get away from me!"

Miles rose. "The water grows cold."

She looked up at him with a slight smile. "Why should I wash? For you? Do you like your women clean and fresh smelling? If so, then I'll never wash! I will grow so dirty I will look like a Nubian slave and my hair will crawl with lice and other vermin that will soil your pretty clothes."

Miles looked at her a moment before speaking. "The tent is surrounded by men and I will be outside. If you try to leave, you will be returned to me." With that, he left her alone.

As Miles knew he would be, Sir Guy was waiting for him outside the tent. Miles nodded

20

once and the giant followed him into the trees.

"I sent two men for the clothes," Sir Guy said. When Miles's father died, Miles was nine and the elder Montgomery's dying wish was that Sir Guy take care of the young boy who was sometimes like a stranger even in his own famlly. Miles talked as much to Sir Guy as he did to anyone.

"Who is she?" Sir Guy asked, his hand on the bark of an enormous old oak tree.

"Elizabeth Chatworth."

Sir Guy nodded once. The moonlight cast eerie shadows on the scar across his face. "I thought as much. Lord Pagnell's sense of humor would run to delivering a Chatworth to a Montgomery." He paused, watching Miles for a long moment. "Do we return her to her brother on the morrow?"

Miles walked away from his man. "What do you know of her brother, Edmund Chatworth?"

Sir Guy spit lustily before answering. "Compared to Chatworth, Pagnell is a saint. Chatworth loved to torture women. He used to tie them up and rape them. On the night he was killed—and bless the man who did the killing—a young woman cut her wrists in his chamber."

Sir Guy watched as Miles clenched and unclenched his fists, and Guy regretted his words. More than anything else in the world, Miles loved women. Hundreds of times Guy had had to pull Miles off a man who'd dared to wrong a woman. As a boy he'd attacked grown men and when his temper was aroused it was all Guy could do to hold him. Last year, Guy had not succeeded in

21

keeping Miles from killing a man who'd slapped his sharp-tongued wife. The king'd almost refused to pardon Miles for that fracas.

"Her brother Roger isn't like Edmund," Sir Guy said.

Miles whirled on him, his eyes black. "Roger Chatworth raped my sister and caused her suicide! Do you forget that?"

Guy knew that the best way to handle Miles's temper was to remain silent on the subject that angered him. "What do you plan to do with the girl?"

Miles turned away, ran his hand down the trunk of a tree. "Do you know that she hates the Montgomery name? We have been innocent in all the hatred between the Montgomerys and Chatworths yet still she hates us." He turned to face Sir Guy. "And she seems to hate me in particular. When I touch her she is repulsed. She wipes where I have touched her with a cloth, as if I'd defiled her."

As soon as Sir Guy closed his open mouth, he almost laughed. If possible, women loved Miles more than he loved them. As a child, he'd spent most of his time surrounded by girls, which is one reason why Miles was put in Sir Guy's charge—to make sure he turned into a man. But Guy had known from the first that there was no doubt of young Miles's masculinity. He just liked women. It was a quirk, rather like the love of a good horse or a sharp sword. At times, Miles's absurdly gentle treatment of women was a bother, such as

his lethally enforced rule of no raping after a battle, but on the whole, Sir Guy'd learned to live with the boy's affliction—he was all right otherwise.

But Sir Guy had never, *never* heard of a woman who wasn't willing to lay down her life for Miles. Young, old, in between, even newborn girls clung to him. And Elizabeth Chatworth wiped away his touch!

Sir Guy tried to put this information into perspective. Perhaps it was like losing your first battle. He reached out and put a big hand on Miles's shoulder. "We all lose now and then. It doesn't make you less of a man. Perhaps the girl hates all men. With her brother for an example—"

Miles shrugged the hand away. "She's been hurt! Badly hurt! Not just her body that's covered with bruises and scratches, but she's built a wall around her of anger and hatred."

Sir Guy felt that he was standing on the edge of a deep ravine. "This girl is a highborn lady," he said quietly. "You can't keep her prisoner. The king has already outlawed your brother. You don't need to provoke him anymore. You must return Lady Elizabeth to her brother."

"Return her to a place where women are tortured? That's where she learned to hate. And if I return her now, what will she think of the Montgomerys? Will she have learned that we aren't evil as her brother was?"

"You can't think to keep her!" Sir Guy was aghast.

Miles seemed to be considering this. "It will be days before anyone learns where she is. Perhaps in that time I can show her—"

"And what of your brothers?" Sir Guy demanded. "They're expecting you home. It won't take Gavin long to find that you hold Elizabeth Chatworth prisoner." He paused, lowering his voice. "The girl will have only good to say about the Montgomerys if you return her unharmed."

Miles's eyes sparkled. "I believe Elizabeth would say she used an ax to force me to return her." He gave a slight smile. "My mind is made up. I will keep her for just a little while, long enough to show her that a Montgomery isn't like her dead brother. Now! I must return and"—he smiled more broadly—"give my dirty little captive a bath. Come on, Guy, don't look like that. It's just for a few days."

Sir Guy kept quiet as he followed his young master back to camp, but he wondered if Elizabeth Chatworth could be conquered in just a few days.

The moment Elizabeth was sure Miles was gone, she ran to the far side of the tent and, lifting the heavy fabric, saw men's feet just outside. She checked the entire perimeter of the tent and there was practically no space between the guards' feet, almost as if they were holding hands to protect themselves against one small woman.

She was scratching her dirty scalp when Miles

24

returned carrying two buckets of steaming water. Instantly, she stiffened her spine, folded her arms across her chest. Even when he sat beside her on the cot she didn't look at him.

Not until he took her hand and began to bathe it with a warm, soapy cloth did she look at him. After a moment's astonishment, she jerked away from him.

He caught her chin in his hand and began to wash her face.

"You'll feel much better when you're clean," he said gently.

She knocked his hand away. "I don't like to be touched. Get away from me!"

Patiently, he recaptured her chin and resumed washing. "You are a lovely woman, Elizabeth, and you should be proud of your looks."

Elizabeth looked at him and decided at that moment that if she didn't already hate Miles Montgomery, she would now. Obviously, he was a man used to women falling over their feet for him. He thought all he had to do was touch a woman's cheek and she would be panting with desire. He was handsome, true, and his voice was sweet, but many men were more handsome and had years of experience behind them—and several of these men had tried unsuccessfully to seduce Elizabeth.

She gazed into his eyes, let hers go liquid and when she saw the little gleam of satisfaction creep into his eyes, she smiled—and then sunk her teeth into the side of his hand.

Miles was so astonished that it took him a moment to react. He grabbed her jaw and buried his fingers into the muscles, forcing her to open her mouth. Obviously still astonished, he flexed his hand, studied the deep teeth marks in his skin. When he looked back at Elizabeth, there was triumph in her eyes.

"Do you think I'm stupid?" she asked. "Do you think I don't know what game you're playing? You hope to gentle the tigress and when you have me eating from your hand, you'll return me to my brother, no doubt carrying another of your bastards. It will be a great triumph for you, both as a Montgomery and as a man."

His eyes held hers for a moment. "You are a clever woman, Elizabeth. Perhaps I would like to prove to you that men are capable of more than savagery."

"And how shall you do that? By holding me prisoner? By forcing me to endure your touch? You can see that I don't tremble with lust every time you get near me. Is it that you hate to admit defeat? Pagnell likes rape and violence. What stirs you? The chase? And once you have the woman do you discard her as used goods?"

She could see that she'd asked him questions he couldn't answer and it disgusted her that her own species had always succumbed to him so easily. "Can't a man, just once, do something decent? Send me to my brother!"

"No!" Miles shouted into her face, then his eyes widened. Never had a woman made him angry before. "Turn around, Elizabeth. I'm going to wash your hair."

She gave him a calculating look. "And if I refuse, will you beat me?"

"I am close to considering it." He grabbed her shoulder and spun her about, pulling her down onto the cot so her long hair hung over the edge.

Elizabeth was quiet while he soaped and rinsed her hair and she wondered if she'd pushed him too far. But his manner infuriated her. He was so quiet, so sure of himself, that she longed to find his feet of clay. She'd already seen that he merely had to hint at an order to his men and they obeyed him. Did women come to him so easily, too?

Perhaps she was wrong to try to anger him. Perhaps he'd release her if she pretended to fall madly in love with him. If she wept prettily on his shoulder he might do as she asked, but besides the disgusting ordeal of voluntarily touching him, she refused to beg to any man.

Miles combed her wet hair with a delicate ivory comb and when he was finished, he left the tent and returned in moments with a lovely gown of red samite, a mixture of silk and wool. There were also underclothes of fine lawn.

"You may finish bathing or not, as you like," he said, "but I would suggest you put the clothes on." With that he left her alone.

Elizabeth did wash, hurriedly, wincing a few times at bruises but hardly noticing them. She was glad for the clothes because they gave her more freedom to carry out her plans to escape.

Miles returned with a loaded tray of food, and he lit candles in the dark tent. "I brought a bit of everything as I have no idea what you like."

She didn't bother to answer him.

"Does the gown please you?" He was watching her closely but she looked away. The gown was an expensive one, trimmed with embroidery done in gold wire. Most women would have been pleased with it, but Elizabeth didn't seem to notice whether she wore silk or russet.

"The food grows cold. Come and eat here at the table with me."

She looked at him. "I have no intention whatsoever of eating anything at your table."

Miles started to speak but closed his mouth instead. "When you grow hungry enough, the food will be here."

Elizabeth sat on the cot, her legs stretched before her, her arms folded, and concentrated on the tall, ornate candlestand in front of her. Tomorrow she would find a way to escape.

Ignoring the smells of the food Miles was eating, she lay down and forced her body to relax. She would need her strength for tomorrow. The long ordeal of the day made her exhausted body quick to fall asleep.

Elizabeth woke in the middle of the night and instantly she tensed, sensing some sort of danger but too sleep-befuddled to remember it. Within minutes, her mind cleared and quietly she moved her head to look at Miles, asleep in the cot on the other side of the tent.

As a child living in a household filled with horrors, she'd learned the art of moving about soundlessly. Stealthily, not allowing the noisy dress to make a sound, she tiptoed toward the back of the tent. No doubt guards were stationed all around, but at the back they'd be less alert.

It took her many minutes to lift the back of the tent enough to crawl under it. She compressed her body into a thin line and rolled, not in one movement, but inch by cautious inch. A guard walked past her but she clung to a bit of shrubbery and faded into its outline. When the guard had his back turned, she ran for the forest, seeking out and using every deep shadow. Only through years of practice, of dodging her brother Edmund and his "friends," was she able to slip away so silently. Roger had chided her, saying she would make an expert spy.

Once inside the forest, she allowed herself to breathe and used her will to calm her racing heart. Forests at night were no stranger to her and she began walking at a brisk, easy pace. It was amazing how little noise she made.

When the sun rose, Elizabeth had been walking for about two hours, and her pace was beginning to slow. She hadn't eaten in over twenty-four hours, and her energy was flagging. As her feet dragged, her skirt caught on shrubs, branches caught in her hair.

After another hour, she was trembling. She sat on a fallen log and tried to compose herself.

Perhaps it was understandable that she didn't have a great deal of strength, since the combination of lack of food and the ordeal of the previous day had taken nearly all of it. The thought of rest made her eyes heavy and she knew that if she didn't, she'd never be able to continue.

Wearily, she lowered herself to the forest floor, ignoring the little crawly things on the underside of the log; it wasn't the first time she'd spent the night in a forest. She made a feeble attempt to cover herself with leaves but was only half finished when she fell back, asleep.

She woke to a sharp poke in the ribs. A big, burly man dressed in little more than rags grinned down at her, one of his front teeth missing. Two other men, filthy men, stood behind him.

"Told you she wasn't dead," the burly man said as he grabbed Elizabeth's arm and pulled her upright.

"Pretty lady," said one of the other men, putting his hand on Elizabeth's shoulder. She went one way and his hand stayed where it was; the dress tore, exposing her shoulder.

"Me first!" gasped the third man.

"A real lady," said the burly man, his hand on Elizabeth's bare shoulder.

"I am Elizabeth Chatworth and if you harm me the Earl of Bayham will have your heads."

" 'Twas a earl that tossed me off my farm," said one man. "Me wife and daughter died of the winter cold. Froze to death." His expression was ugly as he looked at Elizabeth. She would have backed away but the log behind her imprisoned her.

The burly man put his hand to Elizabeth's throat. "I like my women to beg."

"Most men do," she said coolly and the man blinked at her.

"She's a mean one, Bill," said another man. "Let me have her first."

Suddenly, the man's expression changed. He gave a strange gurgle and fell forward onto Elizabeth. Deftly, she sidestepped his falling form and barely gave a look to the arrow protruding from his back. As the two men were gaping at their dead companion, Elizabeth lifted her skirts and leaped over the log.

Out of the forest came Miles. He grabbed Elizabeth's arm and his face made her breath catch. It was contorted with rage, his lips a single line, his eyes black, his brows drawn together, his nostrils flared. "Remain here!" he ordered.

For a moment she obeyed him and because of her hesitation she saw why Miles Montgomery had been awarded his spurs on the field of battle before he was eighteen. The men he faced were not unarmed. One held a spiked ball on a chain and expertly swung it at Miles's head. Miles ducked while wielding his sword at the other man.

Within seconds, he had destroyed both men while barely quickening his own pulse. It did not seem possible that this killer could have washed her hair without so much as creating a single tangle.

Elizabeth didn't waste time contemplating the complexities of her enemy but started running away from the battle area. She knew she could not outrun Miles but she hoped she could outsmart him. At the first low hanging branch, she caught it and swung herself upward.

Within seconds, Miles appeared below her. There was blood on his velvet doublet, blood on his drawn sword. Like a baited bear, he swung his head from side to side, then stopped and listened.

Elizabeth held her breath and didn't make a sound.

After a moment, Miles suddenly turned on his heel and looked up at her. "Come down here, Elizabeth," he said in a deadly voice.

Once, when she was thirteen, this same thing had happened. Then she'd leaped from the tree, straight onto the hideous man pursuing her, knocked him down and before he'd recovered his wind, she escaped. Without another thought, she threw herself onto Miles.

But he did not fall. Instead, he stood steady and held her tightly to him.

"Those men could have killed you," he said, seemingly unaware of her attempt to knock him down. "How did you slip past my guards?"

"Release me!" she demanded, struggling against him, but he held her easily.

"Why didn't you obey me when I told you to wait for me?"

That idiot question stopped her struggles. "Should I have waited for one of those ruffians if he'd commanded me to do so? What's the difference between them and you?''

His eyes showed anger. ''Damn you, Elizabeth! What do you mean that I'm like those scum? Have I harmed you in any way?''

''So you found her,'' came Sir Guy's voice and there was a hint of amusement in it. ''I am Sir Guy Linacre, my lady.''

Elizabeth, her hands pushing hard against Miles's shoulders, nodded at Sir Guy. ''Are you finished mauling me?'' she snapped at Miles.

He released his grip on her so suddenly she almost fell. The quick change of motion was too much for Elizabeth's empty stomach. At once, she put her hand to her forehead and as things grew black, she put out her hand in search of something to steady herself.

It was Sir Guy who caught her and swung her into his arms.

''Do not touch me,'' she whispered from inside the fog she was experiencing.

As Miles took her from Sir Guy, he said, ''At least it isn't *only* me she repulses.'' When Elizabeth opened her eyes, Miles was giving her a look of disgust. ''How long has it been since you've eaten?''

''Not long enough to make me welcome you,'' she answered tartly.

At that Miles laughed, not one of his little half-smiles but a deep-down laugh, and before Elizabeth could react, he bent his head and kissed her lips soundly. ''You are utterly unique, Elizabeth.''

She wiped her mouth with the back of her hand so hard she threatened to remove her skin. "Put me down! I am perfectly capable of walking."

"And let you try and run again? No, I think I'll keep you chained to me from now on."

Miles put Elizabeth on his horse before him and together they rode back to the camp.

Chapter 3

SHE WAS surprised to see that the tents had been taken down and mules were packed and ready to leave. Elizabeth wanted to ask where he was taking her but she kept rigid in the saddle, touching Miles as little as she could, refusing to speak to him.

He led the horse away from the waiting men and into the woods, Sir Guy remaining behind. Inside the forest was set a table laden with several steaming dishes. A small, old man hovered over the array, but left when Miles gave a dismissing motion of his hand.

Dismounting, Miles held up his arms for Elizabeth, but she ignored him and slid to the ground without aid. She did this slowly so as not to repeat her ridiculous act of half fainting.

"My cook has prepared a meal for us," Miles said as he took her hand and led her forward.

She jerked from his touch and glanced at the food. Tiny roasted quails lay upon a bed of rice, surrounded by a cream sauce. A platter contained raw oysters. There were sliced hard-cooked eggs in a saffron sauce, sliced salted ham, fish eggs on twice-baked bread, flounder stuffed with onions and nuts, poached pears, cream tarts, a pie oozing blackberries.

After a look of astonishment, Elizabeth turned away. "You travel well."

Miles caught her arm and when he spun her around, Elizabeth again felt dizzy and clutched at a stool at her feet. "The food is for you," he said, helping her to sit down. "I will not allow you to starve yourself further."

"And what will you do?" she asked wearily. "Put hot coals to the bottoms of my feet? Or perhaps you have your own special ways of forcing women to do what you want."

A frown crossed Miles's face, drawing his brows together. He grabbed her upper arms and pulled her to stand before him. "Yes, I do have my own forms of punishment."

Elizabeth had never seen this look of his, with his eyes just this shade of gray, looking as if tiny blue fires burned behind the gray. Bending, he put his lips to her neck, ignoring her when she stiffened and tried to pull away from him.

"Do you have any idea how desirable you are, Elizabeth?" he murmured against her neck. His lips nibbled upward, barely touching her skin, just enough to impart warmth to her, while his right hand played with the shoulder exposed by her torn dress. His fingers moved inward slowly, caressing the top of her breast while his teeth gently touched her earlobe.

"I would like to make love to you, Elizabeth," he whispered, so low that she felt more than heard his words. "I would like to thaw your cool exterior. I'd like to touch and caress every morsel of you, to look at you, to have you look at me with all the desire I feel for you."

Elizabeth had stood quite still during Miles's touching of her and, as always, she felt nothing. He did not truly repulse her as his breath was not foul and he didn't hurt her, but she felt none of the blood-quickening rush the girls in the convent had giggled about.

"If I swear to eat will you stop this?" she asked coolly.

Miles pulled away from her, studied her face for a moment, and Elizabeth prepared herself for the coming abuse. All men, when they found she was not overwhelmed by their lovemaking, responded by calling her many ugly names.

Miles gave her a quiet smile, caressed her cheek one more time, and offered his arm to lead her to the table. Ignoring his arm, she went to the table alone, not allowing Miles to see her confusion.

He served her himself, placing choice tidbits upon an ornate silver plate, and smiled when she ate her first bite.

"And now you are congratulating yourself on having kept me from starving myself," she said. "My brother will thank you for returning me to him in good condition."

"I am not returning you yet," Miles said softly.

Elizabeth refused to allow him to see how he upset her, but continued eating. "Roger will pay you whatever ransom you ask."

"I will take no money from my sister's murderer," Miles said, the sound coming from a closed throat.

She threw the quail leg she was eating to her plate. "You have said this before. I know nothing of your sister!"

Miles turned toward her and his eyes were the color of steel. "Roger Chatworth tried to take the woman who was promised in marriage to my brother Stephen, and when Stephen fought for his bride, your brother attacked his back."

"No!" Elizabeth gasped, standing.

"Stephen bested Chatworth but refused to kill him, and in retaliation, Chatworth kidnapped my sister and, later, Stephen's bride. He raped my sister and, in horror, she cast herself from a window."

"No! No! No!" Elizabeth shouted, her hands over her ears.

Miles stood, grabbed her hands, held them. "Your brother Brian loved my sister and when she killed herself, he released my sister-in-law and brought the body of my sister to us."

"You are a liar! You are evil! Release me!"

Miles drew her closer, held her loosely in his arms. "It's not pleasant to hear that someone you love has done so much wrong."

Elizabeth'd had much experience in getting

away from men and Miles'd had no experience in women struggling against his grasp. Quickly, she brought her knee up between his legs and instantly he released her.

"Damn you, Elizabeth," he gasped, leaning against the table, cupping himself.

"Damn you, Montgomery," she shot back as she grabbed a pitcher of wine and flung it at his head just before she turned to flee.

He ducked the pitcher and caught her arm in the same motion. "You'll not escape me," he said, pulling her toward him. "I'm going to teach you that the Montgomerys are innocent in this feud, even if I have to die proving it."

"The idea of your death is the first pleasant notion I've heard in days."

For a moment Miles closed his eyes as if in a silent prayer for help. He seemed recovered when he looked back at her. "Now, if you have finished eating, we must ride. We are going to Scotland."

"To—!" she began, but he put a finger to her lips.

"Yes, my angel"—his voice was heavy with sarcasm —"we are going to spend time with my brother and his wife. I want you to get to know my family."

"I know more than enough about your family. They are—"

This time, Miles kissed her and, if she did not react to his touch, when she turned away she was silent.

They rode for many hours at a slow, steady

pace. The many baggage mules behind them bearing furniture, clothing, food, armor, weapons, made their progress ponderous.

Elizabeth was given her own horse but a rope was tied to the saddle and attached to Miles's horse. Twice he tried to make conversation but she refused to speak to him. Her mind was too busy thinking about, and trying not to think about, what Miles had told her about her brother.

For the last two years the only contact she'd had with her family was through Roger's letters and snatches of gossip from traveling musicians. Of course the musicians were aware she was a Chatworth and so had said little either way about her family.

But the extensive Montgomery family was another matter. They were a favorite subject of songs and gossip. The oldest brother, Gavin, had jilted the beautiful Alice Valence and on the rebound she'd married Elizabeth's brother Edmund. Elizabeth had begged Roger to stop the marriage, saying that the poor woman didn't deserve to be shackled to the treacherous Edmund. Roger said there was nothing he could do to prevent the marriage. Only a few months later, Gavin Montgomery had married the magnificently wealthy Revedoune heiress, and after Edmund's murder, the jealous heiress had tossed boiling oil on poor Alice Chatworth's face. Elizabeth had written from the convent and begged Roger to care for her brother's widow and Roger had quickly agreed.

Less than a year later, Roger had written that the Scottish heiress, Bronwyn MacArran, had pleaded to be allowed to marry Roger but Stephen Montgomery was forcing the poor woman to become his bride. Roger had challenged Stephen in an attempt to protect the MacArran woman, and during the fight, Montgomery had cleverly made it appear that Roger attacked his back. As a result, Roger was disgraced.

She wasn't sure why Brian had left his home; Roger would never say. But she was sure it had to do with the Montgomerys. Brian was sensitive and gentle. Perhaps he could no longer stand all the horrors that had been done to his family because of the Montgomerys. But whatever made Brian leave had nothing to do with the lies she'd heard today. She doubted if Roger even knew the Montgomery men had a sister.

All during the long ride, she'd idly been tucking the torn shoulder of her dress inside the high neckline. When Miles called a halt to the procession, she was startled to see that it was growing dark. Her thoughts had kept her occupied for hours.

Before them was an inn, half timbered, old but prosperous-looking. The landlord stood outside, his big red face split by a welcoming grin.

Miles stood beside her. "Elizabeth"—he held up his arms for her—"do not embarrass yourself by refusing me," he said, a twinkle in his eye as he glanced at her raised foot.

Elizabeth considered for a moment, then

allowed him to help her from her horse, but she stepped away from his touch as soon as she was on the ground. Two of his men entered the inn first while Miles caught Elizabeth's arm.

"I have something for you." Watching her closely, he held out a lovely, intricately wrought gold brooch of a pelican, its beak tucked under its outstretched wing, standing on a band of diamonds.

Elizabeth's eyes didn't flicker. "I don't want it."

With a look of exasperation, Miles pinned the shoulder of her gown together. "Come inside, Elizabeth," he said flatly.

Obviously, the innkeeper was expecting them, for the bustle of activity within was enormous. Elizabeth stood to one side as Miles conferred with Sir Guy while the landlord waited for their commands.

It was a large room set with tables and chairs, a big fireplace to one side. For the first time, Elizabeth really looked at Miles's men. There were an even dozen of them and it seemed they gave remarkably little trouble. Now they walked about, opening doors, quietly checking for any hidden danger. Did Miles Montgomery have so many enemies he must always be wary—or was he just cautious?

A pretty young maid curtsied before Miles and he gave her his little half-smile. Elizabeth watched curiously as the maid blushed and preened under Miles's gaze.

"Yes, my lord," she said, smiling, bobbing up and down. "I hope ye like the meal I've cooked."

"I will," Miles said so matter-of-factly that it made his enjoyment seem a sure fact.

With another blush, the girl turned back to the kitchen.

"Are you hungry, Elizabeth?" Miles asked, turning back to her.

"Not for what you seem to inspire." She nodded toward the maid's retreating back.

"How I wish there were jealousy in those words. But I have patience," he added with a smile and gave her a little push toward the table before she could answer.

Miles and she sat at a small table, apart from his men but in the same room. Dish after dish was brought to them but Elizabeth barely ate.

"You don't seem to have a big appetite at best."

"If you were held prisoner would you gorge yourself on your captor's food?"

"I would probably not lose a moment in planning my captor's death," he answered honestly.

Elizabeth glared at him in silence and Miles concentrated on his food.

Halfway through the long, silent meal, Miles caught the hand of one of the maids placing a dish of fresh salmon on the table. As Elizabeth looked up in surprise, she saw that the maid's hands were scratched and raw.

"How have you injured yourself?" Miles asked gently.

"The berry brambles, milord," she answered, half frightened, half fascinated by Miles's attention.

"Landlord!" Miles called. "See that the girl's hands are cared for and she's not to put them in water until they heal."

"But my lord!" the man protested. "She's only a scullery maid. She's serving tonight because my regular girl has the pox."

Sir Guy slowly rose from the head of the table of Miles's retainers, and all that was needed was the size of the giant and the landlord took a step backward.

"Come, girl," the landlord said angrily.

"Thank . . . thank you, my lord," she bobbed a curtsy before she fled the room.

Elizabeth cut herself a slice of French cheese. "Did Sir Guy come to your defense for the girl's sake or his own?"

Miles's expression went from amazement to amusement. He caught her hand and kissed the palm. "Guy doesn't like fights over scullery maids."

"And you do?"

Smiling, he shrugged. "I prefer to avoid fights about anything. I am a peaceful man."

"But you would have fought a fat, congenial landlord over the scratched hands of a worthless girl." It was a statement.

"I do not consider her worthless. Now"—he

dismissed the subject—"you must be tired. Would you like to retire?"

Miles's men all bid her goodnight and she nodded toward them, following Miles and the landlord up the stairs to the single room—and single bed—that awaited them.

"So! You have waited until now to force me to your bed," she said when they were alone. "Perhaps the tent walls were too thin to muffle my cries."

"Elizabeth," he said, taking her hand. "I will sleep on the windowseat and you may have the bed. I cannot allow you to have a room alone because you'd find some way to leave."

"Escape, you mean."

"All right, have it your way, escape. Now come here. I want to talk you." He pulled her to the windowseat, sat down and pulled her to sit beside him. When he drew her back against his chest, she began to protest.

"Relax, Elizabeth. I will leave my hands here about your waist and not move them, but I'll not let you up until you relax and talk to me."

"I can talk sitting up, away from you."

"But I cannot keep from touching you," he said with feeling. "All the time I want to caress you, to soothe away your hurt."

"I am not hurt." She pushed at his arms holding her to him. He was a large man, tall and broad, and the outward curve of his chest just fit the arch of her back.

"But you are hurt, Elizabeth, probably more

than you know."

"Ah yes, I see now. There is something wrong with me because I don't salivate with adoration whenever you are near me."

Miles kissed her neck, chuckling. "Perhaps I deserved that. Hold still or I'll kiss you more." Her abrupt stillness made him wince. "I want you to tell me what you like. Food does not interest you, nor pretty dresses. Gold and diamonds don't even make you blink. Men don't rate a glance from you. What is your weakness?"

"My weakness?" she asked, thinking about it. He was stroking her hair at her temple and in spite of herself, she was beginning to relax. The last two days of tension and anger were draining her strength. His long legs were stretched out on the windowseat and she was between them. "What is your weakness, Montgomery?"

"Women," he murmured, dismissing the question. "Tell me about you."

The muscles in her neck were relaxing and her weight was easing against him. It wasn't a bad feeling to be held so safely by such strong arms when the man wasn't pawing at her, tearing her clothes, hurting her. "I live with my two brothers, both of whom I love and who love me. I am far from being a pauper and I have but to hint at a jewel or gown I'd like and my brother Roger purchases it for me."

"And . . . Roger"—he tripped over the name—"is good to you?"

"He protects me." She smiled and closed her

eyes. Miles was massaging the tight muscles in her neck. "Roger has always protected Brian and me."

"Protected you from what?"

From Edmund, she almost said but caught herself. Her eyes flew open and she sat up. "From men!" she spat. "Men have always liked my looks but Roger kept them away from me."

He kept her hands imprisoned. "You know many tricks for repulsing men and you have wrapped yourself in steel. You are obviously a naturally passionate woman, so what has killed your passion? Was it that perhaps Roger was not always near enough to protect you?"

Elizabeth refused to answer him and she cursed her momentary trustfulness. After a while, Miles gave an exaggerated sigh and released her. Immediately she sprang away from him.

"Go to bed," he said tiredly as he stood, turning his back on her.

Elizabeth didn't trust him to keep his word about not sleeping with her, but she would do nothing to entice him. Fully clothed except for her soft leather shoes, she slipped into the big bed.

Miles blew out the single candle and for a long moment stood silhouetted before the moonlit window.

When Elizabeth heard no sounds from him she quietly turned on her back to watch him. All her body was tense with fear of what was to come. With resignation she watched him undress, and when he was nude she held her breath. But Miles lifted the thin blanket on the windowseat and stretched out—or tried to. He cursed once when his feet hit the paneling at the end of the cushion.

It was some minutes before Elizabeth began to realize that Miles Montgomery was not going to force himself on her. But she suspected that as soon as she was asleep he would pounce. She dozed lightly but every noise woke her. When Miles tried to turn on his narrow bed, he woke her and for a moment she would tense, but when she heard his even breathing of sleep, she'd relax again and sleep—until the next noise woke her.

Chapter 4

"DIDN'T YOU sleep well?" Miles asked the next morning as he pulled on his clothes. Tight black hose gripped his powerful legs, an embroidered jacket barely reaching the tops of his thighs.

"I never sleep well in the presence of my enemies," she retorted.

With a chuckle, he brushed her hands away and braided her hair for her, tying the tail with a bit of ribbon. When he finished, he kissed her neck, causing her to jump away while rubbing her neck.

He held out his arm to her. "I know you will be sad to leave my company but my men wait below for us."

She ignored his arm and left the room ahead of him. It was very early yet, the sun only a warm glow on the horizon. Miles murmured that a meal was waiting for them some distance down the road, and that they would ride for a few hours first.

Miles and Elizabeth stood together on the little

porch of the inn, Sir Guy before them, Miles's knights waiting with the horses and baggage mules behind the giant.

"Everything is ready?" Miles asked Sir Guy. "The innkeeper has been paid?"

Before Sir Guy could answer, a little girl, about four, raggedly dressed, came running out of the inn, swerved to miss Miles and fell down the two steps. Instantly, Miles was on his knees, pulling the child into his arms.

"Hush, sweetheart," he whispered, standing, the child clinging to him.

To Sir Guy and the knights, this was a familiar sight, and they waited patiently, with a bored air, while Miles comforted the child. Elizabeth didn't concern herself with Miles. Her one and only thought was for the injured child. She stretched out her arm, put her hand on the back of the crying child's head.

The child pulled her face away from the hollow in Miles's shoulder, and through tear-blurred eyes she looked at Elizabeth. With a fresh burst of tears she lifted her arms and lunged forward into Elizabeth's grasp.

It was difficult to tell who was more astonished: Miles, Sir Guy or the Montgomery knights. Miles gaped at Elizabeth and for a moment his pride took a beating.

"Hush now," Elizabeth said in a gentle voice such as Miles had never heard before. "If you stop crying Sir Guy will give you a ride on his shoulders."

Miles coughed to cover the laugh that threatened to choke him. Between Sir Guy's size and the hideous scar on his face, most people, and especially women, were terrified of him. He'd never seen anyone dare to volunteer the giant to be a child's horse.

"You'll be so tall," Elizabeth continued, swaying with the child, "you'll be able to reach up and catch a star."

The child gave a sniff, pulled away from Elizabeth and looked at her. "A star?" she hiccuped.

Elizabeth caressed the child's wet cheek. "And when you get the star, you can give it to Sir Miles to repay him for the new dress he's going to purchase for you."

The eyes of Miies's men went to their lord to watch his reaction—and no one dared laugh at his look of indignation.

The child sniffed again and twisted to look at Lord Miles. She gave him a smile, but when she looked at Sir Guy she clung to Elizabeth.

"There's no reason to be afraid of him," Elizabeth said. "He likes children very much, don't you, Sir Guy?"

Sir Guy gave Lady Elizabeth a hard, assessing look. "In truth, my lady, I like children a great deal but they have little use for me."

"We shall remedy that. Now, child, go with Sir Guy for your ride and bring back a star."

The child, a bit hesitant at first, went to Sir Guy and clung to his head when he set her on his shoulders. "I'm the tallest girl in the world," she squealed as Sir Guy walked away with her.

"I've never seen you smile before," Miles said.

Elizabeth's smile disappeared instantly. "I will reimburse you for the child's dress when I am home again." She turned away.

Miles caught her hand and led her away from his men's listening ears. "The child was only a beggar's."

"Oh?" she said offhandedly. "I thought perhaps she was one of yours."

"Mine?" he asked, bewildered. "Do you think I'd allow one of my children to run about in rags, with no supervision?"

She turned on him. "And how do you know where all your children are? Do you keep ledgers full of their names? Their whereabouts?"

Miles's face showed several emotions: disbelief, some anger, amusement. "Elizabeth, how many children do you think I have?"

She put her chin into the air. "I neither know nor care how many bastards you have."

He caught her arm, turning her to face him. "Even my own brothers exaggerate about my children so why should I expect more from outsiders? I have three sons: Christopher, Philip and James. And any day I expect to hear word of another child of mine. I am hoping for a daughter this time."

"You are hoping—" she gasped. "It doesn't bother you about their mothers? That you use the women, then discard them? And what of the children? They must grow up with the label of bastard! Outcasts because of some hideous man's one moment of pleasure.''

His grip tightened on her arm and there was anger in his eyes. ''I do not 'use' women,'' he said through clenched teeth. ''The women who have given me children came to me freely. And all my children live with me, are cared for by competent nurses.''

''Nurses!'' She tried to pull away from him, but couldn't. ''Do you toss the children's mothers into the street? Or do you give them a little money like you did Bridget and send them on their ways?''

''Bridget?'' Miles searched her face for a moment. His rising temper calmed. ''I assume you mean the Bridget who is the mother of my James?'' He didn't wait for her answer. ''I will tell you the truth about Bridget. My brother Gavin sent a message to St. Catherine's convent to ask for some serving girls. He wanted girls of good reputation who wouldn't be tantalizing his men and causing fights. From the moment this Bridget entered our house she pursued me.''

Elizabeth tried to pull away from him. ''You are a liar.''

Miles caught her other arm with his hand. ''Once she told me that she'd heard so much about me that she felt like a child who'd been told not to play with fire. One night I found her in my bed.''

''And you took her.''

"I made love to her, yes, that night and several other nights. When she realized she was going to have my child, I took a lot of ribbing from my brothers."

"And you cast her out—after you took her child away, that is."

He gave her a small smile. "Actually, she cast me aside. I was away for four months and she fell in love with Gavin's second gardener. When I returned I talked with them, told them I'd like to have the child and would raise him to be a knight. Bridget agreed readily."

"And how much money did you give them? Surely you must have offered some consolation to a mother giving up her child."

Miles released her arms, glaring at her. "Did you know Bridget very well? If you did you'd know she was more interested in her pleasures than motherhood. The gardener she was marrying didn't want Bridget or the child and later he asked for money for 'what he was giving up.' I gave him nothing. James is mine."

She was silent for a moment. "And what of your other children's mothers?" she asked quietly.

He walked away from her. "I fell in love with the younger sister of one of Gavin's men when I was just a boy. Christopher was born when both Margaret and I were only sixteen. I would have married her but her brother sent her away. I didn't know about Kit until Margaret died of smallpox a month after Kit's birth."

He looked back at Elizabeth and grinned. "Philip's mother was a dancer, an exotic creature who shared my bed for two"—he sighed—"two very interesting weeks. Then nine months later she sent a messenger with Philip. I've never seen or heard from her since."

Elizabeth was fascinated with his stories. "And this new child?"

Miles ducked his head and if he'd been a woman she would have thought he blushed. "I'm afraid this child may cause some problems. The mother is a distant cousin of mine. I resisted her as long as I could but . . ." He shrugged. "Her father is very angry with me. He says he'll send the child to me but . . . I'm not sure he will."

Elizabeth could only shake her head at him in disbelief. "Surely there must be other children." Her voice was sarcastic.

He frowned slightly. "I don't think so. I try to keep track of my women now and watch for children."

"Rather like gathering eggs," she said, eyes wide.

Miles cocked his head to one side and gave her an intense look. "One moment you condemn me for leaving my children in rags, strewn about the country like so much refuse, and now you damn me for caring for them. I am not a celibate man nor do I intend to be, but I take my responsibilities seriously. I love my children and I provide for them. I should like to have fifty of them."

"You have a good start," she said, sweeping past him.

Miles stood still, watching her walk back toward his men and the horses. She stood a little apart from the men, with that stiff-backed carriage of hers. She wasn't like either of his sisters-in-law, used to authority, at ease with the people who worked for them. Elizabeth Chatworth was rigid whenever she was near men. Yesterday, by accident, one of his men on horseback had brushed against her and Elizabeth had reacted so sharply, pulling her horse's reins so unexpectedly, that her horse had reared. She'd controlled the animal and held her seat but the experience had disgusted Miles. No woman—or man for that matter—should be so frightened of another human's touch.

Sir Guy returned, alone, to the men and at once he searched for Miles, walking toward him when he saw him. "It's getting late. We should ride." He paused. "Or perhaps you've reconsidered about returning the lady to her brother."

Miles was watching Elizabeth, who was now talking to the mother and the little girl who'd fallen earlier. He turned back to Guy. "I want you to send a couple of men to my northern estate. They are to bring Kit to me."

"Your son?" Sir Guy questioned.

"Yes, my son. Send his nurse with him. No! On second thought, bring him alone but with a heavy guard. Lady Elizabeth will be his nurse."

56

"Are you sure of what you're doing?" Sir Guy asked.

"The Lady Elizabeth likes children so I will share one of mine with her. If I can't reach her heart one way, I will use another."

"And what will you do with this woman once you've tamed her? Once, when I was a boy, there was a cat that had lived wild and it claimed the area around a certain shed as its own. Whenever anyone went near the shed, the cat scratched and bit. I set myself the job of taming it. It took many weeks of patience to gain the cat's trust but I felt triumphant when it began to eat from my hand. But later the cat began to follow me everywhere. I tripped over it constantly and it became a major nuisance. After several months I was kicking the cat, hating it because it was no longer the wild thing I'd loved at first, but only another cat, just like all the others."

Miles continued to study Elizabeth. "Perhaps it *is* the chase," he said quietly. "Or perhaps I'm like my brother Raine, who can't stand any injustice. All I know now is that Elizabeth Chatworth fascinates me. Maybe I do want to have her eat from my hand—but maybe when she does, it will be because I'm her slave."

He turned back to Sir Guy. "Elizabeth will like Kit and my son can only benefit from knowing her. And I'd like to see my son as well. Send the message."

Sir Guy nodded once in agreement before leaving Miles alone.

Minutes later they were mounted and ready to leave. Miles didn't try to talk to Elizabeth but silently rode beside her. She was beginning to look tired and by midday, he was of half a mind to return her to her brother.

A half-hour later, she suddenly sprang to life. While Miles had been feeling sorry for her, she'd worked loose the rope attaching their horses. She kicked her horse forward, used the loose end of her reins to slap the rumps of two horses in front of her, and with the rearing horses as a shield, she gained precious seconds to escape. She was half a mile down the rutted, weed-infested road before Miles could get around his men and follow her.

"I will bring her back," he shouted over his shoulder to Sir Guy.

Miles knew the horse Elizabeth rode had little speed in it but she got what she could out of it. He was close enough to catch her when the girth of his saddle slipped and he was sent sliding to one side. "Damn her," he gasped, knowing very well who'd loosened the saddle, but, at the same time, he smiled at her ingenuity.

But Elizabeth Chatworth wasn't prepared for a man who'd grown up with three older brothers. Miles was used to practical jokes such as loosened cinches and he knew how to handle them. Expertly, he shifted his weight to the front of the horse, in essence riding bareback but sitting on the horse's neck, the saddle behind him.

He lost some speed when the horse threatened to revolt at this new position, but Miles controlled the animal.

Elizabeth turned her mount into a corn field when the primitive road disappeared and she was disconcerted to see Miles close on her heels.

He caught her in the corn field, grabbing her about the waist. She fought him wildly and Miles, with no stirrups to anchor himself, started falling. When he went down his arm was still fastened around Elizabeth's waist.

As they both fell, Miles twisted and took most of the jolt, cushioning Elizabeth, putting his arm up to protect her back from a flying hoof. The horses ran for a few more feet then stood, sides heaving.

"Release me," Elizabeth demanded when she caught her breath. She was sprawled on top of Miles.

His arms held her to him. "When did you loosen the cinch?" When she didn't answer he hugged her until her ribs threatened to break.

"At dinner," she gasped.

He moved his hand to the back of her head, forcing it to his shoulder. "Elizabeth, you are so clever. How did you manage to sneak past my men? When did you leave my sight?"

His neck was sweaty and his heart was pounding against her own. The exercise had done away with her tiredness and she was glad for it even if she hadn't succeeded in her escape.

"You gave me a good run," he said, amused. "If my brothers hadn't thought it a great joke to send me out with a loosened cinch, I wouldn't have known how to handle it. Of course *they* were careful that I was on a slow mount so if I fell I wouldn't kill myself.'' He moved to look at her face. ''Would you have been terribly glad to see me break my neck?''

''Yes, very,'' she said, smiling, practically nose to nose with him.

Miles laughed at that, kissed her quickly, pushed her off him and stood, frowning as she wiped the back of her hand across her mouth. ''Come on, there's an inn not far from here and we'll stop for the night.'' He didn't offer to help her up.

When they returned to the men, Sir Guy gave Elizabeth a quick look of admiration and she guessed that he'd be more vigilant from now on. She wouldn't have more chances to toy with the men's gear.

It wasn't until they were mounted again that Elizabeth saw that Miles's forearm was cut and bleeding. She knew it had happened when he'd put his arm between her and the horse's hoof. Sir Guy inspected the cut and bound it while Elizabeth sat on her horse and watched. It seemed odd that this man, a Montgomery, would protect a Chatworth from harm.

Miles saw her watching. ''A smile from you, Elizabeth, would make it heal faster.''

''I hope it poisons your blood and you lose your arm.'' She kicked her horse forward.

They didn't speak again until they arrived at the inn at which, as before, Miles had sent someone ahead to prepare for them. This time, Miles and Elizabeth were given a private dining room.

"Tell me more about your family," he said.

"No," she answered simply, reaching for a dish of snails in garlic sauce.

"Then I will tell you of mine. I have three older brothers and—"

"I know about them. You and your brothers are notorious."

He raised one eyebrow at her. "Tell me what you've heard."

"With pleasure." She cut into a beef and chicken pie. "Your brother Gavin is the eldest. He was to marry Alice Valence but he rejected her so he could marry the rich Judith Revedoune, who is a vicious-tempered woman. Between your brother and his wife they succeeded in driving Alice—now Chatworth—insane."

"Do you know your sister-in-law?"

Elizabeth studied the food on her plate. "She wasn't always as she is now."

"The bitch was born a whore. She rejected my brother. Now, tell me of Stephen."

"He forced a woman who wanted my brother to be his bride."

"And Raine?"

"I know little of the man, except that he's magnificent on a battlefield."

Miles's eyes burned into hers. "After your brother raped my sister and Mary killed herself, Raine led some of the king's men to attack your brother Roger. The king has declared Raine a traitor and my brother lives in a forest with a band of criminals.'' He paused. ''And what of me?''

''You are a lecher, a seducer of young girls.''

''I am flattered that my virility is so overrated. Now let me tell you the truth about my family. Gavin had to take over the raising of three brothers and the managing of estates when he was but sixteen. He barely had time to find out about women. He fell in love with Alice Valence, begged her to marry him, but she refused. He married Judith Revedoune and only after a long while did he realize he loved Judith. Alice tried to scar Judith with hot oil but Alice was the one scarred.''

''You lie constantly,'' Elizabeth said.

''No, I do not lie. Stephen is the peacemaker in our family and he and Gavin are close. And Raine—'' He paused and smiled. ''Raine believes the world's burdens rest upon his big shoulders. He is a good man but unbelievably stubborn.''

''And you?'' Elizabeth asked softly.

He took his time answering. ''I am alone. My brothers seem so sure of what they want. Gavin loves the land, Stephen is a crusader about his Scots, Raine wants to change the world, but I . . .''

She looked up at him and for a moment there was a silent exchange. She too had felt alone in her life. Edmund was evil, Roger was always angry and she'd spent her life escaping Edmund and his friends while trying to protect Brian.

Miles took her hand in his and she didn't pull away. "You and I have had to grow up quickly. Do you remember being a child?"

"All too well," she said flatly, pulling her hand away.

For a while they ate in silence. "Was your home . . . happy?" she asked, as if it didn't matter.

"Yes." He smiled. "Each of us was fostered but we still spent a great deal of time together. It's not easy being the youngest son. You get knocked about a bit. And were you happy?"

"No. I was too busy running from Edmund to think of anything as silly as happiness. I would like to retire now."

Miles followed her to their room and she saw that tonight a cot had been set along one wall.

"No windowseat," he said cheerfully, but Elizabeth didn't laugh. He took both her hands in his. "When are you going to trust me? I am not like Edmund or Pagnell or any other of the disgusting men you know."

"You are holding me prisoner. Do men as good as you think you are hold innocent women captive?"

He kissed her hands. "But if I returned you to your brother, what would you do? Would you wait for Roger to find you a husband and then happily settle down to wedded bliss?"

She pulled away from him. "Roger has given me permission to never marry. I have considered taking vows of the church."

Miles gave her a look of horror. Before she could protest, he pulled her into his arms, stroked her back. "You have so much love to give. How could you think to hide it? Wouldn't you like to have children, to watch them grow? There's nothing like a child looking at you with complete adoration and trust."

She lifted her head from his shoulder. She was growing almost used to his touching and holding of her. "I've never before met a man who loved children. All the men I know care only for fighting, drinking, raping women."

"There's something to be said for a good rousing fight now and then and I've been drunk before, but I like willing women in my bed. Now, let's get you out of this dress."

She jerked away from him, her eyes hostile.

"I plan to sleep on that cold, hard, lonely cot but I think you must be sick of that gown. You'd be more comfortable sleeping without it."

"I am more comfortable *in* my clothes, thank you."

"All right, have your own way." He turned away and began to undress while Elizabeth fled to the protection of her bed.

The single candle was still burning and when Miles wore only his loincloth, he bent over her, pulling the blanket from over her face. She lay stiff, rigid, while he sat on the edge of the bed, his hand caressing the hair at her temple. Not speaking, he simply looked at her, enjoying the feel of her skin.

"Goodnight, Elizabeth," he whispered as he planted a soft kiss on her lips.

Her hand shot out to wipe it away but he caught her wrist. "What would it take to make you love a man?" he murmured.

"I don't think I could," she replied honestly. "At least not as you mean."

"I'm beginning to think I want to test that. Goodnight, my fragile angel."

He kissed her again before she could protest that she was far from fragile, but this time she was able to wipe the kiss away.

Chapter 5

MILES, ELIZABETH, Sir Guy and the Montgomery knights traveled for two more days before reaching the southern border of Scotland. Elizabeth tried once more to escape—at night while Miles slept close to her—but she didn't reach the door before he caught her and led her back to bed.

Elizabeth lay awake a long time after that, thinking about how she was a prisoner and yet not a prisoner. She had never been treated with as much courtesy as Miles Montgomery treated her. He did insist upon touching her at every opportunity but she was growing used to that. It certainly was no pleasure but it was no longer as vile as it'd seemed at first. Once, at an inn where they'd stopped for dinner, a drunk had fallen toward Elizabeth and, as a reflex, she'd stepped nearer to Miles for protection. He had been inordinately pleased by that.

Today he'd told her that from now on they'd

be using his tent as the inns were not as abundant in Scotland. He hinted that once they crossed the mountains, there could be trouble since the Highlanders didn't like the English.

All through supper, he'd seemed preoccupied and had conferred with Sir Guy several times.

"Are the Scots as bloodthirsty as all this?" she asked after he'd left the supper table the second time.

He didn't seem to understand what she was talking about. "I'm meeting someone here and he's late. He should have been here by now."

"One of your brothers—or is it a woman?"

"Neither," he said quickly.

Elizabeth asked no more questions. As she crawled into her bed, wearing the same dress Miles had given her, she turned to her side to watch him on his cot. He tossed and turned every moment.

When a loud knock came on the door, Elizabeth sprang out of bed almost as quickly as Miles. Sir Guy entered, a little boy behind him.

"Kit!" Miles cried, grabbing the child, hugging him fit to crush him. The boy didn't seem to mind as he also clung to Miles.

"What took them so long?" Miles asked Sir Guy.

"They were caught in a rainstorm and lost three horses."

"No men?"

"Everyone was saved but it took a while to replace the horses. Young master Kit held onto his saddle when two knights couldn't," Sir Guy said with pride.

"Is that true?" Miles asked, turning the boy around.

Elizabeth saw a small replica of Miles but with brown eyes instead of gray, a handsome boy, his face solemn.

"Yes, Papa," Kit answered. "Uncle Gavin said that a knight always stays with his horse. Afterward, I helped the men pull the baggage from the water."

"You're a good boy." Miles grinned, hugging Kit once again. "You may go, Guy, and see that the men are fed. We'll leave first thing in the morning."

Kit smiled goodbye to Sir Guy, then whispered loudly to his father. "Who is she?"

Miles stood Kit on the floor. "Lady Elizabeth," he said formally, "may I present Christopher Gavin Montgomery."

"How do you do?" she said, taking the child's extended hand. "I am Lady Elizabeth Chatworth."

"You are very pretty," he said. "My papa likes pretty women."

"Kit—" Miles began, but Elizabeth interrupted him.

"Do you like pretty women?" she asked.

"Oh yes. My nurse is very, very pretty."

"I'm sure she is if your father hired her. Are you hungry? Tired?"

"I ate a whole sackful of sugared plums," Kit said with pride. "Oh Papa! I have a message for you. It's from someone named Simon."

A frown crossed Miles's face, but as he read the message he broke into a grin.

"Good news?" Elizabeth asked, not able to hide her curiosity.

Miles sobered himself as he tossed the note to his rumpled cot. "Yes and no. My cousin has been delivered of my daughter but my Uncle Simon is threatening my life."

Elizabeth wasn't sure whether to laugh or be disgusted. "You have a little sister, Kit," she said at last.

"I have two brothers already. I don't want a sister."

"I believe your father makes those decisions. It's late and I think you should be in bed."

"Kit can take the cot and I'll . . ." Miles began, eyes twinkling.

"Kit will sleep with me," Elizabeth said loftily, offering her hand to the child.

Kit accepted readily and he yawned as she led him around the bed.

Miles watched, smiling a bit triumphantly, as Elizabeth undressed the sleepy little boy down to his underwear. He readily went into her arms as she lifted him into bed. Elizabeth crawled in beside him, pulled Kit to her.

For a moment Miles stood to one side, watching them. With a smile, he bent and kissed both foreheads. "Goodnight," he whispered before going to his cot.

During the next day, it didn't take Miles long to

see that Elizabeth's interest extended only to Kit. And the child took to Elizabeth as if he'd known her forever. All Elizabeth would say was, "I have always liked children and they seem to know this." Whatever the reason, Kit seemed perfectly at ease with Elizabeth. In the afternoon, he rode with her, fell asleep against her. When Miles suggested he take the heavy child, Elizabeth practically snarled at him.

At night they curled up with each other on a single cot and slept peacefully. Miles looked down at them and felt like an outsider.

They traveled for three more days and Elizabeth knew they must be getting close to the MacArrans' land. Miles had been in deep thought all day and twice she'd seen him arguing with Sir Guy. From the frown on Sir Guy's face, Miles was obviously planning something the giant didn't like. But whenever Elizabeth got within hearing distance the men stopped talking.

At midday Miles stopped the entourage of men and mules and asked if she and Kit would like to dine with him. Usually they all ate together, within sight and protection of each other.

"You seem pleased with yourself about something," Elizabeth said, watching him.

"We're within a day's ride of my brother and his wife," Miles said happily, lifting Kit from Elizabeth's horse.

"Uncle Stephen wears a skirt and Lady Bronwyn can ride a horse as fast as the wind," Kit informed her.

"Stephen wears a plaid," Miles amended as he pulled Elizabeth from her horse, ignoring her attempts to brush his hands away. "My cook has laid a meal for us inside the forest."

Kit took Elizabeth's hand and Miles held the child on the other side and together they walked into the forest.

"What do you think of Scotland?" Miles asked as he held her arm as she stepped over a fallen log.

"It's as if the place has been untouched since the beginning of time. It's very rough and . . . untrimmed."

"Rather like its people." Miles laughed. "My brother has let his hair grow to his shoulders and his clothing . . . no, I'll let you see for yourself."

"Aren't we going a bit far from your men?" The primitive forest closed around them and the undergrowth was making it more difficult to walk.

Miles drew an ax from where it was slung across his back and began to hack away a wider path.

With a look of puzzlement, Elizabeth turned to him. He was wearing somber clothes of dark green, a brown cloak about his shoulders—and he was heavily armed. There was a longbow with a quiver of arrows on his back, as well as the ax, his sword on his hip and a dagger at his waist. "Something is wrong, isn't it?"

"Yes," he said, looking about her. "The truth is, Elizabeth, I was given a message to meet someone here, but we've gone too far."

She raised one eyebrow. "You would risk your son's life in this secret meeting?"

He slipped his ax back into its sheath. "My men are all around us. I wanted you close to me rather than leave you and Kit with any of my men."

"Look, Papa!" Kit said excitedly. "There's a deer."

"Shall we go and see the deer?" she said calmly. "Run ahead of us and we'll catch you." Keeping Kit in her sight, she turned to Miles. "I will stay with Kit and you go look for your men. I feel there's been some trick to separate us."

Miles's eyes widened at her ordering of him, but within moments he disappeared into the forest while Elizabeth hurried after Kit. When Miles seemed to take forever before he returned, she looked about with anxious eyes.

"Are you unhappy, Elizabeth?" Kit asked, catching her hand.

She knelt to his level. "I was just wondering where your father is."

"He will return," Kit said confidently. "My papa will take care of us."

Elizabeth tried not to show her disbelief. "I am sure he will. I hear a stream in that direction. Shall we find it?"

They had some trouble breaking through the underbrush but they made it to the stream. It was a wild, rushing body of water, cascading angrily over rocks, tearing at the rocky shore.

"It's cold," Kit said, stepping back. "Do you think there are any fish in it?"

"Salmon, most likely," said Miles from behind Elizabeth, and she jumped. Miles put his arm about her shoulders. "I didn't mean to frighten you."

She stepped away from him. "What about your men?"

He gave a look to Kit who was throwing forest debris into the water and watching it being swept away. He took her hands in his. "My men are gone. There's no sign of them. Elizabeth, you won't panic, will you?"

She looked into his eyes. She was frightened to be in a strange land with a child and this man she didn't trust. "No," she said firmly. "I don't want to frighten Kit."

"Good." He smiled, squeezing her hands. "We are on the southern boundaries of MacArran land now and if we walk due north we should reach some of the crofters' cottages by evening tomorrow."

"But if someone has spirited away your men—"

"My concern now is for you and Kit. If we stay in the forest perhaps we can escape notice. I don't mind a fight, but I don't want you or Kit harmed. Will you help me?"

She didn't pull away from his hands. "Yes," she said softly. "I'll help you."

He released one of her hands. "These mountains are cold even in the summer. Put this around you." He held up a large piece of woolen

73

fabric woven in a deep blue and green tartan.

"Where did you get this?"

"This was all that was left of the meal my cook left. The food was gone but the cloth he spread it on, one of the plaids Bronwyn gave me, was left behind. We'll need this tonight." He kept her hand clasped tightly as she tossed the plaid over her arm and they walked toward Kit.

"Would you like to walk to Uncle Stephen's house?" Miles asked his son.

Kit gave his father a shrewd look. "Where is Sir Guy? A knight doesn't walk."

"A knight does what is necessary to protect his women."

Between the two males passed a long look. Kit might be only four years old but he'd known since birth that he was to be a knight. He'd been given a wooden sword at two and all the stories he'd heard were of chivalry and knighthood. Kit took Elizabeth's hand. "We will protect you, my lady," he said formally and kissed her hand.

Miles touched his son's shoulder in pride. "Now, Kit, run ahead and see what game you can find us. Even a rabbit or two will do."

"Yes, Papa." He grinned and scurried away along the side of the stream.

"Should you let him out of our sight?"

"He won't be. Kit has more sense than to stray too far."

"You seem little concerned about the loss of your men. Were there signs of a battle?"

"None." He seemed to dismiss the subject as

he stooped, plucked a delicate yellow wildflower and slipped it behind her ear. "You look as if you belong in this wild place with your hair down, your torn dress held together with diamonds. I wouldn't mind giving you many diamonds, Elizabeth."

"I would prefer freedom."

He stepped away from her. "You are no longer my prisoner, Elizabeth Chatworth," he declared. "You may leave my presence forever."

She looked about the wild, rough forest. "You are very clever, Montgomery," she said with disgust.

"I take it that means you'll stay with me," he said, eyes twinkling, and before she could answer he lifted her, swirled her about in his arns, planting a kiss on her cheek.

"Release me," she said but there was a hint of a smile about her lips.

He nuzzled her earlobe. "I think you could have me at your feet if you so wished," he whispered.

"Bound and gagged, I'd hope," she retorted, pushing away from him. "Now, do you plan to feed us or do you carry that bow only because it looks good?"

"Papa!" Kit yelled before Miles could answer. "I saw a rabbit!"

"I'm sure it's waiting for me to come and slaughter it," Miles said under his breath as Kit came thrashing toward them.

A sound from Elizabeth that could only be

described as a giggle made Miles turn an astonished face toward her.

Elizabeth refused to look at him. "Where is the rabbit, Kit? Your brave father will face the animal, and perhaps we'll get some supper, if not dinner."

After an hour of walking, with Miles seeming more concerned with toying with Elizabeth's fingers, they saw no more rabbits. It was later than she'd thought and it was growing dark—or perhaps the forest just seemed dark.

"We'll camp here for the night. Kit, gather firewood." When the child was gone, Miles turned to Elizabeth. "Don't let him out of your sight. I'll find us some game." With that he slipped away into the forest.

As soon as Miles was gone, Elizabeth began to feel the isolation of the forest. She followed Kit, loading her arms with dry branches. She hadn't noticed it before, but she felt as if eyes were watching her. In her brother's house she'd learned to develop a sixth sense about men who hid in corners, ready to pounce on her.

"Are you frightened, Elizabeth?" Kit asked, his eyes wide.

"Of course not." She forced a smile but she kept remembering all the stories she'd heard about the savagery of the Scots. They were wild people, torturers of little children.

"My papa will protect you," Kit said. "He was given his spurs when he was just a boy. My Uncle Raine says Papa is one of the greatest knights in

76

England. He won't let anyone get you."

She pulled the boy into her arms. "Your papa is indeed a great fighter. Did you know that three men attacked me a few days ago? Your papa slew them in minutes and he wasn't even hurt." For all the child's bravado, Elizabeth could see that he was frightened. "I think your papa could fight off all the men of Scotland. There's no one anywhere who is as brave and strong as your papa."

A low chuckle made Elizabeth look around to see Miles holding two dead rabbits by their ears. "I thank you for the tribute, my lady."

"Elizabeth was scared," Kit explained.

"And you were right to comfort her. We must always protect our women. Would it be possible that you'd know how to skin rabbits, Elizabeth?"

She lowered Kit and took the rabbits with an air of confidence. "You'll find that a Chatworth is no Montgomery lady to sit about on satin cushions and wait for the servants to bring her food."

"You've described Stephen and Gavin's wives perfectly. Come, Kit, let's see if the Montgomery men can be useful."

In a very short time, Miles and Kit had a fire going and Elizabeth had the rabbits skinned and skewered. Miles used his ax to drive stakes into the ground and set up a turnspit for the rabbits. Leaning back on his elbows, Miles idly watched the fire while Kit turned the meat.

"You seem very relaxed," Elizabeth said, frowning, keeping her voice low. "We're unprotected in a strange land, yet you build a fire. We can be seen for miles.''

He tugged on her skirt until she sat down, a few feet from him. ''This land belongs to my brother and his wife, and if the MacArrans see us they'll recognize the Montgomery leopards on my cloak. The Scots rarely kill women and children outright. You'll be delivered to Stephen and all you'll have to do is explain who you are.''

''But what has happened to your men?''

''Elizabeth, my men are gone with no trace of a fight. I would imagine they were escorted to Larenston, Bronwyn's castle. Right now my concern is for the safety of you and Kit. When we reach Larenston and my men aren't there, then I'll worry. Kit! You're allowing the meat to burn on one side.''

He moved closer to her. ''Elizabeth, you're as safe as you can be. I've scouted this area and seen no one. You're cold,'' he said when she shivered. He took the plaid from the ground behind her, pulled it around both their shoulders and drew her toward him.

''It's only for warmth,'' he said when she struggled against him, and refused to loosen his grip.

''I've heard that before!'' she snapped. ''The warmth is only the beginning. Do you enjoy forcing me?''

''I do not enjoy your hints that I'm like one of your brother's slimy friends,'' he snapped.

Elizabeth stopped struggling. ''Perhaps life with

Edmund *has* distorted my thinking a bit, but I don't like to be pawed."

"You've made that clear enough, but if we're to survive the night I think we need each other's warmth. Kit, break off a leg. It looks done to me."

The rabbits were barely cooked inside, charred outside, but the three of them were too hungry to care.

"I like it, Papa," Kit said. "I like it here in the forest."

"It's awfully cold," Elizabeth said, huddled in the plaid. "If this is summer, what is winter like in Scotland?"

"Bronwyn thinks England is hot. In the winter she wraps herself in one of those plaids and sleeps on the snow."

"No!" Elizabeth breathed. "Is she truly such a barbarian?"

Smiling, Miles turned to his son, saw his eyes drooping.

"Come lay down beside me," Elizabeth said and Kit went to her.

Miles spread his cloak, motioned for Elizabeth and Kit to lie on it, covered them with the plaid. After tossing more wood on the fire, he lifted the plaid and crawled in beside Kit.

"You can't—" she began but stopped. There was nowhere else for him to sleep. Between them, Kit's sleeping body kept them warm. Elizabeth was very aware of Miles so close to her, but instead of frightening her his presence was reassuring.

With her head propped on her arm, she watched the fire. "What was Kit's mother like?" she asked softly. "Did she fall in love with you the first time she saw you in your armor?"

Miles gave a snort of laughter. "Margaret Sidney turned up her pretty little nose at me and refused to speak to me. I did everything I could to try and impress her. Once, when she came to the training field to bring water to her father, I turned to look at her, lost my stirrup and Raine hit me in the side with his lance. I still have the scar."

"But I thought—"

"You thought that I'd sold my soul to the devil and as a result I could have any woman I wanted."

"I had heard that story," she said evenly, not looking at him.

He caught her free hand from Kit's side, kissed her fingertips. "The devil hasn't made an offer for my soul, but if he did, I might think about it."

"You blaspheme!" she said, pulling her hand away. She was quiet for a moment. "But your Margaret Sidney changed her mind."

"She was sixteen and so very beautiful and so in love with Gavin at the time. She wanted nothing to do with a boy like me."

"And what changed her mind?"

He grinned broadly. "I persisted."

Elizabeth stiffened. "And when you got her, how did you celebrate?"

"By asking her to marry me," Miles shot back. "I told you I loved her."

"You give your love lightly. Why didn't Bridget marry you or this cousin who just bore your daughter?"

He was quiet for several moments. "I have loved only one woman; I have made love to many women. I have asked only Kit's mother to marry me and when I ask again, it will be because I love the woman."

"I pity her." Elizabeth sighed. "She will have to put up with your bastards being presented, two and three a year."

"You don't seem to mind this child of mine, and you held the girl at the inn when you thought she was mine."

"But I, happily, am not married to you."

Miles's voice lowered. "If you were my wife, would you mind receiving new children every few months?"

"I wouldn't blame your four children for your past transgressions, but if I should marry any man, which I will not do, and if my husband humiliated me by impregnating every servant girl in England, I believe that I would arrange his death."

"Fair enough," Miles said, an undertone of amusement in his voice. He turned on his side, put his arm over Kit, around Elizabeth's shoulders, and drew both of them to him. "Goodnight, my angel," he whispered and was asleep.

Chapter 6

MILES WAS awakened by Kit's foot in his ribs as the boy painfully climbed over his father. "Be very quiet, Papa," Kit whispered loudly and juicily in the vicinity of Miles's ear. "Don't wake Elizabeth." With that he was over his father and running into the dim forest.

Miles watched his son and rubbed his bruised ribcage.

"Will you live?" Elizabeth asked laughingly from beside him.

He turned and their eyes met. Elizabeth's hair was spread about her and her face was sleep softened. He'd not realized how stern a control she kept on herself. Cautiously, smiling slightly, he moved his hand from her shoulder to her cheek, gently caressed the outline of her jaw.

His breath held when she didn't pull away. It was as if she were a wild animal he was trying to tame and he must move very slowly so as not to frighten her away.

Elizabeth watched Miles, felt his hand on her face with a sense of wonder. His eyes were liquid, his lips full and soft. She'd never allowed a man to touch her before and never wondered what it would be like to feel a man's caress. But now she lay stretched out, facing Miles Montgomery, only inches separating their bodies, and she wondered what it would feel like to touch him. There was a dark growth of beard on his cheeks, emphasizing the sharp cut of them. A curl of dark hair touched his ear.

As if reading her thoughts, Miles lifted Elizabeth's hand, placed it on his cheek. She let it rest there for a moment, her heart pounding. It was as if she were doing something forbidden. After a very long moment, she moved her hand to touch his hair. It was soft and clean and she wondered how it smelled.

Her eyes went back to Miles's and she sensed that he was going to kiss her. Pull away, she thought, but she didn't move.

Slowly, his eyes telling her she could refuse him, he drew near her and when his lips touched hers, she kept her eyes open. What a pleasant feeling, she thought.

He just touched her lips with his and held them there, not forcing her mouth open, not grabbing her and throwing his weight onto her as other men had done, but just the light, highly pleasant kiss.

He was the first to pull away and there was a light of such warmth in his eyes that she began to stiffen. Now would come the pouncing.

"Hush," he soothed, his hand on her cheek. "No one is going to hurt you ever again, my Elizabeth."

"Papa!" Kit yelled and the spell was broken.

"No doubt he's spotted a unicorn this time," Miles said under his breath as he reluctantly rose. His jest was rewarded by the hint of a smile from Elizabeth.

Rising, Elizabeth winced at an ache in her shoulder. She wasn't used to sleeping on the ground.

Acting as if it were the most natural thing in the world, Miles began to knead Elizabeth's shoulders. "What have you found now, Kit?" he called above her head.

"A path," Kit yelled back. "Can I follow it?"

"Not until we get there. Better?" he asked Elizabeth, and when she nodded he kissed her neck and quickly began to gather their few belongings.

"Are you always so free with women?" she asked and there was curiosity in her voice. "When you visit someone's house do you freely kiss all the women?"

Miles didn't pause in burying the dead coals of last night's fire. "I can be civilized, I assure you, and usually I limit my kissing to hands—at least in public." He looked back at her, smiling, eyes sparkling. "But with you, my lovely Elizabeth, from our first . . . ah, meeting, nothing has been done in the usual manner. I can't help but feel that you were a gift to me, a very precious gift, but, nonetheless, something that is mine to keep."

Before she could answer—and, in truth, she was too stunned to answer—he caught her hand and began pulling her to where Kit glared at them impatiently. "Let's go and see where this path takes us."

Miles held her hand as Kit led them down the narrow, long-disused path. "What do you think of my son?"

Elizabeth smiled at the boy who was poking at a mushroom on the ground. As she watched, he straightened and began running ahead of them. "He's very independent, intelligent and quite adult for his age. You must be very proud of him."

Miles's chest swelled visibly. "I have two more at home. Philip Stephen is as exotic-looking as his mother, with a temper that sets his nurse trembling, and he's only a year old."

"And your other boy? Bridget's son?"

"James Raine is exactly opposite of Philip and the two of them are together constantly. I have a feeling it may always be that way. James gives Philip his toys when Philip demands them." He chuckled. "The only thing James will share with no one is his nurse. He screams even if I touch her."

"He must do a great deal of screaming," Elizabeth said sarcastically.

"James is silent practically always," Miles said, laughing. He leaned closer to her. "But then he does go to bed quite early."

She pushed him away playfully.

"Papa," Kit yelled, running to them. "Come and look. It's part of a house but it burned down."

Around the bend was what was left of a burned crofter's cottage, most of the roof collapsed, only one corner standing.

"No, Kit," Miles said when his son started to enter the ruin. Heavy, charred beams slanted from the one standing wall to the ground. "Let me test it first."

Elizabeth and Kit stood together while Miles grabbed one beam after another and swung his weight on it. A few bits of dirt came falling down but the beams held.

"It seems safe enough," Miles said as Kit ran inside the structure and began looking into crevices.

Miles took Elizabeth's arm. "Let's walk up the hill because, if I'm not mistaken, I think those are apple trees."

There was a small orchard on top of the hill and most of the trees were dead, but there were about a dozen scrawny, nearly ripe apples hanging from some of the branches. As Elizabeth reached for one of them, Miles's arm slid about her waist and lifted her. She caught the apple and he slowly lowered her, the front of her body sliding down his. His lips had just reached hers when Kit called out.

"Look what I found, Papa."

Elizabeth turned away to smile at Kit. "What is it?"

With a dramatic sigh, Miles set Elizabeth down.

"It's a swing!" Kit yelled.

"So it is," Miles said, holding Elizabeth's hand. He grabbed the ropes of the swing and gave them a couple of sharp jerks. "Let me see how high you can go," he said to his son.

Elizabeth and Miles stood back as Kit took over the swing, using it in an aggressive way to propel himself upward until his feet touched a tree branch.

"He'll hurt himself," Elizabeth said, but Miles caught her arm.

"Now show Elizabeth what you can do."

She gasped as Kit, still swinging very high, pulled his legs up and stood in the swing.

"Now!" Miles commanded, his arms open wide.

To Elizabeth's disbelief, Kit sent his small body flying through the air and into Miles's arms. As Kit screamed with delight, Elizabeth felt her knees weaken.

Miles put his son down and caught her arm. "Elizabeth, what's wrong? It was only a child's game. When I was Kit's age, I used to jump into my father's arms in just the same way."

"But if you stepped away . . ." she began.

"Stepped away!" He was aghast. "And let Kit fall?" He pulled her into his arms, soothing her. "Did no one play with you as a child?" he asked quietly.

"My parents died soon after I was born.

Edmund was my guardian.''

That simple statement said a great deal to Miles. He pulled her away to look at her. ''Now we shall make up for your lack of a childhood. Get in the swing and I'll push you.''

She was glad to put away her memories of Edmund and she went readily to the swing.

''I will, Papa,'' Kit said, pushing the wooden bottom of the swing and not making much progress. ''She's too heavy,'' Kit whispered loudly.

''Not for me.'' Miles laughed, kissed Elizabeth's ear and took the ropes. ''Wipe it away, Elizabeth,'' he said as he pulled her far back off the ground.

''I can't now, but I will,'' she tossed over her shoulder.

Miles released her and she went flying. Every time she returned, he gave her a push on her bottom instead of the swing's and all Elizabeth did was laugh. Her skirt went up to her knees, she kicked off her shoes and stretched her legs out.

''Jump, Elizabeth!'' Kit commanded.

''I'm too heavy, remember?'' she teased, laughing.

Miles stood to the side of her. The more time he spent with her, the more beautiful she grew. Her head was back and she was laughing as he'd never seen her laugh before.

''Papa can catch you,'' Kit persisted.

''Yes, Papa is more than willing to catch the Lady Elizabeth.'' Miles grinned, standing before her. He saw a look of doubt cross her face. "Trust me, Elizabeth." He was smiling but was deadly earnest at the same time. "I won't step aside; I'll catch you no matter how hard you fall."

Elizabeth didn't play Kit's trick of standing in the swing, but she did release the ropes and go flying headlong into Miles's arms. When she hit him, the breath was almost knocked from her.

Miles clasped her tightly, then with a look of horror he said, "You *are* too heavy, Elizabeth."

His fall was the most ostentatious fake she'd ever encountered, and as he went down with great loud groans she giggled, clinging to him. With a loud, heartfelt, "Uh oh," from Miles, they began rolling down the steep hill. It was a terribly insincere roll. When Miles was on the bottom, he clutched at Elizabeth, his hands running down the length of her and when she was on the bottom, his arms and knees kept her off the ground so that not even a rock jabbed at her.

Elizabeth's giggle turned into a laugh which made her very weak and her hands were quite ineffectual at pushing him away. He'd pause with her on top just long enough for her to push at his arms, then he'd turn and she'd hang on for dear life.

At the bottom of the hill, he stopped, flung his arms outward, closed his eyes. "I'm crushed, Elizabeth," he said in a wounded tone.

Kit, wanting to join the fun, came tearing down the hill and jumped into the middle of his father's stomach, catching him unaware.

The groan Miles gave this time was genuine, and Elizabeth broke into new gales of laughter.

With great show, Miles set his son off his stomach and turned to Elizabeth. "Like to see me in pain, do you?" His voice was serious but his eyes were alive with teasing. "Come on, Kit, let's show Lady Elizabeth she can't laugh at two knights of the realm."

Eyes wide, Elizabeth stood and backed away, but Miles and Kit were too fast for her. Miles caught her shoulders while Kit threw his body weight onto her legs. Elizabeth tripped over her skirt, Miles tripped over his son and Kit just kept pushing. The three of them went down in a laughing heap as Miles began to tickle Elizabeth's ribs and Kit joined his father.

"Enough?" Miles asked, close to Elizabeth's face which was streaming with tears. "Are you willing to admit to our being the best of knights?"

"I . . . never said you weren't," she gasped.

Miles's tickling became more severe. "Tell us what we are."

"The bravest, handsomest knights in all of England—in all the world."

His hands stilled, slipping about her waist, his thumbs just under her breasts. "And what is my name?" he whispered, completely sober.

"Miles," she whispered back, her eyes on his. "Miles Montgomery." Her arms were on his shoulders and now they slipped about his neck, lightly.

Miles bent and kissed her, softly, but there was for the first time a tiny spark between them.

Kit jumped on his father's back and Miles's face slid from Elizabeth's, and he just missed slamming into the dirt.

"Let's swing again, Papa."

"To think that I used to love my son," Miles whispered in Elizabeth's ear before he rose, his son attached to his back.

None of them had noticed that the sky had darkened in the last few minutes, and they each gasped when the first cold drops hit them. The sky opened up and nearly drowned them.

"To the cottage," Miles said, pulling Elizabeth up, his arm about her shoulders, and together they ran for shelter.

"Did you get wet?" he asked as he lowered Kit from his back.

"No, not much." She smiled up at him for just a moment before turning toward Kit.

Miles casually put his hand on Elizabeth's shoulder. "Why don't the two of you build a fire while I find us something to eat?"

Kit agreed enthusiastically while Elizabeth gave a dubious look to the torrential rain outside. "Perhaps you should wait until it slackens."

Miles gave her a smile of delight. "I'll be safe enough. Now, the two of you stay in here and I'll not be far away." With that, he slipped between the charred beams and was gone.

Elizabeth went to the edge of the shelter and looked after him. She was certain Miles

Montgomery had no idea how unusual today had been to her. She'd spent an entire morning with a man and not once had any violence occurred. And the laughter! She'd always loved to laugh but her brothers were so solemn—anyone living in the same house with Edmund Chatworth soon grew to be solemn. But today she'd laughed with a man and he'd not tried to tear her clothes off. Always before, if she even smiled at a man, he'd grabbed her, hurt her.

It wasn't that Elizabeth was so beautiful that she drove men to uncontrollable passion. She knew she was pretty, yes, but if she'd heard correctly she was no match for the Revedoune heiress. What had always made Elizabeth the victim of men's aggressions was her brother Edmund. His distorted sense of humor ran to wagering with his guests as to who could get Elizabeth in bed with him. Edmund hated that Elizabeth wasn't terrified of him. When she was a child he used to bring her home from the convent where she lived most of the time and he'd often hit her, knock her down stairs. But somehow Elizabeth had escaped uninjured.

When she was twelve, she began to stand up for herself. She'd successfully held off Edmund with a lighted torch. After that Edmund's game grew more serious, and Elizabeth grew more wary, more skillful at fending off her attackers. She'd learned how to hurt men who were trying to use her. She'd persuaded Roger to show her how to use an ax, a sword, a dagger. She knew how to defend herself with a razor-sharp tongue.

After weeks with Edmund and the men he surrounded himself with, Elizabeth would escape back to her convent, usually with Roger's help, and she'd be able to rest for a few weeks—until Edmund came for her again.

"I have the fire going, Lady Elizabeth," Kit said from behind her.

She turned a warm smile on him. Children had always been her love. Children were what they seemed, never trying to take from her, always giving freely. "You've done all the work and I've just been standing here." She went to him. "Perhaps you'd like me to tell you a story while we wait for your father."

She sat down, leaning against the wall, her feet toward the fire, her arm around Kit. Tossing Miles's cloak over them, she began to tell Kit about Moses and his people of Israel. Before she was to the Red Sea opening, Kit was asleep, curled up against her.

The rain beat down on the bit of roof over their heads, leaking in three places. While she watched the fire, Miles came in out of the mist, gave her a smile and fed the fire. He was silent as he skinned and dressed a young pig, cut the meat into chunks and set them to roast on sticks.

As she watched, she couldn't help but think what an odd man he was. Or were most men like him? Roger'd always said that Elizabeth only saw the dregs of mankind, and from the way some of the young women at the convent rhapsodized over their lovers, Elizabeth'd often thought that perhaps some men weren't like the ones she fought off.

Miles knelt by the fire, his hands quickly working with the meat. Within reach was his bow, his arrows over his back, his sword never leaving his side. Even as they'd been tumbling down the hill, Miles's sword had been attached to his hip. What sort of man could laugh with a woman and at the same time be prepared for danger?

"What are you thinking?" Miles asked quietly, his eyes intense.

She recovered herself. "That you're so wet you're about to drown the fire."

He stood, stretched. "This is a cold country, isn't it?" With that he slowly began to remove his wet clothes, spreading each piece by the fire.

Elizabeth watched him with detached interest. Nude men weren't unfamiliar to her, and often her brother's men had trained wearing the small loincloths. But she doubted if she'd ever really *looked* at any of the men.

Miles was lean but muscular and when he turned toward her, wearing only the loincloth, she saw he had a great amount of dark hair on his chest, a thick, V-shaped, curling abundance of it. His thighs were large, heavy from training in armor, and his calves were well developed.

"Elizabeth," Miles whispered. "You will have me blushing."

It was Elizabeth who blushed and could not meet his eyes when she heard him chuckle.

"Papa," Kit said, rousing. "I'm hungry."

Reluctantly, Elizabeth released the child. As much as she loved children, there had been few of them in her life. there was nothing quite like a child in her arms, needing her, trusting her, touching her.

"There's pork and a few apples," Miles told his son.

"Are you cold, Papa?" Kit asked.

Miles didn't look at Elizabeth. "I have the warm glances of a lady to keep me warm. Come eat with us, Lady Elizabeth."

Still pink-cheeked, Elizabeth joined them and it wasn't long before she got over her embarrassment. At Kit's insistence, Miles told stories of when he and his brothers were growing up. In every story, he was the hero, saving his brothers, teaching them. Kit's eyes shone like stars.

"And when you took your vows," Elizabeth said innocently, "didn't you foreswear lying?"

Miles's eyes twinkled. "I don't think they extended to impressing one's son or one's . . ." He seemed to search for a word.

"Captive?" she supplied.

"Ah, Elizabeth," he said languidly. "What would a lady think of a man whose older brothers constantly tried to make his life miserable?"

"Did they?"

She was so earnest in her question that he knew she took him literally. "No, not really," he reassured her. "We were left alone at an early age and I guess some of our pranks were a bit hazardous, but we all lived."

"Happily ever after," she said heavily.

"And what was it like living with Edmund Chatworth?" he asked casually.

Elizabeth shifted her legs under her. "He also liked . . . pranks," was all she'd say.

"Did you have enough, Kit?" Miles asked, and as he reached for another piece of pork, she saw the long gash on the inside of his wrist. It had opened again and was bleeding.

Miles never seemed to miss even a glance of hers. "The bow string hit it. You may doctor it if you wish," he said so eagerly, with so much hope, that she laughed at him.

She raised her skirt, tore off a long piece of petticoat and wet it in the rain. Miles sat cross-legged before her, his arm extended as she began to wash away the blood.

"I can't tell you how good it is to see you smile," he said. "Kit! Don't climb on those beams. Take the cloth from inside the quiver and clean my sword. And watch that you don't damage the edge." He looked back at Elizabeth. "I take it as an honor that you smile at me. I'm not sure, but I feel that you don't smile at many men."

"Very few," was all she'd answer.

He lifted her hand from his wrist and kissed her palm. "I'm beginning to think you're as angelic as you look. Kit adores you."

"I have a feeling Kit has never met a stranger, that he adores everyone."

"I don't." He kissed her hand again.

"Stop it!" She pulled away from him. "You are entirely too free with your kisses."

"I am doing very well at limiting myself to kisses. What I'd like to do is make love to you. Kit!" he yelled at his son who was waving the sword above his head. "I'll have your hide if you even consider thrusting that at anything."

In spite of herself, Elizabeth had to laugh as she thrust Miles's cleanly bandaged arm back to him. "I think you should leave your son at home when you try courting."

"Oh no." He smiled. "Kit has accomplished more than I could have in months."

With that cryptic remark, he moved to take his cherished sword from his son's reckless hands.

Chapter 7

THAT NIGHT the three of them slept together again, Kit firmly wedged between them. Elizabeth lay awake for a long time listening to the breathing of Miles and Kit. The past two days had been so unusual, so unlike anything she'd ever experienced before. It was like a bit of sunshine after years of rain.

When she woke she was alone on the cloak, the plaid tucked about her. Sleepily she smiled, snuggled deeper under the covers, and for a second she wished she could always stay in this place, that each day could be filled with laughter.

Turning to her back, stretching, she looked about the little shelter, saw that it was empty. Her senses had dulled over the last few days. Usually, she slept with one ear open, but somehow, Miles and Kit had managed to leave without disturbing her. She listened now for any sounds of them, smiling when she heard slow, quiet footsteps not too far away.

Stealthily, soundlessly, she left the shelter and faded into the surrounding forest. Once inside, hidden, she heard the unmistakable sounds of Kit and Miles to her left. Then who was skulking about in the undergrowth ahead of her?

Using all her years of experience at escaping her brother's friends, she slipped through the forest effortlessly. It was some minutes before she saw who was trying so hard to sneak up on them.

Lying on his stomach, his long, long body held immovable, was Sir Guy, only his head turning from side to side as he scanned the horizon where Kit and Miles scampered.

With no more sound than a breath of air, Elizabeth crept behind Sir Guy. Stooping, she picked up a small, elongated rock and clutched it in her fist. Roger had taught her that even her small, weak fist could carry some power if she held a hard object. With the rock in one hand, she bent and grabbed Sir Guy's small dagger from its sheath at his side.

The giant stood in one fluid, quick movement. "Lady Elizabeth!" he gasped.

Elizabeth stood back, at arm's length from the man. "Why are you following us? Did you betray your master and now you come to kill him?"

The scar across Sir Guy's face whitened but he didn't answer her. Instead, he turned his head in the direction of Miles and gave a high, piercing whistle.

Elizabeth knew Miles would come at the call, that it was a signal between them. If Sir Guy felt free to call his master, then Miles must know something of the reason for the giant's hidden presence.

In a remarkably short time, Miles appeared, sword drawn, alone.

"The lady asks if I mean to kill you," Sir Guy said solemnly.

Miles looked from one to the other. "How did she find you?"

Sir Guy's eyes never left Elizabeth's face. He seemed to be embarrassed and admiring all at once. "I didn't hear her."

Miles's eyes twinkled. "Give him back the dagger, Elizabeth. There needn't be any concern for Guy's loyalty."

Elizabeth didn't move. Her hand clutched the rock, hidden in the folds of her skirt, and at the same time she made note of the flat rock Sir Guy's softly clad foot was resting upon. Feet were vulnerable in even the strongest men.

"Where are your men?" she asked Miles, her eyes on Sir Guy.

"Well . . . Elizabeth," he began. "I thought perhaps . . ."

From the slight changes in Sir Guy's face, Elizabeth knew that whatever had been done had been Miles Montgomery's idea.

"Speak up!" she commanded.

"We're on MacArran land and I knew we'd be safe so I decided to walk with you and Kit. There's never been any danger."

She whirled to face him but kept Sir Guy in her

view. "This was all a trick," she said evenly. "You lied about your men disappearing. You lied about being in danger. You did this all in an attempt to get me alone."

"Elizabeth," he soothed. "We were surrounded by people. I thought perhaps that if we could be alone for a time you might come to know me. And Kit—"

"Don't profane that child's name! He was not in this ugly plot of yours."

"It wasn't a plot," he pleaded, his eyes soft.

"But what of danger? You risked my life and that of your son. These woods are full of savage men!"

Miles smiled patronizingly. "True, but these savages are related to me by marriage. I'm sure we're surrounded by MacArrans even now."

"I've heard no one except this great thrashing boar."

Sir Guy stiffened beside her.

"There was no harm done." Miles smiled at her. "Give me the dagger, Elizabeth."

"No harm except lies given to a woman," she spat at him.

After that, everything seemed to happen in a single flash. She lunged at Miles with the dagger. Sir Guy's hand knocked it from her grasp, and as the little knife went flying, Elizabeth's heel came down on the two smallest toes of Sir Guy's left foot. Miles, as he turned astonished eyes to Sir Guy's cry of pain, didn't see Elizabeth's fist, wrapped about the rock, as it plowed into his

101

stomach. With a great whoosh of pain, Miles bent over.

Elizabeth stepped back, watching as Sir Guy sat on the ground and tried to remove his boot, his face showing his pain. Miles looked as if he might lose his dinner.

"Well done," came a voice from behind her. She whirled about to look into the face of a strikingly beautiful woman, with black hair and blue eyes, as tall as Elizabeth, which was rare. A big dog stood beside her.

"That should teach you, Miles," she continued, "that all women don't appreciate being used as a man sees fit."

Elizabeth's eyes widened as from the trees men began to drop and, coming from the direction of the cottage, an older man was leading Kit by the hand.

"Lady Elizabeth Chatworth," the woman said, "I am Bronwyn MacArran, laird of Clan MacArran and sister-in-law to this scheming young man."

Miles was recovering himself. "Bronwyn, it's good to see you again."

"Tam," Bronwyn said to the older man. "See to Sir Guy's foot. Did you break it?"

"Probably," Elizabeth answered. "When I've done it before I've found it usually breaks the man's smallest toe."

Bronwyn gave her an acknowledging look of appreciation. "These are my men. Douglas." As she called each man's name, he stepped forward, nodded at Lady Elizabeth. "Alex, Jarl and Francis."

Elizabeth gave each man a hard, appraising look. She didn't like being surrounded by men and she moved so Sir Guy was no longer behind her. The many men near her made her feel as if she were locked in a small stone cell.

Miles, rubbing his stomach, noticed the move and came to stand nearer to Elizabeth, and when Tam took a step closer, Miles touched the man's arm, his eyes giving warning. With a quick frown of puzzlement, Tam released Kit and stepped away from Elizabeth, noticing that her eyes were wary, watching.

"And where is my worthless brother?" Miles asked Bronwyn, who was quietly watching the scene before her.

"He is patroling the northern borders but I expect him to meet us before we reach Larenston."

Miles took Elizabeth's arm, tightened his grip when she tried to move away from him. "Bronwyn has a baby," he said aloud. Under his breath, he whispered, "You're safe. Stay close to me."

Elizabeth gave him a withering look that said she didn't feel he was safer than any other man, but she didn't move from his side. The men who stood close to Bronwyn were wildly dressed, their knees bare, their hair down to their shoulders, great long wide swords at their belts.

Bronwyn felt there was more wrong than just

Miles's childish trick played on Elizabeth, but she had no idea what it was. Perhaps when they returned to Larenston she could find out what this tension in the air meant. "Shall we ride?"

Elizabeth stood still, not moving until Bronwyn's men were in front of her. There was a long walk to where the horses were hidden and the men were a silent group. Sir Guy hobbled along slowly, leaning on a thick staff.

"I want to ride behind the men," Elizabeth said to Miles, her jaw set.

He started to protest but stopped, murmured something to Bronwyn and at her nod, the Scotsmen and Sir Guy rode ahead, Kit settled with Tam.

"Elizabeth," Miles began from atop the horse beside her. "Bronwyn's men mean you no harm. There's no reason to fear them."

She glared at him. "Am I to take your word for their trustworthiness? You who have lied to me? You who are of a family that is at war with my family?"

Miles glanced heavenward for a moment. "Perhaps I was wrong to play the trick on you, but if I'd asked you to spend a few days frolicking in the forest with Kit and me, what would have been your answer?"

She looked away from him.

"Elizabeth, you must admit you enjoyed yourself. There, for a few hours, you weren't afraid of men."

"I am *never* afraid of men," she snapped. "I

have merely learned to be cautious.''

"Your caution overtakes your entire life," he said sternly. "Look at us now, eating the dust of Bronwyn's men because you fear that one of them will attack you if you don't have him in your sight.''

"I have learned—'' she began.

"You have learned only the bad part of life! Most men are not like Edmund Chatworth or Pagnell. While we're here in Scotland you're going to learn that some men can be trusted. No!'' he said, his eyes locking with hers. "You are going to learn that *I* can be trusted.'' With that he spurred his horse forward to ride beside Sir Guy, leaving Elizabeth alone.

Bronwyn glanced back at Elizabeth, then turned her horse to ride beside the blonde woman. They were a striking pair: Elizabeth with her delicate fair features; Bronwyn's strong, sculptured features.

"A lovers' quarrel?'' Bronwyn asked, her eyes searching Elizabeth's face.

"We are not lovers," Elizabeth said coolly.

Bronwyn raised her eyebrows at that, thinking that it must be a first for Miles to spend any time with a woman and not possess her. "And how does a Chatworth come to ride with a Montgomery?'' she asked in the same tone as Elizabeth had used with her,

Elizabeth gave Bronwyn a scathing look. "If you plan to pour out venom about my brother Roger, you should think twice.''

Bronwyn and Elizabeth faced each other across the horses and after a moment—in which many signals passed between them—Bronwyn gave a curt nod. "Ask your brother about his Scots relatives," she said frigidly before reining her horse away, leaving Elizabeth to herself.

"And have you angered Bronwyn?" Miles asked when he once again rode beside her.

"Am I to listen to all manner of evilness against my own brother? That woman swore to marry Roger but went back on her word. And as a result—"

"As a result Roger Chatworth attacked my brother's back," Miles interrupted. He paused, leaned across her horse to take her hand in his. "Give us a chance, Elizabeth," he said softly, his eyes meltingly imploring. "All I ask is that you give all of us time to show you that we can be trusted."

Before Elizabeth could answer, the sound of thundering hooves came to them. With a glance up, she saw that every man had his claymore drawn, and before she could protest, Bronwyn's Scots had encircled the two women. Miles moved his horse closer to Elizabeth.

"It's that idiot husband of mine," Bronwyn said, and her pleased tone was completely at odds with her words.

Five men came to a halt before them, the leader a tall man with dark blond hair that came to his shoulders, a good-looking man who was obviously enjoying the sparks his wife was shooting at him.

"You're getting old, Tam," the blond man said lazily, leaning on the front of his saddle.

Tam merely gave a grunt and resheathed his claymore.

"Damn you, Stephen," Bronwyn hissed. "Why were you riding along the cliff like that? And why didn't you give any warning of your approach?"

Slowly, he dismounted his horse, tossed the reins to one of the men behind him and walked toward his wife. Casually, he put his hand on her ankle and started traveling upward.

Bronwyn kicked out at him. "Let me go!" she demanded. "I have more important duties than to play games with you."

With lightning quickness, Stephen caught her waist and hauled her out of the saddle. "Did you worry about me riding along the cliff?" he murmured, pulling her to him.

"Tam!" Bronwyn gasped, pushing at Stephen.

"The lad needs no help from me," Tam answered.

"But I would be willing to help," Miles said quietly.

Stephen released his wife abruptly. "Miles," he gasped, and hugged his brother when Miles was dismounted. "When did you arrive? Why are you in Scotland? I thought you were with Uncle Simon—and what's this I hear about Uncle Simon wanting your head on a platter?"

Miles gave a bit of a smile and a shrug to his brother.

Stephen grimaced as he knew he wasn't likely to

get anything from his younger brother. Miles was so closemouthed it was infuriating.

"Miles brought Elizabeth Chatworth," Bronwyn said flatly.

Stephen turned to look through the men and upwards to see Elizabeth. For all her soft features, she looked rigid, unbending, as she sat stiffly in the saddle. Stephen started toward her but Miles caught his arm.

"Do not touch her," Miles said conversationally as he moved toward Elizabeth.

After a second's astonishment, Stephen grinned. He well understood jealousy; he'd just never seen it in his brother before.

As Miles put his arms up to Elizabeth and she hesitated, he said, "Stephen will not harm you and he'll be expecting the same courtesy." there was a twinkle in Miles's eyes.

Elizabeth couldn't help a slight smile as she glanced at Sir Guy, who had shot a couple of glances toward her that said she was part monster, part witch. They had to wait to be introduced to Stephen because Kit, who'd fallen asleep against Tam, had wakened and launched himself onto his beloved uncle. Stephen had Kit settled on one arm as he extended his hand to Elizabeth.

Elizabeth stood rigid and did not take his hand.

Miles sent his brother a look of warning and Stephen, with a knowing smile, dropped his hand.

"You are welcome to our home," Stephen said.

"I am a Chatworth."

"And I am a Montgomery *and*"—he glanced at

Bronwyn—"a MacArran. You *are* welcome. Shall we walk along the cliff? It's steep and can sometimes be frightening."

"I can ride a horse," Elizabeth said flatly.

Miles took her arm, raised her fingers to his lips. "Of course you can. My clumsy brother is only trying to make an excuse to talk to you."

"Uncle Stephen!" Kit said. He'd been trying so hard to wait until the adults were finished speaking. "Lady Elizabeth hit Papa and made Sir Guy limp and we slept in the forest without a tent or anything." He smiled at Elizabeth who winked back at him.

"Made Sir Guy limp?" Stephen laughed. "Somehow I doubt that."

"Lady Elizabeth Chatworth broke Sir Guy's toes," Bronwyn said coolly.

Stephen narrowed his eyes at his wife. "I'm not sure I like your tone."

Miles spoke quickly to get his brother's attention. "How are the MacGregors?"

What followed was half-description, half-argument as Bronwyn and Stephen talked of the clan that had been the enemy of Clan MacArran for centuries—until a few months ago when a truce had been made. Bronwyn's brother Davy had married the daughter of the MacGregor.

As they talked, they walked along the treacherous cliff road, one side high rock, the other a sheer drop. Elizabeth, caught close to Miles, beside Stephen, Bronwyn ahead of them, listened with no little fascination to the exchange

109

between the married couple. They argued heatedly but with absolutely no animosity. The men behind them talked among themselves, so this bantering was obviously not new to them. Bronwyn taunted Stephen, called him several names and Stephen merely smiled at her and told her her ideas were ridiculous. Of all the marriages Elizabeth had seen, the husband would have blackened the wife's eye if she'd said half what Bronwyn was saying.

Elizabeth glanced at Miles, saw he was smiling benignly at Bronwyn and his brother. Kit began to enter the argument, taking Bronwyn's side, running ahead to grab her hand.

"He's your son." Stephen laughed, looking at his brother.

Because Stephen looked toward Miles, toward the rock wall, he saw the rocks tumbling from above—aiming for Elizabeth. With a knight's instincts, he acted as quickly as he thought, making a leaping grab for Elizabeth. The two of them slammed into the rock wall, Stephen's big body pinning Elizabeth, crushing her as the rock fell behind him.

Elizabeth also reacted without thinking. For a few moments, her guard had been down, but with men behind her, beside her, she'd remained nervous. Her senses did not register the reason for Stephen's abrupt attack but only knew that once again a man was threatening her.

She panicked. Not just a small uproar, but Elizabeth let out a scream that startled the already

110

nervous horses. And she didn't stop with one scream, but she began clawing and kicking like a caged wild animal.

Stephen, stunned by her reaction, tried to catch her shoulders. "Elizabeth," he shouted into her terrified face.

Miles had been struck on the shoulder and back by falling stones, knocking him to his knees. The moment he heard Elizabeth's screams he went to her.

"Goddamn you!" he bellowed at his brother. "I told you not to touch her." With a hard push he shoved Stephen away, tried to catch Elizabeth.

"Quiet!" he commanded.

Elizabeth was still in a frenzy, scratching Miles, trying to tear away from him.

He caught her shoulders, gave her a sharp shake. "Elizabeth," he said patiently, loudly. "You are safe. Do you hear me? Safe." It took another shake before she turned eyes to his—eyes such as Miles had never seen before, frightened, terrified, helpless eyes. For a moment they looked at each other and Miles used all his strength of character to will her into peacefulness. "You are safe now, my love. You'll always be safe with me."

Her body began trembling and he pulled her into his arms, held her close to him, stroked her hair. When he glanced at Stephen standing near them, he said, "Leave a horse. We'll follow later."

Elizabeth was hardly aware of the funeral-quiet procession passing them. Her fear had made her weak and all she could do was lean against Miles for support, while he stroked her cheek, her neck, her arm. After many minutes, she pulled away from him.

"I have made an ass of myself," she said with such despair that Miles smiled at her.

"Stephen didn't understand when I told him not to touch you. I'm sure he thought it was mere jealousy."

"You are not jealous?" she asked, pulling away, trying to change the subject.

"Perhaps. But your fears are more important than my jealousy."

"My fears, as you call them, are none of your concern." She succeeded in pulling completely away from him.

"Elizabeth." His voice was pleading, very low. "Don't keep all this inside you. I've told you I'm a good listener. Talk to me. Tell me what has made you so afraid."

She caught the rock wall with her hands behind her. The solid mass felt good, gave her a feeling of reality. "Why have you sent the others away?"

A flicker of anger crossed his eyes. "So I'd have no witnesses when I ravished you. Why else?" When he saw that she wasn't sure he was being sarcastic, he threw up his hands in despair. "Come on, let's go to Larenston." He grabbed her arm much too hard. "You know what you need, Elizabeth? You need someone to make love to you, to show you that your fear is much worse than the reality."

"I've had many volunteers for the task," she hissed at him.

"From what I've seen, you've known only rapists—not lovers."

With that, he practically tossed her into the saddle and mounted behind her.

Chapter 8

ELIZABETH PUT her hand to her forehead and opened her eyes slowly. The big room where she lay upon the bed was empty, dark. It had been many hours since she and Miles had ridden into the fortress of Clan MacArran. It was an ancient place, set on the edge of a cliff like some giant eagle using its talons to hold on. Some woman who looked as old as the castle handed Elizabeth a hot drink laced with herbs, and when the woman's back was turned, Elizabeth dumped the drink into the rushes behind a bench. Elizabeth had a knowledge of herbs and she had a good guess as to what the drink contained.

The gnarled little woman, whom Bronwyn called Morag, watched Elizabeth with sharp eyes and after a few moments Elizabeth feigned sleepiness and lay upon the bed.

"She needs the rest," Bronwyn said over her. "I've never seen anyone go insane quite as she did when Stephen pulled her from under the falling

114

rocks. It was as if demons had suddenly entered her body.''

Morag gave a little snort. "Ye fought Stephen long and hard when ye first met him.''

"It wasn't the same," Bronwyn insisted. "Miles calmed her but only after a long time of shaking her. Did you know she broke Sir Guy's toes?''

"And I heard the two of ye quarreled," Morag snapped.

Bronwyn straightened defensively. "She dares to defend Roger Chatworth to me. After what he has done—''

"He's her brother!" Morag spat. "Ye would expect her to be loyal yet ye seem to think she should see your way at once. Bronwyn, there is more than one way of things in the world." She bent and spread a large blue and green plaid over Elizabeth's quiet form. "Let's leave her in peace. A messenger has come from Stephen's eldest brother.''

"Why didn't you tell me?" Bronwyn said, angry at being treated as a child and more angry because she deserved the treatment.

Elizabeth lay perfectly still after the door had closed, listening for anyone's breathing. Sometimes men had pretended they'd left a room but in truth they were actually only hiding in dark corners. When she was sure she was alone, she turned over and cautiously opened her eyes. She was indeed alone.

She sprang from the bed and went to the window. It was just growing dark outside, the moonlight beginning to silver the steep walls of the gray stone castle. Now was the time to escape, now before a routine was set, before all the MacArrans were informed she was a prisoner.

As she watched, on the ground below, four men walked past, their bodies sheathed in plaids. With a smile, Elizabeth began to form a plan. A quick, silent search of the room revealed a chest of men's clothes. She pulled up the silk skirt of her gown, tied it about her waist, then pulled on a voluminous men's shirt and slipped into heavy wool socks. For just a second, she looked down at her knees, blinked at the idea of appearing in public so very bare—nude almost. There were no shoes so she had to make do with her own soft shoes, her toes tightly jammed with the added bulk of the socks. Rolling the plaid about her so it formed a short skirt and could be tossed across a shoulder took several attempts, and she was sure she still didn't have it right when she tied a belt about her waist. It was much too long to buckle.

With her breath held, she cautiously opened the door, praying that as yet no guard had been posted outside her door. Her luck held and she slipped through a narrow opening and out into the dim hall. She'd memorized the way out of the castle when Miles had led her to the room and now, as she paused to get her bearings, she listened for sounds.

Far away, to her left and below, she could hear voices. Slowly, melting into the wall, she glided down the stairs toward the main exit. Just as she was moving past the room where people were gathered, she heard the name Chatworth. She glanced toward the door to the outside but at the same time she wanted information. With no more noise than a shadow, she moved to where she could hear.

Stephen was speaking. "Damn *both* of you, Miles!" Anger permeated his voice. "Gavin has no more sense than you do. The two of you are helping Chatworth accomplish what he wants. He's coming close to destroying our family."

Miles remained silent.

Bronwyn put her hand on Miles's arm. "Please release her. Lady Elizabeth can return to England with an armed guard and when Gavin hears she's released, he'll let Roger Chatworth go."

Still Miles did not speak.

"Goddamn you!" Stephen bellowed. "Answer us!"

Miles's eyes ignited. "I will not release Elizabeth. What Gavin does with Roger Chatworth is my brother's business. Elizabeth is mine."

"If you weren't my brother—" Stephen began.

"If I weren't your brother, what I did would have no effect on you." Miles was quite calm, only his eyes showing his anger.

Stephen threw up his hands in despair. "You talk to him," he said to Bronwyn. "None of my brothers has any sense at all."

Bronwyn planted herself before her husband. "Once you fought Roger Chatworth for what you believed to be yours. Now Miles is doing exactly the same thing and yet you rage at him.''

''It was different then,'' Stephen said sullenly. ''You were given to me by the king.''

''And Elizabeth was given to me!'' Miles interjected with great passion. ''Bronwyn, am I welcome here? If not I and my men will leave—with Lady Elizabeth.''

''You know you are welcome,'' Bronwyn said softly. ''Unless Chatworth is prepared for war, he'll not attack the MacArrans.'' She turned to Stephen. ''And as for Gavin holding Chatworth prisoner, I'm glad for it. Do you forget what Chatworth did to your sister Mary or that he held me prisoner for a month?''

Elizabeth slipped away after hearing those words. They were going to find that she wasn't the docile captive they assumed she would be.

Outside, a fog was rolling in from the sea and she smiled in secret thanks for the Lord's help. Her first necessity was to get a horse because she could not walk out of Scotland. Standing still, she listened, stiffly intent, trying to ascertain where the stables were.

Elizabeth was quite good at stealing horses; she'd had a great deal of practice in her short lifetime. Horses were like children. They needed to be talked to quietly, simply, with no quick movements. There were two men at one end of the stables, laughing, talking in low tones about the latest women they'd bedded.

With great stealth, Elizabeth eased a bridled

horse from the far end of the long stable. She pulled a saddle from the stall wall and waited until she was outside before saddling the animal. She thanked heaven for the relative noisiness of so many people living together on a few acres of land. A creaky cart went by; a man leading four horses tied the animals not far from the stables and two of the horses started nipping each other. As a consequence, three men began shouting and cracking whips. None of the people milling about even glanced at the slight figure in the shadows, a plaid covering the person's head.

When Elizabeth mounted, she lazily followed the cart out the open gates of Larenston and, like the cart driver, raised her hand in silent greeting to the guards above her. The guards were there to keep people from entering; people leaving were of little interest to them.

The only way to reach the MacArran fortress was across a frighteningly narrow bit of land. Elizabeth's already racing heart threatened to break her ribs. The cart in front of her was unusually narrow and, even so, its wheels rode just on the edges of the road—inches in either direction and the man, cart and horse would be over the side.

When she reached the end of the road, she breathed a sigh of relief for several reasons—the end of the treacherous path and, so far, no alarm had been sounded.

The cart driver looked over his shoulder and grinned at her. "Always glad when I come off that path. Are ye goin' this way?"

Straight ahead was the easy way, through the crofters' farms where people would see her and could give a search party directions. To the right was the cliff road, the one she and Miles had ridden on. To ride along the cliff at night . . .

"Nay!" she said in her huskiest voice to the cart driver. Obviously the man would want to talk if she rode with him. She pointed a plaid-covered arm toward the cliff.

"You young'uns!" The man chuckled. "Well, good luck to ye, lad. There's plenty of moonlight, but watch yer step." With that he clucked to his horse and drove away.

Elizabeth lost no time in contemplating her fear but urged her mare toward the black emptiness before her. At night the road looked worse than she remembered. Her horse fidgeted and after only a second's hesitation, she dismounted and began to lead her.

"Damn Miles Montgomery!" she muttered. Why did he have to come to a savage place like this? If he were going to hold someone captive, he should have done it in civilized surroundings.

The howl of a wolf directly overhead made her stop muttering. Silhouetted atop the cliff were three wolves, heads low, watching her. The horse danced about and Elizabeth wrapped the reins around her wrist. As she moved, the wolves moved with her. Another one joined the pack.

It seemed to Elizabeth that she had traveled for miles but she couldn't even see the end of the cliff road. For a moment, she leaned against the rock wall, tried to calm her racing heart.

The wolves, seeming to believe their victim was admitting defeat, growled collectively. The horse reared, tore the reins from Elizabeth's hands. She made a leap for the horse, lost her footing and fell half over the edge of the cliff. The freed horse went tearing down the path.

She lay still for a moment, trying to regain her composure and to figure out how to free herself. Precariously, she clung to the edge of the cliff, one leg dangling with no support, her other foot straining to hold on. Her arms were hugging rock, her chin pressing downward. She moved her left arm, and as she did, rock crumbled from under her. With a gasp of terror she began to move her right leg to search for a foothold—but found none. Another bit of rock crumbled and she knew she had to do something.

Using every bit of strength in her arms, she tried to push herself up, inching her hips to the left. When her left knee caught on the solid rock road, she had to blink away tears of relief. Inch by slow inch, she moved her aching, bruised body back onto the road.

On hands and knees she crawled to the safety of the rock wall and sat there, tears rolling down her cheeks, her chest heaving. Blood trickled down her arms and her raw knees burned.

Above her came a great cry of animals fighting. Pushing herself away from the wall, she saw an animal attacking the wolves. "That great dog of

Bronwyn's," she gasped and closed her eyes in silent prayer for a moment.

She didn't sit there long. Soon her disappearance would be discovered and she needed to be well ahead of her Montgomery enemies.

When she stood, she realized she was hurt worse than she thought. Her left leg was stiff, her ankle painful. When she wiped away the tears from her cheeks, her hand showed bloody in the moonlight. With raw palms, she began to feel her way along the road, not trusting her sight to guide her but needing the solid rock for direction.

The moon had set by the time she reached the end of the road, but instead of being frightening, the black open space was welcome to her. She pulled the plaid closer about her, ignored her weak legs and began walking.

When two pinpoints of light shone at her, chest height, she gasped, stopped, looked about for some weapon. For several moments she locked eyes with the animal, whatever it was, before it moved. The animal was almost touching her before she realized it was Bronwyn's dog.

The dog cocked its head at her quizzically and Elizabeth wanted to cry with relief.

"You killed the wolves, didn't you?" she said. "Good boy. Are you friendly?" Tentatively, she put out her hand, palm up, and was rewarded with a lick of the dog's tongue. As she began stroking the animal's big head, it nudged her hand, pushing her back toward the cliff road.

"No, boy," she whispered. Her standing still was making her feel her cuts and bruises more. And it seemed like days since she'd slept. "I want to go this way, not back to Bronwyn."

The dog gave a sharp yip at his mistress's name.

"No!" she said firmly.

The dog watched her for a moment as if considering her words, then turned toward the forest ahead of them.

"Good boy." She smiled. "Maybe you can lead me out of this place. Lead me to another clan that will return me to my brother for the reward he'll pay."

She walked behind the dog, but as she began to stumble, it stopped, nudging under her arm until she began to lean on it. "What's your name, boy?" she whispered tiredly. "Is it George or Oliver or is it some Scots name I've never heard?"

The dog slowed its step even more for her.

"How about Charlie?" she said. "I rather like the name Charlie."

With that she collapsed in a heap beside the dog, asleep, or perhaps in a faint.

The dog nudged her, sniffed her, licked her bloody face, and when nothing made her rise he settled beside her and slept.

The sun was high overhead when Elizabeth woke and looked up at the massive, shaggy head of the dog. The animal's eyes were questioning, as concerned about her as a human. There was an ugly cut covered with dried blood under one of the dog's eyes.

"Get that from fighting the wolves?" She smiled up at the dog, scratching its ears. As she started to rise, her legs gave way under her and she clutched the dog. "It's a good thing you're strong, Charlie," she said, using the dog's back to brace herself.

When she was at last on her feet, she looked down at herself and groaned. Her skirt was half tied up, half hanging down to her ankles. Her left knee was cut, scraped, still oozing blood, while her right knee was merely raw. With determination, she tossed the plaid over her arms, not wanting to see the damage done to them. When she touched her hair she felt dried bits of blood so she moved her hand away.

"Can you find some water, Charlie?" she asked the dog. "Water?"

The dog took off instantly across the rocky landscape, returning when Elizabeth could follow only at a snail's pace. The newly healed scabs had opened and there were warm trickles of blood on her body.

The dog led her to a small stream where she washed as best she could. When she met her liberators, she wanted to be as presentable as possible.

She and the dog walked for hours, staying close to the rocks and the few trees. Once they heard horses and instinctively Elizabeth hid, pulling the dog to her side. There was no way she could have held the big dog had it decided to leave her, but for the moment the animal seemed content to stay with her.

By sundown, what little strength she had left was gone, and it didn't seem to matter when the dog began barking at something she couldn't see. "No doubt it's Miles or your mistress," she said heavily and slid to the ground, closing her eyes.

When she opened them again a man she'd never seen before stood over her, legs wide, hands on hips. The dying sunlight haloed his gray hair, made shadows on his strong jaw.

"Well, Rab," he said in a deep voice, stroking the dog, "what have you brought me this time?"

"Don't touch me," Elizabeth whispered as the man bent toward her.

"If you're worried I'll harm you in any way, young woman, you needn't be. I'm the MacGregor and you're on my land. Why is Bronwyn's dog with *you?*" He eyed her English clothes.

Elizabeth was tired, weak, hungry, but she wasn't dead. The way this man said Bronwyn told her they were friends. Tears began falling down her cheeks. Now she'd never get home. No friend of the MacArrans would return her to England, and Roger's capture by a Montgomery could start a private war.

"Don't greet so, lass," the MacGregor said. "Soon you'll be in a nice safe place. Someone will tend to your cuts and we'll feed you and— What the hell!"

Elizabeth, as the man leaned closer, had pulled his dirk from its sheath and aimed for his stomach. Sheer weakness had made her miss.

Lachlan MacGregor sidestepped, took the dirk from her and flung her over his shoulder in one quick movement. "Give me no more trouble, lass," he commanded when she started to struggle. "In Scotland we don't repay kindness by stabbing someone."

He tossed Elizabeth on his horse, whistled for Rab to follow and the three of them set off at a furious pace.

Chapter 9

Elizabeth sat alone in a big room in the Mac-Gregor castle, the oak door barred. The room was mostly bare except for an enormous bed, a chest and three chairs. A fireplace was along one wall, filled with logs, but no fire warmed the cold stones.

Elizabeth huddled in one of the chairs, the plaid from Bronwyn wrapped about her, her sore knees drawn in to her chest. It had been several hours since the MacGregor had tossed her in the room without so much as a backward glance. No food had been sent to her, no water for washing, and the dog, Rab, had bounded away at the first sight of the MacGregor fortress. Elizabeth was too tired to sleep, her mind in too much of a turmoil to allow her much rest.

When she first heard the familiar voice, muffled through the heavy door, her first reaction was one of relief. But she quickly recovered from that. Miles Montgomery was as much her enemy as anyone else.

When Miles opened the door and walked in boldly, she was ready for him. She sent a copper and silver goblet from the mantelpiece flying at his head.

Miles caught the object in his left hand and kept walking toward her.

She threw a small shield from the wall at him and he caught that in his right hand.

With a little smile of triumph, Elizabeth grabbed a battered helmet from the mantel and drew back her arm to throw it. He had no more hands with which to catch this object.

But before she could throw the helmet, Miles was before her, his arms drawing her close to him.

"I was very worried about you," he whispered, his face buried against her cheek. "Why did you run away like that? Scotland isn't like England. It's treacherous country."

He didn't hold her very tightly, at least not enough to cause her to want to struggle, but instead she almost wished he'd pull her closer. As it was, she had to stand very still or else his arms might drop away altogether. At his idiot words, though, she did move away. "I am attacked by wolves, nearly fall into the sea and some man throws me about like a sack of grain and *you* tell *me* this is treacherous country!"

Miles touched her temple and she did not move away from him. There was an unusual light in his eyes. "Elizabeth, you make your own problems."

"I did not ask to be delivered into my enemy's hands nor to be brought as a prisoner into this hostile country and as for that man—"

Miles interrupted her. "The MacGregor was quite angry at your taking a knife to him. A few months ago he nearly died from Bronwyn's using a knife on him."

"But they seemed to be friends."

Before she could speak another word, the chamber door opened and in walked two brawny Scotsmen carrying an oak tub. Behind them came a dozen women bearing buckets of hot water. The last woman held a tray with three decanters and two goblets.

"Knowing your propensity for not bathing, I have taken the liberty of ordering a bath." Miles smiled at her.

Elizabeth didn't answer him but put her nose into the air and turned toward the cold fireplace.

When the room was empty of people except for the two of them, Miles put his hand on her shoulder. "Come and bathe while the water is hot, Elizabeth."

She whirled on him. "Why should you think that I'd do for you what I haven't done for other men? I ran away from you at Larenston and now you seem to think I'll leap into your arms because you've shown up here. What difference does it make whether I'm held prisoner by the MacGregor or a Montgomery? If the truth be known, I prefer the MacGregor."

Miles's jaw hardened and his eyes darkened. "I think it's time some things were made clear between us. I have been more than patient with you. I have stood by silently while you hurt Sir Guy. I have shared my son with you. I have watched as you put the entire Clan MacArran in turmoil and now you've come close to injuring the MacGregor. The peace between the MacGregors and MacArrans is too new and fragile. You could have destroyed what it's taken Stephen a year to build. And look at you, Elizabeth! Have you seen yourself? There is dried blood all over you, you're obviously exhausted and you've lost much weight. I think it's time I stopped letting you have your own way."

"My . . . !" she sputtered. "I do not want to be held prisoner! Do you understand me? Can I get anything through your thick head? I want to go home to my brothers and I will do whatever I can to get there."

"Home!" Miles said through clenched teeth. "Do you have any idea what the word means? Where did you learn how to break men's toes? How to use a knife so efficiently? What made you decide all men were evil creatures? Why can't you abide any man's touch?"

Elizabeth just looked at him sullenly. "Edmund is dead," she said after a while.

"Will you always live under a cloud, Elizabeth?" he whispered, his eyes soft. "Will you always see only what you want to see?" After a long sigh, he held out his hand to her. "Come and bathe before the water cools."

"No," she said slowly. "I don't want to bathe."

She should have been used to Miles's extraordinary quickness, but as usual she was unprepared for it.

"I've had enough of this, Elizabeth," he said before tossing the damp plaid from her. "I've been patient and kind but from now on you're going to learn a little obedience—and trust. I am not going to harm you; I have *never* harmed any woman but I cannot stand by and allow you to hurt yourself."

With that, he tore the front of her dress away, exposing her breasts.

Elizabeth gasped, crossed her arms in front of her and jumped back.

Easily, Miles caught her, and in two swift tears he had her nude. He didn't seem to pay any attention to her body as he picked her up and carried her to the tub where he gently set her into the water.

Without a word, he picked up a cloth, soaped it and began to gently wash her face. "Struggle and the soap will be in your eyes," he said, making her hold still.

She refused to speak to him while he washed the upper half of her body, glad for the soap that hid her red face as his hands glided lingeringly over her high, firm breasts.

"How did you hurt yourself?" he asked conversationally as he soaped her left leg, careful of the ugly cuts and scrapes on her knee.

The water was relaxing her and there was no reason not to tell him. She lay back in the tub,

131

closed her eyes and told him of the night she'd spent along the cliff road. Halfway through the story, a glass of wine touched her hand and she drank of it thirstily. The intoxicant immediately went to her head and, dreamily, she kept talking.

"Rab stayed with me," she concluded, drinking more wine. "The dog understood that I didn't want to go to Bronwyn, but instead he led me to Bronwyn's friend." The wine was making her so relaxed she didn't even feel angry at the dog or the MacGregor or anyone else.

"Miles," she said conversationally, unaware of the pleasure she gave him in using his Christian name. "Why *don't* you strike women? I don't believe I've met a man who doesn't use force to get his way."

He was gently washing her toes. "Perhaps I use a different kind of force."

That was all he was going to say and for a while they were silent. Elizabeth didn't realize that he kept her glass full of wine and by now she had drunk nearly an entire decanterful.

"Why didn't you speak up to your brother this morning? Or was it yesterday morning?"

Miles's momentary pause in washing her was his only sign that he understood her question. She'd never really asked something so personal before, as if she were interested in him.

"My three elder brothers are very pig-headed men. Gavin's never heard anyone's opinion except his own and Raine likes to imagine himself as a martyr for all lost causes."

"And Stephen?" she asked, drinking more wine, watching him through lowered lashes. His hands on her felt so very, very good.

"Stephen fools people into believing he's a willing compromiser, but when it comes to the point, he insists upon his own way. Only for Bronwyn was he willing to look at someone else's view, and she had to fight him—and still fights—for everything. He makes jests about what to her is life and death."

Elizabeth considered this for a moment. "And you are their little brother. No doubt they will always consider you someone to be instructed, someone who must be taken care of."

"And is that the way you are treated also?" he half whispered.

The drink, the hot water, made her loosen her tongue. "Roger thinks I have only a quarter of a brain. Half is missing because I am a woman, half of that gone because he remembers me in swaddling clothes. When I told him some of what Edmund was doing to me, he wasn't sure whether to believe me or not. Or perhaps he didn't want to see the things his own brother did or allowed to happen.

"Damn!" she said, half rising from the tub. With a violent jerk she threw the goblet across the room, slamming it into the stone wall. "I *am* half a woman. Do you know what it feels like to watch Bronwyn and your brother, to see them laugh and love? The two of them sneak little touches when they think no one is looking. Whenever a man touches me, I—"

She broke off, her eyes wide, her head reeling from the drink. "Make love to me, Miles Montgomery," she whispered huskily. "Make me not afraid."

"I had planned to," he said throatily as he pulled her into his arms.

She still stood in the tub, and as Miles's mouth came down on hers, she kissed him back—kissed him with all the passion, all the anger she felt at having been cheated of a normal attitude toward love. While other women were learning how to flirt, Elizabeth's brother had been gambling, promising his little sister's virginity to the winner, and Elizabeth had learned to use a knife. She had preserved her precious virginity and for what? The convent? For a life where she grew harder and angrier every year until she turned to stone—an unloved, useless old woman?

Miles pulled back from her slightly, controlling the kiss, keeping her from hurting herself as she tried to grind her lips against his teeth. His hands were playing up and down her wet back, his fingertips caressing the indentation of her spine.

His lips moved to the corner of her mouth, his tongue touching the tip of hers before he trailed to her cheek, kissing her while his hands toyed with her skin.

Elizabeth tilted her head back and to one side as Miles's teeth ran along her neck and to her shoulder. Perhaps this was the true reason why she'd never allowed a man to touch her. Maybe she'd always known that unless she fought like a demon she'd succumb like this—wantonly, unashamedly.

"Miles," she whispered. "Miles."

"Always," he murmured, nibbling her ear.

With one swift motion he lifted her from the tub and carried her to the bed. Her body was wet, her hair cold and clinging to her, but Miles wrapped a towel about her and began rubbing. The briskness of his rubbing sent new warmth through her and everywhere, every time he touched her she wanted more. She had a whole lifetime of touching to make up for.

Suddenly Miles was beside her, nude, his glorious skin warm, dark, inviting.

"I am yours, Elizabeth, as you are mine," he whispered as he placed her hand on his chest.

"So much hair." She giggled. "So very much hair." She buried her fingers in the short black curling stuff and pulled. Obediently, Miles rolled closer to her, snuggled her golden body to the length of him.

"What does it feel like?" she asked anxiously.

"You'll not know for a long while." He smiled. "When we become one, there'll be no fear in your eyes."

"Become one," she whispered as Miles again began to kiss her neck. He kissed her neck for a very long time before he moved to her arm, his tongue making little swirling motions inside her elbow. It was odd how little vibrations seemed to be traveling from her fingertips, across her breasts to her other fingertips.

She lay still, eyes closed, arms open, legs open as Miles touched her. Those big hands that could wield a sword, could protect a child from harm, could control an unruly horse, were tenderly, slowly setting her body on fire.

When his hand moved from her throat to her cheek, she turned her head and kissed the palm, put both her hands on his and began to make love to that hard delicate hand, scraping it against her teeth, tasting his skin, running her tongue around and around the hairs on the back of his hand.

She was rewarded by a primitive sound from Miles that set her heart racing.

"Elizabeth," he groaned. "Elizabeth. How I have waited."

Elizabeth decided she wasn't really in the mood for more waiting. Instinctively she tried to wiggle further under Miles, but he refused to allow that. Instead, he brought his mouth to her breast and Elizabeth nearly came off the bed.

Miles chuckled at her reaction and she felt his laughter all along the length of her. Love and laughter, she thought. That's what Miles had added to her life.

Miles's lips on her breasts soon made her stop thinking. He straddled her hips, on his knees, his hands about her waist, squeezing, caressing, and gradually he began using his fingers to guide her hips into a slow, undulating rhythm.

She caught the rhythm easily. Her breathing deepened and her hands on Miles's arms tightened, her fingers digging into his muscles. His body surrounding her, warm, hard, sculptured, was all she was aware of as her whole body began to move sensuously.

"Miles," she whispered, her hands moving to his hair. She was not gentle as she pulled his face to hers, sought his lips in a kiss such as she'd never dreamed of before. There was sweat on both of them, salty, hot sweat.

Elizabeth drew her knees up, clutched Miles's hips and when she did, he entered her.

There was no pain as she was more than ready for him, but for a moment she trembled with the force of her reaction. Miles held still, also slightly trembling, until Elizabeth started the slow rhythm he'd taught her with his hands.

Slowly, together, they made love. After only moments, Elizabeth lost herself in a sea of passion she'd never known existed before. As Miles increased his speed, she locked her legs about him and gave herself up to her senses. With one blinding flash, Elizabeth's body convulsed and her legs began to shake violently.

"Hush," Miles soothed as he lifted onto one elbow and stroked her temple. "Hush, my angel. You're safe now."

He withdrew from her, pulled her into his arms. "My promised angel," he whispered. "My angel of rain and lightning."

Elizabeth didn't understand his words completely but she did, perhaps for the first time in her life, feel safe. She fell asleep instantly, her body so close to Miles's that she could scarcely breathe.

When Elizabeth awoke, she stretched luxuriously feeling each and every muscle of her body, wincing when she pulled the torn skin of her knees. Her eyes opened and the first thing she saw was a long table covered with steaming food. She was sure she'd never been so hungry in her life. Grabbing Bronwyn's plaid from the floor, she tossed it about her body haphazardly and went to the table.

Her mouth was full of a bit of poached salmon when the door opened and Miles walked in. Elizabeth froze, her hand halfway to her mouth as she began to remember the previous night. There was such a disgustingly *knowing* look in Miles's dark eyes that Elizabeth began to grow angry. Before she could even sort her feelings, Miles casually began to discard the Scots clothes he wore.

What right did he—! Elizabeth thought, choking on the salmon as she tried to speak. But he did have a right. After the way she'd acted last night, he had every right to believe the very worst of her. But still she'd like to wipe that expression off his face.

Elizabeth didn't really consider what she did, but beside her were two heaping platters of warm, soft tarts, baked to a golden turn, heavy with summer fruit. With a smile, her eyes locked with Miles's, she slipped her hand under a tart and, still smiling, sent it flying toward him.

He wasn't expecting missiles sent at him and the pie hit his collar bone, splashing his cheek, running down his chest in a warm ooze of cherries and juice.

Elizabeth knew that whatever happened now it was worth it for the look on Miles's face. He was totally, completely, shocked. With her hand over her mouth to cover a giggle, Elizabeth sent two more pies flying at him, hitting his bare hip with the first one, the chair behind him with the other one.

Miles looked at Elizabeth with an odd expression, discarded the rest of his clothes and kept walking toward her.

The plaid Elizabeth had worn fell from her body and Elizabeth, eyes wide, began to throw pies in earnest, using both hands. She wasn't sure but she thought she saw murder in those gray eyes.

Miles kept coming, only moving when a tart came flying at his face. His entire body was covered in a mixture of peaches, cherries, apples, dates, plums, all running down his muscular body in a glorious riot of colors—and flavors, Elizabeth thought irrelevantly.

When he reached the table, his piercing eyes held hers and she didn't dare move. He bolted over the table to stand besider her and Elizabeth, breath held, looked up at him. But as she looked, a cherry, plump and juicy, ran down his forehead, his nose, and hung for just a second before plopping down onto the floor. Another giggle escaped Elizabeth.

Slowly, tenderly, Miles drew her into his arms. "Ah, Elizabeth," he said, "you are such a joy."

As his lips came near hers, she closed her eyes, remembering all too well the sensations of last night. He bent her backward in his arms and Elizabeth gave herself over to the strength of him. He had power over her. All he had to do was touch her and she began to tremble.

But lips did not touch hers. Instead, she received a face full of juicy, syrupy peach pie. As peaches ran into her ears, her eyes flew open. Gasping, she looked up into Miles's devilish face.

Before she could even protest, with a wicked little smile, he lifted her and set her on the table—smack in the middle of the second platter of tarts. Fruit juice oozed over her legs, somehow did the impossible and traveled up her spine. Her hands were covered, peaches dripped off her chin, her hair was glued to her body.

With utter disgust, she lifted her hands, brushed them against each other, saw that did no good whatever, and on second thought, she ate two apple slices from the back of her wrist.

"A little too sweet," she said seriously, looking at Miles. "Perhaps we should complain to the cook."

Miles, nude before her, showed that his mind was not on the cook. Elizabeth's eyes widened in mock dismay. It was difficult, if not impossible, to retain one's composure while sitting in a puddle of fruit pies. She opened her arms to her sticky lover and he came to her.

When Elizabeth kissed Miles's neck and came away choking on a cherry pit, their laughter began. Miles noisily began eating peaches from her forehead while Elizabeth nibbled plums from Miles's shoulder.

Miles grabbed her, rolled onto his back amid a great clatter of dishes and the squish of food, and set her down on his swollen manhood. There was no more laughter as their thoughts turned serious and they made love with vigor, twice changing positions, ending with Miles on the bottom.

Elizabeth lay quite still on top of him, weak, exhausted, thinking she might die before she had energy to rouse herself.

But Miles, with a grunt, lifted both of them and removed a small earthenware bowl that had once contained a sauce of some sort from the small of his back, and flung it to the floor.

Elizabeth raised herself and absently scratched her thigh. "You are a sight, Miles Montgomery," she said, smiling, brushing a poached egg from his hair. The yellow was working its way down toward his scalp.

"You are not exactly presentable at court." With another groan of pain, he removed a serving fork from under his buttocks.

"What do you think your MacGregor is going to think of this?" Elizabeth asked, moving off Miles. She sat up, cross-legged beside him and surveyed the room. The walls, floors, furniture were covered with smashed tarts, and the table was a disaster, everything overturned, dripping, running together—except for a couple of dishes at the very end of the table. On her hands and knees, Elizabeth crawled toward the undisturbed food, squealed once when Miles gave her buttocks a sweet caress, but came back with a bowl of chicken cooked with almonds and a small loaf of wheat bread.

Miles, still stretched on his back on the table, raised himself on his hand. "Still hungry?" he teased.

"Starved." She grabbed a spoon from under Miles's ankle and dug into the stew, and when Miles turned soulful, forlorn eyes up to her, she began to feed him also. "Don't get used to this," she commanded as she shoveled more food into his mouth.

Miles merely smiled at her and occasionally kissed her fingers.

All in all, they found quite a bit of undestroyed food on the table. Elizabeth hung over the side, with Miles holding an ankle and a wrist, and retrieved a whole roast partridge which had caught on the leg stretchers. Miles refused to feed himself and Elizabeth was "forced" to feed him, even to stripping the meat from the partridge bones.

"Worthless is what you are," Elizabeth said, scratching. The food on her body was beginning to dry and it *itched!*

"What you need," Miles murmured, running

nibbling kisses up her arm, "is—"

"I don't want to hear any of your suggestions, Montgomery!" she warned. "Last night you got me drunk and pounced on me in a tub and now . . . this!" There were no words to describe the fragrant mess about them. "Damn!" she cursed, using both hands to scratch her thigh. "Is there nothing normal about you?"

"Nothing," he reassured her as he lazily stepped down from the table and began to dress. "There's a lake not far from here. How about a swim?"

"I have no idea how to swim."

He caught her waist and lifted her from the table. "I'll teach you," he said so lewdly that Elizabeth laughed and pushed against him.

"Underwater?" she said, and when Miles seemed to consider this seriously, she nearly ran from him, slipping once on an ooze of cod livers but catching herself on the table edge. In record time, she'd slipped into a tartan skirt, a saffron-colored shirt and tossed a plaid about her shoulders. The skirt had been in the line of fire of a cheese tart.

"Do I look as bad as you?" she asked as he pulled food from his hair.

"Worse. But no one will see us." With that cryptic sentence, he walked toward a tapestry on the far wall, pulled it aside and revealed a staircase built inside the thick stone walls. He took Elizabeth's hand and led her into the dark, cold passage.

Chapter 10

Two HOURS later they were washed and Miles was drying Elizabeth with a plaid.

"Quite useful, aren't they?" she murmured, wrapping the tartan cloth about her cool body. The Scots summer was not conducive to lying about nude.

"Many things about the Scots are practical as well as pleasant—if you'd give them half a chance."

She stopped drying her hair. "What does it matter to you whether I like the Scots or not? I understand your wanting to get me into your bed but I don't understand this constant . . . interest, I guess, in my welfare."

"Elizabeth, if I'd merely wanted you in my bed I could have taken you that first day when you were delivered to me."

"And you would have lost part of yourself to my ax blade," she snapped.

After a moment's surprise, Miles began to

laugh. "You and that ax! Oh Elizabeth, you were such a charming sight with your leg sticking out and surrounded by so much hair. You were—"

"You do not have to laugh *quite* so hard," she said stiffly. "It was not humorous to me. And I may yet escape you."

That sobered him. He pulled her down to the ground beside him. "I don't want to have to go through more nights like those. Rab was missing and we found dead wolves along the cliff and the mare you rode came back limping. We were really afraid you'd fallen over the cliff."

She pushed at him because he was holding her so tightly she couldn't breathe. As she looked up at him, she frowned. She'd always thought that if a man did take her virtue, she would hate him, but hate was far removed from what she felt for Miles. Between them now was a soft sense of sharing, as if they'd always been here and always would be.

"Is it always like this?" she whispered, looking up at the trees overhead.

There was a pause before Miles answered. "No," he said so softly it could have been the wind.

She knew he understood what she meant. Perhaps he was lying to her, perhaps tomorrow he'd again be her enemy, but right now he wasn't.

"There were never days like this when my brother was alive," she began, and when she started she couldn't stop. Although she'd fought Miles at every opportunity, she now knew that in

145

truth she'd never been in any real danger—not the danger she'd experienced for most of her life. In the last few weeks she'd seen courtesy; she'd seen love between Bronwyn and Stephen, Miles and his son—and love that asked very little in return was something she'd not seen in her lifetime.

Instead of telling a horror tale of all the atrocities Edmund had committed, she talked of the way she and her two other brothers had bound themselves together. Roger had not been very old when his parents died and he'd been turned over to the rule of his treacherous brother. He'd done all he could to save his younger siblings but at the same time he wanted to live his own life. Every time that Roger slipped in his vigilance, Elizabeth was summoned from her convent and used in Edmund's nasty games. Roger, in remorse and guilt over his lapse, would strike out and renew his vows to protect Brian and Elizabeth, but always, Edmund's slimy ways would undermine Roger's good intentions.

"He's never had anyone but us," Elizabeth said. "Roger is twenty-seven but he's never been in love, never even had the time to while away a summer afternoon. He was old by the time he was twelve."

"And what of you?" Miles asked. "Didn't you consider that you deserved some time for laughter?"

"Laughter." She smiled, snuggling against him. "I don't think I remember any laughter in my life until a certain young man rolled down

146

a hill with me."

"Kit is a delightful child," Miles said with pride.

"Kit, ha! It was someone larger who, even as he rolled, protected his fine sword."

"Noticed that, did you?" he said softly, tucking a strand of her hair behind her ear.

For a moment they were silent, with Elizabeth looking at him in puzzled silence. "You are not a kidnapper," she said at last. "I have seen you with men and with women and if you are nothing else in life, you are kind to women. So why do you not release me? Is it because, as you said, I have so many . . . problems?" She said the last stiffly.

He did not take her question lightly and it was a while before he answered. "All my life I've seemed to enjoy the company of women. I like nothing better than to lie about with a beautiful woman in my arms. My brothers seemed to think this made me less of a man but I don't guess one can change how one is. As for you, Elizabeth, I saw something I'd never seen before—a man's hatred and anger. My sister-in-law Judith could probably organize all of England, yet she needs my brother's strength and love. Bronwyn loves people and could make anyone do her bidding, but she's unsure of herself and needs Stephen's stubborn belief in himself to back her."

He paused. "But you, Elizabeth, are different. You could probably exist alone and you wouldn't even know there was more to life."

"Then why . . ." she began. "Why hold someone like me prisoner? Surely some soft, docile woman would be more to your liking."

He smiled at the insult in her tone. "Passion, Elizabeth. I think you are surely the most passionate human on earth. You hate violently and I am sure you will love just as violently."

She tried to move away but he pinned her to the ground, his face near hers. "You'll love only once in your life," he said. "You'll take your time in giving your love but once it is given, no power on earth—or hell—will break that love."

She lay still under him, gazing up into those deep gray orbs that burned into her.

"I want to be that man," he said softly. "I want more than your body, Elizabeth Chatworth. I want your love, your mind, your soul."

When he bent to kiss her, she turned her head away. "You don't ask much, do you, Montgomery? You've had more than I've given any other man—but I don't think I have more to give. My soul belongs to God, my mind to myself and my love goes to my family."

He rolled away from her and began to dress. "You asked me why I keep you prisoner and I've told you. Now we'll return to the MacGregor's and you will meet his men. The MacGregor is angered over your taking a knife to him and you will apologize."

She did not like his attitude. "He is a friend to the MacArrans who are related to my enemies, the Montgomerys"—she smiled sweetly—"therefore I

148

had every right to try and protect myself.''

''True,'' he agreed, handing her her clothes, ''but if the MacGregor isn't appeased, it could cause problems between the clans.''

She began to dress sullenly. ''I don't like this,'' she muttered. ''And I'll not enter a hall of strange men without a weapon.''

''Elizabeth,'' Miles said patiently. ''You cannot wield an ax at every gathering of men you enter. Besides, these Scots have some beautiful women of their own. Perhaps they won't be so enraptured with your charms that they're driven to insane acts of lust.''

''I didn't mean that!'' she snapped, turning away from him. ''Must you laugh at . . . ?''

He put his hand on her shoulder. ''I don't mean to laugh at you, but you have to begin to realize what is normal and what isn't. I'll be there to protect you.''

''And who will protect me from you?''

At that, his eyes lit and he ran his hand down the side of her breast. ''You will be pleased to know that no one will protect you from me.''

She pulled away from him and finished dressing.

What Miles had planned for Elizabeth was, to her, sheer torture. He clamped his fingers down on her elbow until pain shot up her arm, and he forced her to shake hands with over a hundred of the MacGregor men. When she finished, she collapsed in a chair against the wall and shakily drank the wine Miles handed her. When he complimented her as if she were a dog that'd performed a trick correctly, she sneered at him, which made him kiss her fingers and laugh.

"It will get easier," he said confidently.

Indeed, it did get easier, but it took weeks. Miles never let up on her for a moment. He refused to let her walk behind the men and when she turned constantly to check the men's whereabouts, he made her be still. They rode on a hunt and once Elizabeth was separated from Miles. Three MacGregors found her, were quite cordial to her, but by the time she reached Miles, there was terror in her eyes. Instantly, he pulled her onto his horse, held her and soothed her and when that wasn't enough, he made love to her under a beech tree.

There was one man at the MacGregors who Miles warned her against: Davy MacArran, Bronwyn's brother. Miles had a fierce dislike for the boy who was actually older than himself. Miles said, with great contempt, that Davy had tried to kill his own sister.

"For all the arrogance of my brothers," Miles said, "they would give their lives for me as I would for them. I have no use for men who go against their families."

"As you are asking me to do?" she retorted. "You are asking me to forsake my brothers and give myself body and soul to you."

There was a flicker of anger in Miles's eyes before he left her alone in the room they shared.

Elizabeth went to the window to look down at the men in the courtyard below. It was an odd feeling to know that if she wanted she could walk in that courtyard and not be molested. She need have no fear that she would have to fight for her life. There was no urge on her part to test her knowledge but it was pleasant to consider.

The MacGregor walked by and the powerful strut of the big man almost made her smile. His vanity had taken a beating at Bronwyn's hands and again at Elizabeth's, and when Miles had practically pushed Elizabeth before him, the MacGregor'd hardly looked at her. This had *never* happened to her before and before she knew what she was doing, she found herself practically coaxing him to talk to her. It had taken only minutes before she felt him twining about her fingers. He liked pretty women and he was old enough that he was beginning to wonder whether pretty women liked him. Elizabeth soon dispelled that idea.

Later Miles looked at her in disgust. "You changed quickly from the frightened rabbit to the temptress."

"Do you think I make a good temptress?" she taunted. "Lachlan MacGregor is a widower. Perhaps—"

She didn't finish because Miles kissed her so hard he nearly bruised her lips. With her fingertips on her lower lip, she watched his broad back as he moved away from her—and smiled. She was beginning to realize that she had some power over Miles, but as yet she didn't know the extent of her power.

Now, as she watched the courtyard, men, wearing the MacArran cockade, rode into the area. The MacGregors falsely acted with nonchalance, but Elizabeth saw that all the men's hands were very close to their sword belts. Miles came from inside the MacGregor's stone house and talked to the MacArrans.

Elizabeth watched for only a moment before turning back to the room with a sigh, and she began to gather Miles's belongings. She knew without a doubt that they would be leaving.

Miles opened the door, paused for a moment, saw what she was doing and began to help her. "My brother Gavin has come to Larenston."

"With Roger?" She paused with her hand on a velvet cape.

"No, your brother has escaped."

She whirled to face him. "Unharmed? With all his body parts?"

Miles's eyes widened for a moment. "As far as I know, everything is attached." He caught her hands. "Elizabeth . . ."

She pulled away. "Perhaps you should have one of the MacGregor's beautiful lasses to pack your fine belongings." With that she fled to the stairs behind the tapestry.

In spite of everything she could do, tears began to fall. She tripped in the black darkness, barely caught herself from falling and ended up sitting down hard on a stone stair as several rats squealed in protest at her disturbance.

Sitting there, crying as if her life were over, she knew she had no reason to cry. Her brother was no longer a prisoner as she was; he was unharmed. And now Gavin Montgomery had come, no doubt to force his younger brother to release her. By this time tomorrow she'd probably be on her way home. No more would she have to shake hands with strange men. No more would she be a captive, but she'd be free to go home to her own family.

A sound on the stairs above her made her turn and although she couldn't see him, she knew Miles was there. Instinctively, she held her arms out to him.

Miles grabbed her so hard she knew her ribs would crack, and all she did was cling to him all the more tightly. They were like two children hiding from their parents, frightened of tomorrow, making the most of now.

To them there was no dust or filth, no angry little eyes watching them as they fumbled with each other's clothes, their lips joined, never parting. The violence with which they came together was new to Elizabeth, as Miles had always been gentle with her, but when her nails dug into his back, he reacted. The stairs bit into the back of her as Miles lifted her hips and took her with a blinding, fierce passion, but with no more fierceness than Elizabeth sought him. She braced her feet against the stairs and pushed upward with all the force of her strong young body.

The flash of light that tore through them left them both weak, trembling, holding onto each other as if to let go meant they'd die.

Miles was the first to recover. "We must go," he whispered tiredly. "They wait below for us."

"Yes," she said. "Big brother calls." Even in the darkness, she could feel Miles's eyes on her.

"Don't be afraid of Gavin, Elizabeth."

"The day a Chatworth is afraid of a Montgomery—" she began but Miles kissed her to silence.

"That's what I like! Now if you can keep your hands off me long enough, we'll ride to Larenston."

"You!" She started to strike him but he bolted up the stairs before she could, and when Elizabeth tried to move, she winced at a hundred bruised places. She emerged from behind the tapestry bent over, her hand to her back. Miles's conceited chuckle made her straighten painfully. "If women didn't always have to be on the bottom—" she snapped, then stopped when she saw the MacGregor leaning against a chest.

"I was going to say I hoped you enjoyed your visit, Lady Elizabeth." The big man's eyes twinkled so merrily that Elizabeth busied herself in packing, pointedly ignoring him, so pointedly that she didn't hear him move behind her. When his hands touched her shoulder, she gasped, but Miles caught her arm, warned her with his eyes.

"We've enjoyed ye, Elizabeth," the MacGregor said as he removed the crude pin she wore at her shoulder and replaced it with a large round silver one, bearing the MacGregor standard.

"Thank you," she said quietly, and to the amazement of all three of them, she quickly kissed the MacGregor's cheek.

Miles's hand on her arm tightened and he looked at her with such pleasure that his whole body fairly glowed.

"Sweet lass, come and see me again."

"I will," she said and smiled genuinely because she meant her words.

Together the three of them walked down to the courtyard and the waiting horses. Elizabeth looked at all the MacGregor men with curiosity because she knew she was going to miss them. With a sense of wonder at what she was doing, she voluntarily shook hands with some of the men. Miles stayed close to her and she was well aware of his presence, and grateful for it, but her fear at touching the men and being touched by them was only just that—fear, not terror.

She was glad when she came to the end of the line and could mount her horse. Behind her were Bronwyn's men, strangers to her, and she could have cried out at the injustice of having to leave a place she was just beginning to trust.

Miles leaned across and squeezed her hand. "Remember that I am here," he said.

She nodded once, kicked her horse forward and they were off.

For how long will you be here? she wanted to ask. She knew much about Gavin Montgomery.

He was a greedy, treacherous man whose jilting of Alice Chatworth had nearly driven her insane. And Gavin was the head of the Montgomery family. For all Miles's bravado, he was only twenty years old and Gavin had the guardianship of his young brother. Would Gavin take her away, use her in his own games against the Chatworth family? Miles believed Roger'd killed Mary Montgomery. Would this Gavin use Elizabeth to repay the Chatworths?

"Elizabeth," Miles said. "What are you planning?"

She didn't bother to answer him, but kept her head high as they entered Larenston.

Miles helped her from her horse. "No doubt my eldest brother is inside, waiting to get his hands on me," Miles said, eyes twinkling.

"How can you laugh about this?"

"The only way to deal with my brother is to laugh," he said seriously. "I'll come to you later."

"No!" she gasped. "I'll meet your brother with you."

Miles cocked his head, studied her. "I do believe you mean to protect me from my brother."

"You are a gentle man and—"

At that Miles laughed so loud, he startled the horses. He kissed her cheek heartily. "You are a dear, sweet child. Come along then and protect me if you want, but I'll keep an eye on Gavin's toes."

Gavin, Stephen and Sir Guy waited for them in the upstairs solar. Gavin was as tall as Miles but his face was more sculptured, hawklike, and his expression was of pure unadulterated rage.

"Is this Elizabeth Chatworth?" Gavin said through clenched teeth. He didn't wait for an answer. "Send her away. Guy, see to her."

"She stays," Miles said in a cool voice, not bothering to look at either of his brothers. "Sit, Elizabeth."

She obeyed him, sinking into a chair that dwarfed her.

After one angry glance at Elizabeth, Gavin turned to Miles who was pouring himself a glass of wine. "Goddamn you to hell and back, Miles!" Gavin bellowed. "You walk in here as if you hadn't nearly caused a private war between our families and you bring this . . . this . . ."

"Lady," Miles said, his eyes growing dark.

"If she were a lady, I'd swear she isn't now after having spent weeks with you."

Miles's eyes turned black. His hand went to his sword but Sir Guy's hand made him pause.

"Gavin," Stephen warned, "you have no right to make insults. Say what you have to."

Gavin moved closer to Miles. "Do you know what your little escapade is costing our family? Raine can't even show his face but must hide in a forest, and I have spent the last month in the company of that bastard Chatworth—all in an attempt to save your worthless japing hide."

Elizabeth waited for Miles to retort that Raine's

157

outlawing was not Miles's fault, but Miles remained silent, his eyes still dark, locked on his eldest brother.

A muscle in Gavin's jaw worked frantically. "You will release her to me and I will return her to her brother. I'd hoped that by now you'd come to your senses and let her go. I'm sure you've taken her virginity and that will no doubt cost me much, but . . ."

"Will it cost you or Judith?" Miles asked calmly, turning his back on his brother.

A silence fell on the room and even Elizabeth held her breath.

"Stop it, both of you," Stephen interceded. "And for God's sake, Gavin, calm down! You know how Miles is when you insult his woman-of-the-moment. And you, Miles, you're pushing Gavin too far. Miles, Gavin has held Chatworth in order to give you some time to release Lady Elizabeth, and you can imagine that he was, ah, disappointed when Chatworth escaped and still you held Elizabeth. All you have to do is send her back with Gavin and all will be well."

Elizabeth again held her breath as she watched Miles's back and after a moment she felt Gavin watching her. It was then she decided she didn't like the man. She returned his arrogant look with one of her own. She looked away to see Miles watching them.

"I will not release her," Miles said softly.

"No!" Gavin bellowed. "Does the family mean nothing to you? Would you rather risk our name, the name of generations of Montgomerys, merely for the spread of a woman's thighs?''

Gavin wasn't expecting the fist that plowed into his face, but it didn't take him but seconds to recover and leap at Miles.

Chapter 11

STEPHEN AND Sir Guy used all their strength to restrain the two men.

It was Gavin who calmed first. He shook Stephen's arms away, walked toward the window and when he looked back, he had control over himself. "Send Lady Elizabeth away," he said quietly.

Sir Guy released Miles and Miles nodded to Elizabeth. She started to protest but knew that now was not the time. Miles was not going to turn her over to his brother, of that she was sure.

When the men were alone, Gavin sank into a chair. "Brother against brother," he said heavily. "Chatworth would love to know what he's doing to us. Stephen, pour me some wine."

When he held the cup, he continued. "King Henry has ordered this feud between the Montgomerys and Chatworths to cease. I have pleaded that our family is innocent in everything. Raine attacked Chatworth because of what had been done to Mary and I know you are innocent in the kidnapping of this Elizabeth.''

Gavin drank deeply. He was used to these one-sided conversations with his young brother. Getting words from Miles was much worse than teeth pulling. ''Has your Elizabeth told you of the young singer who was with her when Pagnell rolled her in a carpet? You should ask her because that singer has recently married Raine.''

Miles's eyes widened slightly.

''Ah! At last I get some response from my brother.''

''Gavin,'' Stephen warned. ''How is Raine's wife involved in all this?''

Gavin waved his hand. ''Pagnell was after her for some reason, tossed her in a dungeon and Elizabeth Chatworth tried to save her. In so doing, the Chatworth woman got caught and in jest was delivered to our lecherous little brother. God's teeth, why didn't you return her to Chatworth as soon as you found out who she was?''

''As he returned my sister?'' Miles asked quietly. ''When did you start being such a peacemaker?''

''Since I have seen my family torn apart by this hatred. Hasn't it occurred to you that the king will have some say in all this? He's punished Raine by outlawing him and Chatworth has been heavily fined. What will he do to you when he hears that you hold the Chatworth woman?''

''Miles,'' Stephen said. ''Gavin's concern is for

you. I know you've grown to care for the girl but there's more here than you think."

"Elizabeth deserves more than to be sent back to that hellhole of Chatworth's," Miles said.

At that, Gavin groaned, closed his eyes for a moment. "You've been around Raine too long. Whatever you think of Chatworth, no matter what he's done, he's done it with the belief that he was in the right. I've spent weeks with him and—"

"You are well known to side with the Chatworths," Miles said evenly, referring to Gavin's long affair with Alice Chatworth. "I'll not release her and no words from anyone will make me do so. The woman is mine. Now, if you will excuse me, I'd like to see Bronwyn."

In spite of her surety that she would be allowed to stay with Miles, Elizabeth still paced the floor. She cursed herself because she knew that she wanted to stay in Scotland, wanted to stay in a place where she could learn to be unafraid. Roger, she thought, dear, protective, angry Roger was in England somewhere, looking for her, frantic to find her, yet she hoped with all her heart that he'd not succeed.

"Just a little more time," she whispered. "If I can but have one more month I'll leave readily. And I shall have memories to last me a lifetime."

She was so absorbed in her own thoughts that she didn't hear the door open behind her, and when she heard the light footsteps, she whirled about, ready to do battle.

"Did . . . did you enjoy the MacGregors?" Kit stammered, unsure of what the fury on her face meant.

Instantly, Elizabeth's face changed. She knelt, opened her arms to the child and held him very, very close.

"I missed you so much, Kit," she whispered. When her eyes cleared, she held him away from her. "I stayed in a big room with a secret staircase behind a tapestry and your papa and I had a pie fight and we went swimming in a very cold lake."

"Bronwyn gave me a pony," Kit answered, "and Uncle Stephen took me riding and what kind of pies?" He leaned forward and whispered loudly, "Did you make Papa angry?"

"No." She smiled. "Not even when I hit him square in the face with a cherry tart. Come and sit down by me and I'll tell you about how Bronwyn's dog saved me from wolves."

It was some time later that Miles found them together, asleep, both looking perfectly content. For a long time Miles stood over them, quietly watching. When he heard the muffled sounds of horses in the courtyard below and knew it was Gavin leaving, he bent and kissed Elizabeth's forehead. "I'll give you more children, Elizabeth," he murmured, touching Kit's cheek. "See if I don't."

"I most certainly will not!" Elizabeth said to Miles, her face set grimly. "I have nearly killed myself doing what you want but I will not remain

163

here alone while you chase about the countryside having a good time."

"Elizabeth," Miles said patiently, "I am going hunting and you will not be here alone. All the MacArrans—"

"MacArrans!" she shot at him. "All those men near me for three days! No, I will not stay here. I'll go on the hunt with you."

"You know I'd love to have you but I think you need to stay here. There will be times when I can't be with you and you need to learn . . ." He stopped when she turned away.

"I don't need you or any other man, Montgomery," she said, shoulders stiff.

Miles touched her but she moved away. "Elizabeth, we've been through too much together to let this come between us. I think you should stay here with Kit and the men and try to conquer some of your fear. If you don't think you can do that, tell me and of course you can go with me. I'll be downstairs."

Elizabeth didn't look at him before he left the room. Nearly two months had passed since that day Gavin had first arrived, and during that time Elizabeth had found out what happiness was. She and Miles and Kit had spent lovely, long days together, playing in the newly fallen snow, laughing together. And Christmas had been such as she'd never experienced before—a family together.

Bronwyn had taught her a great deal, not by lectures but by example. Elizabeth rode with

Bronwyn a few times and visited some of the crofters. There were a few instances of panic and once when Elizabeth drew a knife on a man who was following her too closely, Bronwyn had interceded and calmed Elizabeth. After that there was no more of the initial hostility between the women. Bronwyn seemed to adopt Elizabeth as a young sister rather than look on her as a potential rival. When Bronwyn started ordering Elizabeth about just as she did everyone else, Miles and Stephen relaxed. Three times Elizabeth told Bronwyn she could drop herself off the cliff road and Bronwyn had laughed heartily.

Rab also seemed to have adopted Elizabeth and quite often he'd refuse to obey either woman, skulking off into the shadows instead. When Stephen called the dog a coward, both women turned on him.

And daily, Miles and Elizabeth drew closer. Sometimes, while she watched Miles training, the upper part of his body bare, glistening with sweat, she felt her knees go weak. *Always,* Miles sensed her presence during those times and the hot looks he turned on her would make her tremble. Once, Stephen's lance had just missed Miles's head because Miles was concentrating on Elizabeth's lustful looks. Stephen had been so angry he'd started choking Miles.

"Another inch and I could have killed you," Stephen screeched in rage.

Both Bronwyn and Elizabeth, as well as Rab and Sir Guy, entered into that fracas. Stephen, his entire body red with fury, had demanded that Miles take Elizabeth away from the training ground. Miles, completely unruffled by his brother's anger, had agreed readily. And what a memorable afternoon that had been! In spite of Miles's outward calm, Stephen's unusual anger had upset him and he alternately attacked Elizabeth and clung to her. They made love in the bed, across a chair, the arm nearly breaking her back, and against a wall. Unfortunately, Miles slammed Elizabeth against a tapestry and she grabbed it. The heavy, dusty rug fell on them, knocked them to the floor—but they kept on until they started coughing. Locked together, they crawled from under the tapestry and continued on the cold stone floor. When they appeared for supper that night, flushed and exhausted, the entire Clan MacArran set up a howl of laughter. Stephen was still angry and all he'd say was to issue an order for Elizabeth to stay away from the training ground.

Two whole months and one week together, almost five months since her "capture," she thought.

But now she knew that time was running out.

Gavin sent a messenger to Miles. Roger Chatworth and Pagnell had gone to the king together and Roger'd told King Henry that Raine Montgomery was trying to raise an army against the king, and that Miles was holding Elizabeth in bondage. The king declared that if Miles did not release Elizabeth, he'd be declared a traitor and all his lands confiscated. As for Raine, the king threatened to burn the forest.

Gavin had pleaded with Miles to release Elizabeth. Miles spent days hardly speaking, but sometimes looking at her with great longing, and Elizabeth began to realize that their days together were numbered. Miles began to push her to spend time with the MacArrans, almost as if he were trying to prepare her for the future—a future without him.

Elizabeth was torn both ways. She did want to learn how to cope with her terror of men, but at the same time she wanted to spend every moment with Kit and Miles.

"Damn!" she muttered, alone in the room. How had she come so far from independence to utter dependence?

Gavin had come to Scotland again, this time in a rage that made his first one seem mild, and for the first time Elizabeth felt some guilt at wanting to stay in the peaceful MacArran household. When Miles came to their room, she asked him to allow her to leave with Gavin. She'd planned to say she wanted to save both his family as well as hers but Miles never gave her a chance. Both Stephen and Gavin's rages together were nothing compared to Miles's. He cursed in three languages, he threw things, tore a chair apart with his bare hands, took an ax to a table. It took both Tam and Sir Guy to hold him.

Gavin and Stephen had obviously seen their little brother like this before. Even Gavin gave up and went home after Miles's display. And Elizabeth was left weakened, looking down at the drugged Miles with tears in her eyes. Roger and Miles, she thought over and over, Roger and Miles. She had a home with two brothers, one of whom was tearing the Isles upside down to find her, yet she sat and cried over her enemy, a man who'd also protected her, who'd shown her patience and kindness and taught her that life could be good.

Drowsily, Miles opened his eyes. "Did I frighten you?" he asked huskily.

She could only nod.

"I frighten myself. They don't happen too often." He caught her hand, held it to his cheek like a child's toy. "Don't leave me again, Elizabeth. You were given to me; you are mine." With that often repeated refrain, he slipped away into sleep.

That had been four days ago, a mere short four days ago, but now he was planning to leave her alone for three days while he and Stephen went boar hunting. Perhaps Miles didn't sense her feeling of dread. Perhaps he was just sure enough of himself that he thought he could always keep her at his side. But Roger was on his way to Scotland and when he arrived with his army, what would she do? Could she stand by and see the MacArrans fight her brother? Could she watch a personal fight between Roger and Miles? Would she hold Kit in her arms and watch Miles die or would she hold Miles at night and taste the blood of her brother?

"Elizabeth?" Bronwyn asked from the doorway. "Miles said you're not going on the hunt."

"No," she said with some bitterness. "I'm to stay here and surround myself with men. Men behind me, men beside me, men watching my every move."

Bronwyn was silent for a moment, watching the blond woman. "Are you worried about Miles or your brother?"

"Both," Elizabeth replied honestly. "And were you ever worried about bringing an English husband into the midst of your Scotsmen? Did you wonder if you could trust him?"

Bronwyn's eyes danced with mirth. "The thought crossed my mind. All Stephen wanted was for me to admit that I loved him. But I was sure there was more to love than just some undefinable feeling."

"And is there?"

"Yes," Bronwyn said. "For some women I think they love a man in spite of what he is, but for me I had to know Stephen was what my clan needed as well as what I wanted."

"What if you'd loved him, loved him deeply, but your clan hated him? What if your staying with Stephen meant you would have alienated your clan?"

"I would have chosen my clan," Bronwyn answered, watching Elizabeth intently. "I would give up many things, even my own life, to keep from starting a war within my family."

"And that's what you think I should do!" she spat. "You think I should return to my brother. Now, while Miles is gone, is a perfect time. If I could have a few of your men I could . . ." She stopped as she locked eyes with Bronwyn.

At last Bronwyn spoke. "I honor my husband's brother. I will not help you to escape."

Elizabeth put her arms around Bronwyn. "What am I to do? You saw how Miles acted when I said I should return to Roger. Should I try to escape again? Oh Lord!" She pushed away. "You are my enemy as well."

"No." Bronwyn smiled. "I'm not your enemy, nor are any of the Montgomerys. We've all grown to love you. Kit would follow you to the ends of the earth. But the time will come when you'll have to choose. Until that moment arrives, no one can help you. Now come downstairs and kiss Miles goodbye before he starts wrecking more of my furniture. We have little enough as it is. And, by the way, how did that tapestry get on the floor?"

Elizabeth's red face made Bronwyn laugh loudly as they descended the stairs.

"Elizabeth." Miles laughed, pulling her into a darkened corner where she kissed him enthusiastically. "I'll only be gone for three days. Will you miss me so much?"

"You are the lesser of evils. If you come back and half-a-dozen men have their toes broken, it will be your fault."

He caressed her cheek. "After Sir Guy's

170

experience, I don't think they would mind."

"What do you mean?"

"Bronwyn put that ugly giant in the care of some little flirt and now the two are inseparable. She has him fetching water for her and no doubt if he could hold a needle, he'd embroider her shirt collars."

Elizabeth almost kicked Miles at that because the shirt he wore under the Scots plaid was one she'd embroidered for him.

"Here, my little captive, behave yourself or I'll send you home."

Her eyes hardened at that, but Miles only laughed and nuzzled her neck. "What you feel is in your eyes. Now kiss me again and I'll be back very soon."

Minutes later she stood with empty arms and a heavy heart. Something was going to happen and she knew it. Her first impulse was to hide in her room, to remain there for three days, but she knew Miles was right. Now was a good time to try and overcome some of her fears.

By early afternoon she'd arranged an expedition of her own. She and Kit would ride out with ten MacArran men, Tam included, to a ruin Bronwyn had told her about. Kit could go exploring and she could work on swallowing her fear.

By the time they reached the ruin, Elizabeth's heart was pounding but she was able to smile at Tam as he helped her from her horse. When she heard a man behind her, she didn't turn quickly but tried to act in a normal manner. As she turned to face Jarl, she was rewarded with a smile of great pride from the young man, and Elizabeth let out a small laugh.

"Does everyone know about me?" she asked Tam.

"My clan has a great respect for you because you can slip about the woods as well as any Scotswoman, and we like people who are fighters."

"Fighters! But I have submitted to my enemies."

"Nay, lass." Tam laughed. "Ye've only come to your senses and seen what fine people we Scots are—and to a lesser degree, the Montgomerys."

Elizabeth joined in the laughter with him, as did the men around them.

Later, as Elizabeth sat on a stone of the ancient fallen-down castle, she watched the men below her, realized that she wasn't really afraid of them and thought how good that felt. She owed much to Miles Montgomery.

Because she was so intent upon the sight before her and perhaps because her wariness had dulled in the last few months, she didn't at first hear the whistle coming from the trees behind her. When it did penetrate her peace-drugged brain, every cell of her body came alert. First she looked to see if any of the MacArrans had heard the sound. Kit was playing with young Alex and making a great deal of noise while the others looked on fondly.

Slowly, as if she were going nowhere really, Elizabeth left the boulders and disappeared into the trees with all the noise of a puff of smoke. Once inside, she stood still and waited and her mind was taken back to the days of her childhood.

Brian had always been the one to be protected. Older than Elizabeth but seeming younger, he'd never been able to develop the protective techniques that Elizabeth had. If a man attacked Elizabeth, she had no qualms about drawing a knife on him, but Brian couldn't. Time after time Elizabeth had rescued Brian from some gaggle of men Edmund had brought to their home. While Edmund roared with laughter, shouting insults at his weakling of a brother, Roger and Elizabeth had soothed the young, crippled Brian.

There had been so many days that Brian had spent in hiding, without food or drink, that they'd devised a way of signaling. Roger and Elizabeth were the only ones who knew the high-pitched whistle and they'd always come when Brian called.

Now, Elizabeth stood still, waiting for Brian to appear. Was he alone or with Roger?

The young man who stepped into the clearing was a stranger to Elizabeth and for a moment she could only gape at him. He'd always been handsome in a delicate way, but now he looked wraithlike and his face was that of some terrible specter.

"Brian?" she whispered.

He gave her a curt nod. "You look healthy. Does captivity agree with you?"

Elizabeth was nearly knocked speechless by this. She'd never heard her young brother say such a thing to anyone, much less to her. "Is . . . is Roger with you?"

Brian's sunken features darkened even more. "Do not say that vile name in my presence."

"What?" she gasped, moving toward him. "What are you talking about?"

For a moment, his eyes softened and he lifted a hand to caress Elizabeth's temple, but fell away before he touched her. "Many things have happened since we last saw each other."

"Tell me," she whispered.

Brian moved away from her. "Roger kidnapped Mary Montgomery."

"I had heard that but I can't imagine Roger . . ."

Brian turned on her with eyes like hot coals. "Do you think he's related to Edmund with no taint of blood? Do you think any of us escaped the evil that controlled our eldest brother?"

"But Roger . . ." she began.

"Do not even speak the name to me. I loved the woman Mary, loved her such as I could never love again. She was good and kind without a single wish to harm, but he—your brother—raped her and she cast herself from a window in horror."

"No," Elizabeth said calmly. "I cannot believe it. Roger is good. He doesn't harm people. He never wanted this war between the Montgomerys and Chatworths. He took in Alice when her own family wouldn't have her. And he—"

"He attacked Stephen Montgomery's back. He lied to Bronwyn MacArran and held her prisoner for a while. When Mary died, I released Bronwyn and took Mary back to Gavin. Did they tell you of the rage of Miles Montgomery when he saw his sister? It lasted for days."

"No," Elizabeth whispered, vividly imagining Miles's fury. "They have said little about any of the war." After the first few days, it seemed to be a silent mutual agreement that she and Miles would not speak of their families' problems.

"Brian," she said softly. "You look tired and worn. Come back to Larenston with me and rest. Bronwyn will—"

"I'll not rest as long as my brother is alive."

Elizabeth gaped at him. "Brian, you cannot mean what you say. We'll contact Roger, then we'll sit down and talk about this."

"You don't understand, do you? I mean to kill Roger Chatworth."

"Brian! You can't forget a lifetime of good in one day. Remember how Roger always protected us? Remember how he risked his life to save you the day Edmund ran you down and crushed your leg?"

Brian's face didn't lose any of its hardness. "I loved Mary and Roger killed her. Someday you'll understand what that means."

"I may love a hundred people but that will not make me stop loving Roger, who has done so much for me. Even now he searches for me."

Brian looked at her in question. "You slipped away easily enough from your guard. If you're held so loosely, why don't you escape and go to Roger?"

Elizabeth moved away from him but Brian caught her arm. "Do the Montgomery men hold such attraction for you? Which is it? The married one or the boy?"

"Miles is far from being a boy!" she snorted. "Sometimes age is deceptive." She ceased when she saw Brian's expression.

"Do you forget that I was there at the Montgomery estate? So it's Miles you've come to love. A good choice. He's a man with enough fire to match your own."

"What I feel for any Montgomery doesn't change what I feel for Roger."

"And that is? What keeps you from going to him? These Scots can't be too difficult to escape. You deceived Edmund for years."

She was silent for a moment. "It isn't just Miles. There's a peacefulness here that I've never known before. No one puts knives to my throat. There are no distant screams at Larenston. I can walk down a corridor and not have to slide from shadow to shadow."

"I saw a glimpse of that once," Brian whispered, "but Roger killed it and now I mean to kill him."

"Brian! You must rest and think what you're saying."

He ignored her. "Do you know where Raine

Montgomery is?"

"No," she said, startled. "He's in a forest somewhere. I met a singer who'd been with him."

"Do you know where I can find her?"

"Why do you care where this Raine is? Has he done something to you?"

"I plan to beg him to teach me how to fight."

"Not to fight Roger?" she gasped, then smiled. "Brian, Roger will never fight you, and look at you. You aren't half the size of Roger and you look as if you've lost weight. Stay here and rest a few days and we'll—"

"Don't patronize me, Elizabeth. I know what I'm doing. Raine Montgomery is strong and knows how to train. He'll teach me what I need to know."

"Do you really expect me to help you?" she asked angrily. "Do you honestly think I'd tell you where this Montgomery was even if I knew? I'll not aid you in your madness."

"Elizabeth," he said softly. "I came to say goodbye. I have waited in these woods for weeks, waiting for a time to see you, but you're always heavily guarded. Now that I have seen you I can leave. I will fight Roger and one of us will die."

"Brian, please, you have to reconsider."

As if he were an old man, he kissed her forehead. "Live in peace, my little sister, and remember me kindly."

Elizabeth was too stunned to reply, but as Brian turned away, Scotsmen began to drop from the trees. Stephen Montgomery, sword drawn, planted himself before Brian Chatworth.

Chapter 12

"Do NOT hurt him," Elizabeth said heavily, without the least fear that Stephen would harm her young brother.

Stephen caught her tone and resheathed his sword. "Go with my men and they'll feed you," he said to Brian.

With one last look at Elizabeth, Brian left the clearing, surrounded by MacArrans.

Elizabeth stood glaring at Stephen for a moment and in that time she understood a great deal.

Stephen had the courtesy to look somewhat embarrassed. With a sheepish grin, he leaned against a tree, took the dirk from the sheath on his calf and began to whittle on a stick. "Miles knows nothing about this," he began.

"You used me as bait to capture my brother, didn't you?" she blurted.

"I guess you could say that. He's been in the woods for days, skulking about, living on bare sustenance, and we were curious as to who he was and what he wanted. Twice while you were with Miles he came near but my men frightened him away. We decided to let you go to him. You were never alone; my men and I were directly overhead, swords and arrows drawn."

Elizabeth sat down on a large rock. "I don't much like being used like this."

"Would you rather we killed him on sight? A few years ago a lone Englishman couldn't have ridden onto MacArran land and lived to tell of it. But the boy seemed so . . . frantic that we wanted to find out about him."

She considered this a moment. She didn't like what he'd done but she knew he was right. "And now that you have him, what do you plan to do with him?" Her head came up. "Does Bronwyn know of this cat-and-mouse game of yours?"

She wasn't sure, but she believed Stephen's mouth whitened a bit. "As I love life, I am thankful she does not," he said with great feeling. "Bronwyn does not do things in secret—at least not too many anyway. She would have hauled the boy into Larenston and Miles . . ." He broke off.

"Miles's hatred of the Chatworths runs deep," she finished.

"Only of the men." He smiled. "Roger Chatworth caused our sister's death and Miles isn't likely to forgive that. You've only seen the side of him he shows to women. When confronted with a man who's hurt a woman, he is unreasonable."

"You were sure Brian was a Chatworth then?"

"He has that look about him."

Elizabeth was quiet for a moment. Brian *had* had some of Roger's look just now, a look of defiance and anger, covered by an expression of I-don't-care. "You heard what Brian said. Can we hold him here and keep him away from Roger?"

"I think he might go mad. He doesn't look too far from that now."

"No," she said heavily. "He doesn't." She looked up at Stephen expectantly.

"I believe I'll do just what Brian asks: I'll take him to my brother Raine."

"No!" Elizabeth said, standing up. "Raine Montgomery will kill him. Didn't he attack Roger?"

"Elizabeth," Stephen soothed. "Raine will take to the boy because Brian helped Mary. If Raine is nothing else, he's fair. And besides that," Stephen said with a little smile, "my brother will work Brian so hard the young man won't have time to hate. Within three days Brian will be so tired, all he'll think of is sleeping."

She studied him a moment. "Why should you help a Chatworth? Mary was your sister also."

"I thought you believed we Montgomerys lied about your brother's involvement in her death."

"If Miles killed a stranger's sister, would you hate your brother without so much as asking Miles why? Perhaps Roger was involved, but perhaps there were reasons for his actions. I do not and will not hate either of my brothers

180

without just cause."

"Well said." Stephen nodded. "I do not bear any love for your brother Roger for what he's done, but my quarrel is with him, not with his family. My brothers don't feel the same way, which is why Gavin was so rude to you. To him family is everything."

"And is Raine the same way? Will he hate Brian on sight?"

"Perhaps, which is why I'm going with Brian. I'll be able to talk to Raine, and if I know my brother, he'll end by adopting your young Brian." He tossed the stick away and resheathed his knife. "And now I must be off. It will take us days to find my brother."

"Now?" she asked. "You'll leave before Bronwyn and Miles return from the hunt?"

"Oh yes." He grimaced. "I don't relish being around when my lovely wife finds out I tricked her into leaving Larenston so I could tend to this English trespasser alone."

"Or Miles," she said, eyes sparkling. "I don't believe he'll take this calmly."

Stephen groaned, making her laugh. "You, Montgomery, are a coward," she pointed out.

"Of the worst sort," he agreed readily, then turned serious. "Will you pray for me while I'm gone? Perhaps if Raine and Brian get along, we can make some progress in ending this war."

"I would like that," she answered. "Brian is a sweet, gentle man and Roger loves him very much. Stephen," she said in a low voice, "if I ask

181

you a question, will you answer me honestly?"

"I owe you that much."

"Has anyone seen Roger?"

"No," Stephen answered. "He's disappeared. The MacGregors are looking for him and my men are always alert. We nearly lost you once and it won't happen again. But no, so far there is no sign of Roger Chatworth."

For a moment they stood quietly, looking at each other. A few months ago this man was her enemy, as were all men. With one step forward, she came close to him, reached up and put her hand to his cheek.

Stephen seemed to understand the full impact of the honor she was bestowing upon him. He caught her hand, kissed the palm. "We Montgomerys are heartbreakers," he said with dancing eyes. "We'll end this feud with love words instead of swords."

She pulled away from him as if she were insulted, but her laughter escaped. "I will indeed pray for you. Now go before my Miles finds you and gives you a good thrashing."

He lifted one eyebrow at that. "Poor little brother, when some woman decides she owns him." With that he left her alone in the clearing.

Elizabeth sat alone for quite some time and now that she was listening carefully to the sounds around her, she could hear the MacArrans. There were still two men in the trees above her. Far off she could hear Kit's laughter and Tam's deep rumbling answer.

In the last months her senses had dulled greatly. Before her swam the angry face of Brian and she knew that once she, too, had felt such hatred. She hoped with all her being that Stephen would be able to take some of Brian's hate away, or perhaps this Raine Montgomery could do it.

With a heavy heart, she returned to the ruins and the laughter of Kit. In a few days, she'd have Miles's anger to deal with and that would take her mind off her problems.

Bronwyn returned to Larenston the next day and went first to her five-month-old son, Alexander. The child had a wet nurse as Bronwyn was too often away to feed him, but she made sure the boy knew who his mother was. As she was contentedly cuddling her son, Rab at her feet, Elizabeth told her about Brian and how Stephen had taken him to Raine.

For a moment, Bronwyn's eyes flashed. "Damn him!" she muttered but calmed when Alex let out a yowl. "Hush, love," she cooed. When Alexander was quiet, she looked back at Elizabeth. "I don't like that he used you. He should have brought your brother here. Stephen forgets that Brian Chatworth released me from your brother's clutches. I wouldn't have harmed the boy."

"I think Stephen was more concerned about Miles— that *he* might harm Brian." Elizabeth leaned forward and caressed Alex's silky head.

Bronwyn's keen eyes missed nothing. "And

when is your child due?'' she asked evenly.

Elizabeth met Bronwyn's eyes.

Bronwyn stood, carried her son to his cradle. ''Morag told me you've had no flow since you've been here. You've not been ill?''

''Not at all. I wasn't sure what was wrong with me at first, but it didn't take long to understand. Who have you told?''

''No one. Not even Stephen. Especially not Stephen. No doubt he'd want to celebrate. Are you planning to marry Miles?''

Elizabeth tucked the soft plaid around Alex's feet. ''He hasn't asked me, but even if he did, there is more between us than marrying and having babies. Roger won't give up merely because I become a Montgomery. He'd have to know I go of my own free will and that I wasn't forced.''

''And would Miles have to force you?'' Bronwyn asked quietly.

Elizabeth smiled. ''You know as well as I that he's forced me in nothing. But I don't think Miles would like marriage to me. I'd demand fidelity from my husband and Miles Montgomery doesn't know the meaning of the word.''

''I wouldn't underestimate any of the Montgomery men,'' Bronwyn answered. ''They may seem to be an arrogant, inflexible lot but there's more to them than pretty faces and virile bodies.''

''They are indeed that.'' Elizabeth laughed as they left the room.

The next day Bronwyn returned to the hunt and it was while Elizabeth was being a helpless maiden in distress and Kit was saving her from a three-headed, fire-breathing dragon that Elizabeth suddenly stopped.

"Elizabeth!" Kit said impatiently, wooden sword brandished over his head.

She couldn't explain what was wrong with her but chills were covering her body. "Miles," she whispered. "Here!" she said to the woman holding Alex. "Take care of Kit."

With that she tore toward the stairs, down and out into the courtyard. When she reached the stables, she had her hand on a saddle before Douglas was beside her.

"I can't let you leave," Douglas said, regret in his voice.

"Out of my way, you fool," she spat at him. "Miles is in trouble and I'm going to him."

Douglas didn't waste time asking her how she knew this since no messenger had come from the hunting party, but he stepped out of the stables, gave three low whistles and in seconds two of his brothers were there.

Elizabeth wasn't used to saddling her own horse and it was a slow process, but the men didn't help her. Douglas checked the tightness of her cinch before catching her foot and practically tossing her into the saddle. Elizabeth didn't even flinch when he touched her.

As they started off, Elizabeth gave no thought as to where she was going but cleared her mind, visualized Miles and set off at a frightening pace, Douglas, Jarl and Francis behind her. The four horses thundered down the narrow, steep-sided road out of Larenston, turned right and headed along the cliff.

Elizabeth had no fear of the road nor did she worry about the men behind her. Once she was again on flat land, she paused only seconds. To the left was the MacGregors, and to the right was unknown territory. She kicked her horse to the right, somehow knowing this was the way.

One of the men yelled at her in warning once and she flattened herself against the horse's sweaty neck as she barely missed being hit by a tree branch. Other than that, the men were silent as they rode hard to keep up with her.

After a long time of riding, Rab came bounding from the underbrush, barking hard. He seemed to expect Elizabeth and had come to guide her the last part of the way.

Elizabeth was forced to slow her horse to a brisk walk as the four of them and Rab made their way through thick undergrowth into a clump of trees so dense the sunlight was hidden.

Rab began to bark again before the people came into view. Bronwyn and her men were standing in a group, looking down at something on the ground. Sir Guy was kneeling.

Bronwyn turned at her dog's bark and lifted surprised eyes to Elizabeth.

Her horse was still moving as Elizabeth slid to

the ground and ran forward, pushing through the people.

Miles lay on the ground, eyes closed, his entire body covered in blood. His clothes were torn and she could see great gashes in his flesh, in his left thigh, in his right side.

She pushed Sir Guy away, knelt, pulled Miles's head into her lap and began to wipe the blood from his face with the hem of her skirt.

"Wake up, Montgomery," she said firmly with no sympathy or pity in her voice. "Wake up and look at me."

It seemed an eternity before Miles's lashes fluttered. When he did look at her he gave a little smile, let his eyes shut again. "Angel," he whispered and was silent.

"Water," Elizabeth said to the stunned faces over her. "I'll need water to wash his wounds, and is there a crofter's house near here?" Bronwyn only had time to nod before Elizabeth continued. "Go and clear the place out. Take the crofters to Larenston but leave me alone with him. Send Morag and her herbs and I'll need sharp steel needles and thread. Guy! Fetch a big plaid and we'll carry him to the hut. Well!" she snapped. "Get busy, all of you."

Instantly, men went off in all directions.

Bronwyn flashed Elizabeth a quick grin. "Are you sure you aren't a Scot?" With that she was off toward Larenston.

Elizabeth, alone for a few moments, held Miles. "You'll be all right, Montgomery," she whispered. "I'll see to it."

She wasted no more time on sentimentality but took the dagger that lay on the ground beside him and began cutting away his clothes in order to examine his wounds. There seemed to be more blood on him than a man's body could hold.

Rab came up to her as she was slicing away Miles's shirt. "Where's the blood from, Rab?" she asked. "Go and find what did this to Miles."

With two great barks, the dog left them alone. To Elizabeth's relief there was only the one gash on Miles's upper body, and that wasn't deep but would have to be sewn. There were several long bloody cuts on his left arm but nothing serious. His legs were another matter. The wound on his thigh was deep and ugly and there were more cuts on one ankle.

She shifted him once to try to see his underside to look for wounds.

With a groan of pain, Miles opened his eyes, looked at her. "You'll have to get on top, Elizabeth, or else I'll bleed all over you," he said with a glance down at his bare body.

"Quiet!" she commanded. "Save your strength to get well."

As she spoke, Rab began pulling the carcass of an enormous, long-tusked boar into the clearing. The dead animal's face was covered in blood and there were several knife wounds in its side.

"So you won a fight with a boar," she said in disgust, tenderly wrapping him in the plaid she wore about her shoulders. "I don't guess it occurred to you not to ride out alone."

Before she could say another word, Rab dragged another boar carcass to lie beside the first one, this one also slashed.

Elizabeth began to wipe Miles's dirty face. "We're going to take you not far from here where it's warm and where it'll be quiet. Now I want you to rest."

Sir Guy with a man and woman came thrashing through the undergrowth, their arms slung with great heavy plaids.

"There's a strong barley broth on the fire," the woman said, "and oatcakes on the hearth. Bronwyn'll send more plaids if ye need them."

Sir Guy, kneeling, pulled the plaid off Miles's body and studied the wounds, looking up in surprise when Rab pulled a third boar carcass into the clearing.

"How many of them are there?" Elizabeth asked.

"Five," Sir Guy said. "His horse must have thrown him into a family of them. He had only his sword and the little dagger but he killed all five of them and managed to drag himself here. Rab led us to the boars but ran off before we found Lord Miles."

"He came to get me," Elizabeth said. "Can you carry Miles?"

Without much show of effort, Sir Guy carefully picked up his young master as if he were a chlld. Instantly, his wounds began to renew their vigor in bleeding.

"Careful!" Elizabeth half screeched, and the look Guy gave her made her quiet.

Sir Guy led the way as he carried Miles through the trees toward the crofters' cottage, and laid him gently on a cot against one wall. It was a tiny, dark, one-room hut, the open hearth the only source of light. There was a crude table and two chairs and no other furniture besides the cot. A pot of water simmered over the fire. Immediately, Elizabeth dipped clean cloths that had been left for her in the water and started washing Miles. Sir Guy lifted him, helped her remove the shreds of his clothes from under him. To Elizabeth's relief, there were no more wounds on the back of him other than minor cuts and bruises.

She had him almost washed when Morag and Bronwyn arrived together, Morag carrying a big basket of medicines.

"I can't see as well as I used to," Morag said, looking down at Miles, nude, the two wounds gaping redly. "One of ye will have to tend to him."

"I will," Elizabeth said quickly. "Tell me what to do and I can do it."

Sewing a man's flesh was far different from sewing on cloth, Elizabeth soon discovered. The muscles of her body tightened each time she slid the needle inside Miles's skin.

Miles lay still, not moving, barely breathing, his body pale from the loss of blood as Elizabeth stitched. Bronwyn threaded the needles, cut and helped to knot.

When Elizabeth finished at last, she was trembling.

"Drink this," Bronwyn ordered.

"What is it?" Elizabeth asked.

"Lord only knows. I learned long ago not to ask what Morag puts into her concoctions. Whatever it is, it'll taste vile but it will make you feel better."

Elizabeth drank the brew, leaning against the wall, her eyes on Miles. When Morag started to hold a cup to Miles's pale lips, she thrust her mug at Bronwyn and went to him.

"Drink this," she whispered, holding his head. "You must get your strength back."

His eyes moved, his lashes barely parted as he looked up at her. "Worth it," he whispered as he drank Morag's brew.

Morag gave a derisive snort. "He'll stay on his back for a year if ye pamper him."

"Well, let him!" Elizabeth snapped back.

Bronwyn laughed. "Come sit down, Elizabeth, and rest. I want to know how you knew Miles had been wounded. We'd only just found him when you rode up."

Elizabeth sat on the floor by Miles's head, leaned back and shrugged. She had no idea how she'd known he was injured—but she had.

Her moments of rest were short-lived. Seemingly seconds later, Morag had something else for Elizabeth to feed Miles.

Night came and Bronwyn went back to

Larenston. Elizabeth sat beside Miles, watching him, knowing that he didn't sleep, while Morag nodded in a chair.

"What . . ." Miles whispered. "What is Raine's wife like?"

Elizabeth thought he was delirious since she'd never met Raine or his wife.

"Singer," Miles said. "Pagnell."

Those words were enough of a key to make her understand. She was surprised that one of the Montgomery lords would marry a lowly little singer. Elizabeth told Miles the story of meeting Alyxandria Blackett, of hearing her extraordinary voice and later her attempt to rescue the singer from Pagnell's clutches which led to Elizabeth's own capture.

Miles smiled at that and searched for her hand. Still touching her, he fell asleep just as the sun began to rise.

Morag woke and began to mix another batch of herbs, dried mushrooms and several things Elizabeth didn't recognize.

Together they changed the bloody bandages on Miles's wounds and Morag applied warm, wet, herb-filled poultices over the sewn cuts.

Miles slept again in the afternoon and Elizabeth left the little cottage for the first time. Sir Guy sat outside under a tree and only looked up in question when he saw her.

"He's resting," she said.

Sir Guy nodded and stared off into space. "Not many boys could fall into a pack of five boars and come out alive," he said with pride.

There were tears in Elizabeth's eyes as she placed a trembling hand on the giant's shoulder. "I will do all in my power to see that he gets well."

Sir Guy nodded, not looking at her. "You have no reason to help him. We've treated you badly."

"No," she answered. "I have been given more than courtesy; I have been given love." With that she turned away toward the stream that ran through the MacArran land. She washed, tidied her hair, sat down for a moment's rest, wrapped in her plaid, and when she woke it was night. Sir Guy sat not far away from her.

Sleep-dazed, she hurried back to the cottage.

Miles was awake and the frown he wore disappeared when he saw her.

"There she is," Morag scolded. "Now maybe you'll drink some of this."

"Elizabeth," Miles said.

She went to him, held his head while he drank nearly a cup of the brew and continued to hold him until he fell asleep.

Chapter 13

"You will not walk," Elizabeth said to Miles with steely firmness. "I have lost too many nights' sleep in trying to heal your wounds without watching you break them open."

He looked up at her with meltingly soft eyes. "Please, Elizabeth."

For a moment she almost relented, but stopped herself with a laugh. "You are a treacherous man. Now be still or I'll tie you to the bed."

"Oh?" he said, eyebrows raised.

Elizabeth blushed at what he was obviously thinking. "Behave yourself! I want you to eat more. You'll never get well if you don't eat."

He caught her hand and, with surprising strength, pulled her down beside him. Or perhaps it was that Elizabeth had no will to resist him. He was half sitting up, propped on pillows against the corner of the room, his legs on the cot before him. Carefully, she stretched beside him. It had been four days since Miles had been gored but his youth and natural resistance had made him recover quickly. He was still weak, still in pain, but he was starting to heal.

"Why have you stayed with me?" he asked. "One of Bronwyn's women could have tended me."

"And have her jump in bed with you and tear your stitches?" she asked indignantly.

"I'll tear my stitches if you make me laugh. How could I have touched another woman when you're so close?"

"When I'm gone, I'm sure you'll manage to gather your courage."

His hand tangled in her hair, pulled her head back and his mouth took hers possessively. "Haven't you learned yet that you're mine?" he half growled. "When are you going to admit that?"

He didn't give her a chance to answer as he kissed her again, and much of the worry Elizabeth'd felt in the last days went into that kiss to make it one of desperation.

The touch of cold steel against Miles's throat made them break apart. Instinctively, he reached for his own sword but met only bare flesh under the plaid he wore.

Over them stood Roger Chatworth, his eyes full of hate, his sword pressing against the vein in Miles's neck.

"Do not," Elizabeth said, moving away from Miles. "Do not harm him."

"I would like to kill all the Montgomerys,"

Roger Chatworth said.

Miles, in one quick motion, moved sideways, caught Chatworth's wrist.

"No!" Elizabeth screamed and clung to her brother's arm.

Miles's bandages began to redden.

"He's hurt," Elizabeth said. "Would you kill a man who can't fight back?"

Roger turned his full attention to her. "Have you become one of them? Have the Montgomerys poisoned you against your own blood relations?"

"No, Roger, of course not." She tried to remain calm. There was such a wild look in Roger's eyes that she feared to anger him. Miles lay against the wall, panting, but she knew that at any moment he'd leap again and tear his wounds further. "Have you come for me?"

There was a sudden hush in the little room as both men watched her. She had to leave with Roger. If she did not, he'd kill Miles. She knew that very well. Roger was tired, angry, beyond all rational thinking.

"It will be good to go home," she said, forcing a smile.

"Elizabeth!" Miles warned.

She ignored him. "Come, Roger, what are you waiting for?" Her heart was pounding so hard she could barely hear her own voice.

"Elizabeth!" Miles shouted at her, his hand clutching at the hole in his chest.

For a moment Roger looked from one to the other, hesitating.

"I'm growing impatient, Roger! Haven't I been away long enough?" She turned on her heel to leave, paused at the door. Her eyes stayed on Roger's, not daring to look at Miles. She couldn't risk even one look at him or she'd lose her resolve.

Slowly, puzzled, Roger began to follow her. A horse waited obediently not far from the cottage. Elizabeth kept her eyes on the animal, not daring to look around because she knew she'd see the body of Sir Guy. Only his death would have kept the giant from protecting his master.

Another shout, stone-shaking, came from the cottage. "ELIZABETH!!"

Swallowing the lump in her throat, Elizabeth allowed Roger to help her on his horse.

"We must have food," Roger said and turned away from her.

"Roger!" she yelled after him. "If you harm him I—" she began and saw that he was ignoring her. She dismounted in a flash and was after him—but not in time.

Roger Chatworth ran his sword through Miles's arm and as Miles lay there bleeding, Roger said, "Raine's wife spared my life and it's to her that you owe your filthy life now." He turned to Elizabeth in the doorway. "Get on the horse or I'll finish the job, if he doesn't bleed to death as it is."

Trembling, feeling very ill, Elizabeth left the cottage and mounted the horse. Within seconds, Roger was behind her and they set off at a grueling pace.

Elizabeth sat before her embroidery frame, working on an altar cover of St. George slaying the dragon. In one corner was a boy who looked remarkably like Kit and St. George . . . the saint had some of the look of Miles Montgomery. Elizabeth stopped for a moment as the child in her womb kicked her.

Alice Chatworth sat across from her, a mirror held to reflect the unscarred half of her face. "I was so beautiful then," Alice was saying. "Absolutely no man could resist me. All of them were ready to lay down their lives for me. All I had to do was hint at something I wanted and it was given to me."

She switched the mirror to the misshapen side of her face. "Until the Montgomerys did this!" she hissed. "Judith Revedoune was jealous of my beauty. She is such an ugly, freckled, red-haired thing that she was worried over my dear Gavin's love. And well she should have been."

Elizabeth gave an exaggerated yawn, ignored Alice's look of hate and turned to Roger, who was standing by the fireplace, mug of wine in hand, his face brooding. "Roger, would you like to go for a walk with me in the gardens?"

As usual, Roger looked at her stomach before he looked back at her face.

"No, I have to talk to my steward," he half mumbled, his eyes searching her face.

She could feel what he wanted to say, what

he'd said many, many times: You've changed.

She'd been back with her brother and her "family" for two weeks and it brought home to her how much she *had* changed in her five months with the Montgomerys. The time had not been enough to make any changes in the Chatworth household, but it was enough for Elizabeth to have started the makings of a new person.

For all her insistence that Roger was different from Edmund, she saw that Roger had actually not enforced his own beliefs within his household. In many ways, the Chatworth house was the same as when Edmund was alive. The reason Roger could easily have Alice live with him was that he was oblivious to her. Roger lived with such inner turmoil, with all his love and care given to Elizabeth and Brian, that he was truly unaware of a great deal that went on around him.

Elizabeth had no more than dismounted her horse, tired after days of travel, when two of Roger's men, who had once been with Edmund, began to make snide comments to her. They hinted that they could hardly wait to catch her alone.

Elizabeth's first reaction had been fear. It had been as if she'd never left the Chatworth estates. Her mind raced over her repertoire of debilitating tricks to use on the men. But her thoughts went back to Sir Guy and how she'd broken his toes, how he'd hobbled for weeks—and later she'd sat with him, saw tears of worry gathering in his eyes over a man they both loved.

She would not return to her skulking, fearful ways. She'd come a long way in conquering her fear of men and she wasn't going to throw all she'd learned away.

She'd turned to Roger and demanded that he send the men away immediately.

Roger'd been very surprised and had quickly hustled her out of the stables. He'd tried to patronize her but Elizabeth wouldn't listen to him. The idea that his dear little sister would talk back to him shocked as well as hurt him. To his mind, he'd just rescued her from a hellhole and she was ungratefully complaining.

For the first time in her life, Elizabeth told her brother the whole truth about Edmund. Roger's face had drained of blood, he'd staggered backward into a chair and looked as if someone had beaten him. All these years he'd thought he'd protected his dear little sister but, in truth, she'd lived in hell. He had no idea Edmund had summoned her from her convent whenever Roger left the estates. He didn't know that she'd had to defend herself from his men.

By the time Elizabeth finished, Roger was ready to kill the men in the stables.

Roger Chatworth's fury was something to be reckoned with. Within three days, he'd put fear in the hearts of his household. Many men were dismissed and if a man so much as looked at Elizabeth with slanted eyes, she went to Roger. No more was she going to stand for such insolence. Before, she'd not known how a lady should be treated, as her only experience was with Edmund, but now she'd had five months in a place where she didn't have to be afraid of walking in a garden alone.

Roger had been taken aback by her demands and she realized how she and Brian had always protected him. Roger could be so kind and at the same time so cruel. She tried only once to talk to him about the Montgomerys, but Roger'd exploded with such hatred, she feared for his life.

Since it had been months since he'd seen her, he quickly noticed the changes in her body, remarked that she'd put on weight. Elizabeth had put her chin in the air and, with no regret, stated that she carried Miles Montgomery's child.

She had expected rage—she was prepared for rage but the deep, deep hurt in Roger's eyes threw her off balance.

"Go. Leave me," he'd whispered and she obeyed.

Alone in her room, Elizabeth'd cried herself to sleep as she had every night since leaving Miles. Would Miles realize she'd gone with Roger to save her lover? Or would Miles hate her? What would they tell Kit about where Elizabeth had gone? She lay on her bed and thought of all the people she'd come to care about in Scotland.

She longed to send a message to someone in Scotland but there was no one she could trust to deliver it. But yesterday, as she took her afternoon walk, an old woman she'd never seen before offered her a basket of bread. She started to refuse it until the woman lifted the cloth and showed a MacArran cockade. Elizabeth grabbed the basket quickly and the old woman was gone before Elizabeth could thank her. Greedily, she tore into the basket.

There was a message from Bronwyn saying she well understood why Elizabeth'd returned with Roger—but Miles didn't. Sir Guy had been hit with three arrows but they thought he'd live. While Miles was untended, he'd gone into a rage, torn all his stitches apart. When Morag found him he was in a fever and for three days they didn't believe he'd live. Stephen had returned from Raine's outlaw camp as soon as he heard Miles had been injured. He bore the news that Raine was taking young Brian under his wing and Stephen had every hope of there soon being peace between the two families. Bronwyn added that Miles was recovering slowly and he refused to mention Elizabeth's name.

Today, as Elizabeth thought of that last sentence, her skin grew cold, making her shiver.

"You should have a cloak," Roger said from behind her.

"No," she murmured, "my plaid is enough."

"Why do you flaunt that thing in front of me?" Roger exploded. "Isn't it enough that you carry a Montgomery within you? Do you have to slap me in the face every time I see you?"

"Roger, I want this hatred to end. I want—"

"You want to be my enemy's whore!" he snarled.

With one quick angry look she turned away from him.

He caught her arm, his eyes soft as he looked at her. "Can you see this from my side? I spent months in hell looking for you. I went to Raine Montgomery to ask where you were, yet he drew a sword on me. If his new wife hadn't stepped between us I'd be dead now. I went to the king on my knees and do you think that was easy? I bear no love for the man since he's fined me so heavily for what happened to Mary Montgomery, but for you I'd have gone on my knees before the devil."

He paused, put his hands on both her arms. "And getting in and out of Scotland was no easy task either, yet when I found you you were cuddled beside Montgomery as if you wanted to become a part of him. And the playacting you did! I felt as if I were the enemy because I was rescuing my own sister from a man who'd held her captive and taken her virtue. Explain all this to me, Elizabeth," he whispered.

She leaned her head forward to touch his chest. "How can I? How can I tell you what has happened to me in the last few months? I've seen love and—"

"Love!" he said. "Do you think that if a man takes you to his bed, he loves you? Has Montgomery sworn undying love to you? Has he asked to make a Chatworth his wife?"

"No, but—" she began.

"Elizabeth, you know so little of men. You were a pawn in this feud. Don't you know that the Montgomerys are laughing because a Chatworth bears a Montgomery child? They'll think they've won."

"Won!" she spat at him, pulling away. "I hate this all being thought of as a game. What should I tell my child, that he was a chess piece, used by two families in their silly war?"

"Silly? How can you say that when Brian is out there somewhere, possibly hating me because of the Montgomerys?"

She hadn't told him of seeing Brian in Scotland. "Did it ever occur to you, Roger, that perhaps you caused Brian to leave? I would like to hear your side of what happened to Mary Montgomery."

He turned away from her. "I was drunk. It was a hideous . . . accident." He turned back, his eyes pleading. "I can't bring the woman back and the king has punished me more than enough with his fines. Brian has left me and you return from my enemy bloated with his child, and instead of the love you once gave me, now all you do is question me, doubt me. What more punishment do you intend for me?"

"I'm sorry, Roger," she said softly. "Perhaps I have changed. I don't know if Miles loves me. I don't know if he'd want to marry me to give our child a name, but I do know that I love him and if he asked me, I'm sure I'd follow him wherever he led."

Only Roger's eyes showed the pain he felt at her words. "How could you turn against me so completely? Is this man so good in bed that your screams of pleasure make you forget the love I bear you and have always had for you? Does five months with him wipe out eighteen years with me?''

"No, Roger. I love you. I will always love you, but I want you both.''

He smiled at that. "How very young you are, Elizabeth. You want a man who, I hear, is also wanted by half the women of England. You want a man who takes you to his bed, gets you with child and never speaks of marriage. And what kind of marriage would it be? Will you care for all his bastards as you have for his eldest son?''

"What do you know of Kit?''

"I know a great deal about my enemies. Miles Montgomery likes women. You are one of many to him and I respect the man for at least not lying to you and saying you were going to be his one and only love.''

He touched her arm. "Elizabeth, if you want a husband, I can find someone for you. I know several men who'd take you bearing another man's child, and they'd be good to you. With this youngest Montgomery you'd be miserable inside a year.''

"Perhaps,'' she said, trying to think rationally. Maybe Miles's hands on her had made her lose reason. He'd always been kind to her, but then he'd been kind to serving girls. If she did desert her brother for a Montgomery, Roger would hate her, and what would she feel for Miles years from now? What if, as a practical joke, someone else "gave" him a pretty young girl? Would he decide she belonged to him also? Would he bring her home to Elizabeth, smiling, expecting her to care for the girl as she did for his bastard children?

"Let me find someone for you. I'll bring many men for your approval and you can choose who you want. At least look at them. If you want to remain unmarried, you can."

She looked at him with love. He'd be laughed at for allowing his sister to bear a child out of wedlock. Some would say she should be killed if she refused to wed. Roger had suffered much disgrace over the last few years, yet he was willing to risk more for her sake.

At her smile, he grinned, and for the first time he looked as if he had a reason for living.

"Yes, I'll look at your men," she said from her heart. She would try with all her might to fall in love with one of them. She'd have a kind, loving husband, children to love and her brothers, because somehow she'd reunite Brian and Roger.

Elizabeth learned a great deal about love in the next few days. Never, before she met Miles, had she had any idea what love was. She'd never even considered loving a man, but then Miles came along and changed that. Within five months of his patience and humor he'd made her love him. She knew she'd always have a soft spot for Miles but there were many men who were good and kind in the world. All she had to do was fall in love with one of them and it would solve everything.

But Elizabeth underestimated herself.

Roger began parading men before her like so many studs ready to service her. There were tall men, short men, thin men, fat men, ugly men, men so handsome you merely gaped at them, swaggering men, bold men, men who made her laugh, one who sang beautifully. On and on they came.

At first Elizabeth was flattered by their attentions, but after just a few days, her old fears began to return. A man touched her shoulder and she jumped high, put her hand on her eating dagger at her side. After a week, she was finding excuses to remain in her room, or else she was always in Roger's company.

Then suddenly, Roger left the estates. He said nothing to her but rode out with eight men at a furious pace. A servant said Roger'd received a message from a dirty, black-toothed man and within seconds Roger'd left. The message was tossed into the fire.

Elizabeth was close to tears knowing that there were eleven male guests below and she was their hostess. She couldn't talk to one man with any coherence because she was always concerned with where the other men were. All Miles's months of patient training were disappearing. Once she brought a brass vase down on the head of a man who'd dared to walk up behind her.

With her skirts flying about her, she fled to her room and refused to return to the hall.

She lay on her bed a long time and all she could remember was Miles. Every time she met a man, she compared him to Miles. Some utterly splendid man would be introduced to her and all she'd think was, he moves his hands too quickly or some other such nonsense. And one night, she'd allowed a man to kiss her in the garden. She'd caught herself just before she brought her heel down on his little toes, but she couldn't keep herself from wiping her mouth with the back of her hand. The poor man'd been terribly insulted.

Elizabeth tried very hard, but not a single man even interested her. As the days passed, she wished she could see Bronwyn and ask advice. She was considering writing a letter when the bottom dropped out of her world.

A haggard, wasted Roger returned bearing the mutilated body of Brian.

Elizabeth greeted him but Roger merely looked through her as he tenderly carried Brian's body upstairs and locked himself in a room. For two days he stayed locked inside with Brian's body and when he emerged, his eyes were sunken and black.

"Your Montgomerys did that," he said hoarsely as he strode past Elizabeth and Alice.

They buried Brian that afternoon but Roger didn't reappear. Elizabeth planted roses on the grave and shed tears for both her brothers.

Alice hounded Elizabeth mercilessly, screeching that the Montgomerys should die for all they'd done. She was fascinated by lamps full of hot oil and waved them around maniacally. She said Elizabeth's child would be born with the mark of Satan and would be cursed for all eternity.

One by one, the male guests left the bereaved and somewhat insane household and Elizabeth was left alone with her sister-in-law.

In early March a messenger wearing full regalia came from the king.

It was a day before the men Elizabeth sent out could find Roger where he'd been—alone in a shepherd's stone hut. He looked to be a skeleton of himself, his cheeks gaunt under a beard, his hair long and dirty, his eyes wild and frightening.

He silently read the message in Elizabeth's presence, then tossed it into the fireplace.

"Tell the king no," he said calmly before leaving the room.

Elizabeth could only gasp, and wonder what message the king had sent. With as much calmness as she could muster, she dismissed the king's men and sat down to wait. Whatever Roger had refused to do would no doubt soon be known to them when the king heard of the refusal. She put her hand on her growing belly and wondered if her child would live to worry about being called a bastard.

Chapter 14

SIX DAYS after the king's messenger had come and gone, Elizabeth was alone in the garden. She had not seen or heard from Roger in days and Brian's death was making Alice lose what sanity she had. It wasn't that the woman cared for Brian but it was the fact that a Montgomery had killed him. Elizabeth thought of this Raine with hatred.

A shadow moved across her path and involuntarily she gasped before looking up—into the dark, intense eyes of Miles Montgomery. His eyes contemptuously swept her up and down, made note of the ivory satin of her gown, the double rows of pearls, the blood-red ruby at her breast.

Elizabeth felt she wanted to drink in all of him, that she couldn't get enough of him. There were dark, faintly yellow shadows under his eyes and he was thinner. Obviously he wasn't fully recovered from his fever.

"Come," he said hoarsely.

Elizabeth didn't hesitate as she followed him

through the garden and into the forest park of the Chatworth estates. Supposedly these boundaries were guarded, but somehow Miles had entered undetected.

He didn't speak to her, didn't look at her and it wasn't until they reached the two waiting horses that she realized what was wrong: He hated her. His rigid body, his cold eyes all screamed it.

She became rigid herself when they reached the horses. "Where are you taking me?"

He turned toward her. "The king has ordered us to marry. Your brother has refused the order. If we disobey, both your brother and I will be declared traitors and our lands confiscated." His eyes touched on the ruby. "You need have no fear. After the marriage I will return you to your precious brother, but even you would not like to have all the things that mean so much to you taken away."

He turned away from her. Elizabeth tried to mount her horse but her long skirt and trembling body made that impossible. Miles came up behind her and, touching her as little as possible, flung her into the saddle.

Elizabeth was too stunned, too much in a state of shock, to even think as they set off quickly to the north. Her eyes were so dry they burned and all she thought of was the way the horse's mane whipped in the wind.

They halted less than an hour later on the outskirts of a small village, before a pleasant little house beside a church. Miles dismounted, didn't look at her as she struggled to get down from her horse.

A priest opened the door to them. "So this is the lovely bride, Miles," he said. "Come along, I know how impatient you are."

As Miles strode ahead, ignoring Elizabeth, she ran after him, caught his arm. The look he gave her as he glanced from her hand to her face made her breath catch. She dropped her hand. "After this is over, could we talk?" she whispered.

"If it doesn't take too long," he said coolly. "My brother is waiting for me."

"No," she said, trying to regain her dignity. "I'll not keep you long." With that, she gathered her skirts and walked ahead of him.

The marriage was over in minutes. There were no witnesses from either family, only a few strangers whom the priest knew. For all the feeling either participant put into the words, they could have been negotiating a grain contract.

When they were pronounced man and wife, Miles turned toward her and Elizabeth held her breath. "I believe we can talk in the vestry," was all he said. Chin up, Elizabeth led the way.

When they were alone in the room, he lazily leaned against the wall. "Now you have your chance to say what you want."

Her first impulse was to tell him where he could spend the rest of his life but she calmed herself. "I didn't know of the king's order that we marry. If I had I would not have refused. I would do a great deal to settle this feud."

"Even to sleeping with your enemy?" he taunted.

She gritted her teeth. "Roger has been very upset at Brian's death." For a moment her eyes flashed fire.

Miles's nostrils flared. "Perhaps you hadn't heard that Raine survived your brother's poison."

"Poison!" she gasped. "Now what do you accuse Roger of?"

"Not Roger," Miles said. "Your brother Brian poisoned Raine."

"Well, Brian certainly paid for the attempt! I hear Raine is a large man. Did he enjoy tearing my slight brother apart? Did he enjoy hearing Brian's frail bones snap?"

Miles's eyes hardened. "I see that once again you have heard only one side. Did Roger say Raine killed Brian?"

"Not in so many words, but . . ."

Miles came away from the wall. "Ask him then. Have your perfect brother tell you the truth about who killed Brian Chatworth. Now, if you have nothing else to accuse me of, I must go."

"Wait!" she called. "Please, tell me the news. How is Sir Guy?"

Miles's eyes turned black. "What the hell do you care? Since when have you cared about anyone except your treacherous brother? Guy nearly died from your brother's arrows. Perhaps he should practice his marksmanship. Another inch and he'd have reached Guy's heart."

"And Kit?" she whispered.

"Kit!" Miles said through clenched teeth. "Kit cried for three days after you left but now he won't even allow Philip's nurse in the same room. The nurse's name is Elizabeth."

"I never meant . . ." she began. "I love Kit."

"No, Elizabeth, you don't. We were nothing to you. You repaid us all for holding you against your will. You are, after all, a Chatworth."

Her anger exploded in her. "I'll not stand for more of your insinuations! What was I supposed to do when my brother held a sword at your throat? Should I have stayed with you? He would have killed you! Can't you understand that I left with him in order to save your ungrateful life?"

"Am I supposed to believe that?" he said, low. "You stand before me dripping pearls, wearing a ruby that costs more than all I own and tell me you followed your brother in order to save me? What has made you think I'm stupid?"

"Tell me then," she shot back, "what should I have done?"

His eyes narrowed. "You claim your brother loves you so much, you should have told him you wanted to stay with me."

She threw up her hands at that. "Oh yes, that would have worked so well. Roger no doubt would have resheathed his sword and gone home docilely. Roger's temper is second only to yours. And, Montgomery, how was I to know you *wanted* me to remain with you?"

He was silent for a moment. "My wants have always been clear. I hear you have been sleeping

214

with many men lately. I'm sure your marital status won't interfere with your activities, although my child will curb you for a while at least."

Very calmly, very slowly, Elizabeth stepped close to him and slapped him across the face.

Miles's head snapped to one side and when he looked back at her, his eyes were ablaze. With one quick, violent gesture he caught both her hands in one of his, pushed her back against the stone wall. His lips came down on hers hard, plundering.

Elizabeth reacted with all her pent-up desires and pushed her body into his hungrily.

His lips made a hot trail down her neck. "You love me, don't you, Elizabeth?"

"Yes," she murmured.

"How much?" he whispered, touching her earlobe with the tip of his tongue.

"Miles," she murmured, "please." Her hands were held against the wall, above her head, and she desperately wanted to put her arms around him. "Please," she repeated.

Abruptly, he pulled away from her, dropped her hands. "How does it feel to be turned down?" he said coldly, but a vein in his neck pounded. "How does it feel to love someone and be rejected? I pleaded with you to stay with me but you chose your brother. Now see if he can give you what you need. Goodbye, Elizabeth . . . Montgomery." With that he left the room, closing the door behind him.

For a long while Elizabeth was too weak to

move, but she finally managed to make her way to a chair and sit on it. She was there, in a daze, when the priest entered, obviously agitated.

"Lord Miles had to leave but an escort awaits you outside. And this was left for you." When Elizabeth didn't react, the priest took her hand and closed it around something cold and heavy. "Take your time, dear, the men will wait."

It was several minutes before Elizabeth gathered her strength enough to stand. The object in her hand fell and clanged against the stone floor. Kneeling, she picked it up. It was a heavy gold ring, sized small enough to fit her hand, set with a large emerald that was incised with three Montgomery leopards.

Her first impulse was to toss the ring across the room, but with a grimace of resignation, she slipped it on her left hand and left the room to go to the guard waiting for her.

Roger met her a half-mile from the estate with an armed guard, swords drawn. She kicked her horse ahead to meet him.

"Death to all Montgomerys!" he cried.

Elizabeth grabbed his horse's bridle, succeeding in nearly pulling her arm from its socket and making Roger's horse rear. Both of them fought their horses for a moment.

"Why do you come riding with Montgomerys?" Roger bellowed.

"Because *I* am a Montgomery," she shouted back.

That statement successfully made Roger pause.

"How dare you not tell me of the king's order that I marry Miles!" she yelled at him. "What else have you lied to me about? Who killed my brother Brian?"

Roger's anger made his face turn red. "A Montgomery—" he began.

"No! I want the truth!"

Roger looked at the guard of men behind her as if he were planning their deaths.

"You tell me the truth here and now or I ride with them back to Scotland. I have just been married to a Montgomery and my child has every right to be raised as one."

Roger was breathing so hard, his chest was swelling to barrel size. "*I* killed Brian," he shouted, then quietened. "I killed my own brother. Is that what you wanted to hear?"

Elizabeth had expected any answer but that one and she felt deflated. "Come back to the house, Roger, and we'll talk."

When they were alone in the solar, Elizabeth demanded that Roger tell her everything about the wars between the Chatworths and the Montgomerys. It wasn't an easy story to listen to and it was even harder to get Roger to tell the unbiased truth. Roger's view of the events was colored by his emotions.

In Scotland he'd seen a chance to marry Bronwyn MacArran, which would have been an excellent match for him. He did tell the woman a few falsehoods in order to make him appear more favorable to her—but what were a few lies in courtship? He'd even maneuvered Stephen Montgomery into fighting for her, but when Stephen won so easily Roger'd been enraged and attacked Stephen's back. Roger's humiliation at that had been too much to bear. He'd kidnapped Bronwyn and Mary merely to show the Montgomerys he was a power to be reckoned with. He never meant the women any harm.

"But you did harm Mary," Elizabeth said angrily.

"Brian wanted to marry her!" Roger defended himself. "After all I'd suffered at the hands of the Montgomerys and then Brian wanted to marry their old, plain, spiritless daughter. No one else in England would have her. Can you imagine how the Chatworths would have been laughed at?"

"Your pride sickens me. Brian lies dead rather than married. Did you get what you wanted?"

"No," he whispered.

"Neither have I." She sat down. "Roger, I want you to listen to me and listen well. The anger between the Montgomerys and Chatworths is over. My name is now Montgomery and my child will be a Montgomery. There will be no more fighting."

"If he tries again to take you—" Roger began.

"Take me!" She stood so fast the chair fell over. "This morning I begged Miles Montgomery to take me with him, but he refused. And I don't blame him! His family has lost someone they loved because of you, yet they have not killed you as probably they should have."

218

"Brian—"

"*You* killed Brian!" she shouted. "You have caused all of this and so help me God, if you so much as look at a Montgomery wrong, I'll take a sword to you myself." With that she left the room, nearly tripping over Alice who, as usual, was eavesdropping.

It was three days before Elizabeth could control her anger enough to even think. When she did think, she decided to look at what she had and do something with it. She was not going to have her child growing up as she had. She would probably never live with Miles so the closest thing to a father her child would have was going to be Roger.

She found Roger brooding before the fireplace and if she'd been a man, she would have pulled him out of his chair and given his backside a good swift kick.

"Roger," she said in a voice filled with honey, "I never noticed before, but you're getting a roll about your middle."

He put his hand to his flat stomach in surprise. Elizabeth had to repress her smile. Roger was a very good-looking man and he was used to women noticing him. "Perhaps at your age," she continued, "a man should grow stout and his muscles weak."

"I'm not so old," he said, standing, sucking in his stomach,

"That was one thing I liked about Scotland. The

men were so trim and fit."

He cocked his head at her. "What are you trying to do, Elizabeth?"

"I'm trying to keep you from living in a world of self-pity. Brian is dead and even if you fall in bed drunk every night for the rest of your life, you won't be able to bring him back. Now go get those lazy knights of yours and put them to work."

There was just a hint of a smile in his eyes. "Perhaps I do need some exercise," he said before leaving the room.

Six weeks later, Elizabeth was delivered of a very large, healthy baby boy whom she named Nicholas Roger. The child showed right away that he had inherited Gavin Montgomery's high cheekbones. Roger took to the child as if he were his own.

When she was up from her childbed, she began to work on making a home for little Nicholas. The first thing she did was order a guard near the baby at all times because Alice seemed to think the child was Judith and Gavin's and Elizabeth didn't trust the crazy woman's actions.

Nicholas was barely a month old when the first letter arrived from Judith Montgomery. It was a reserved letter inquiring after the child, saying Judith regretted not meeting Elizabeth but Bronwyn sang her praises. There was no mention of Miles.

Instantly, Elizabeth wrote back, raving about little Nick, saying he looked like Gavin and did

Judith have any advice for a new mother?

Judith responded with a trunkful of exquisite baby clothes that her son, now ten months old, had outgrown.

Elizabeth, with a bit of defiance, showed the clothes to Roger and told him she'd started a correspondence with Judith Montgomery. Roger, sweat-drenched from the training field, said nothing—but Alice had a great deal to say, all of which was ignored by everyone.

It wasn't until Judith's fifth letter that she mentioned Miles and then seemingly only in passing. She said Miles was living with Raine, both men were without their wives and both men were miserable. That news made Elizabeth's whole week seem wonderful. She laughed at Nick and told him all about his father and his stepbrother Kit.

In September, Elizabeth sent Judith bulbs for her garden, and tucked away inside was a doublet, very adult-looking, that Elizabeth had made for Kit. Judith wrote back that Kit loved the doublet but both he and Miles were under the impression Judith had made it, which made Gavin laugh because Judith was always too busy to have the patience to sew.

Just after Christmas, Judith sent a long, serious letter. Raine and his wife had reunited and Miles had come to visit them before returning to his own estates. Judith was appalled at the change in Miles. He'd always been a loner but now he rarely spoke at all. And worst of all, his love of women seemed to have disappeared. The women were still drawn to him but he looked at them suspiciously and without the least concern. Judith had tried to talk to him but all he'd said was, "I'm a married man, remember? Husbands and wives should remain faithful to each other." With that, he laughed and walked away. Judith pleaded with Elizabeth to forgive Miles and she also warned Elizabeth that all the Montgomery men were insanely jealous.

Elizabeth replied with a long, long letter of anger. Miles was the only man who'd ever touched her; she'd begged him to take her with him when they were married but he refused. She told how she'd gone with Roger only to save Miles's life. She ranted for pages about what a fool she'd been to believe in her brother so blindly, but it was Miles who was keeping them apart, not her.

As soon as Elizabeth sent the letter off with the messenger, she wanted it back. In truth, she'd never met Judith Montgomery. If just a small portion of what Alice thought was wrong with the woman was right, Judith was a monster. She could hurt Elizabeth's chances with Miles.

The month before an answer came nearly drove Elizabeth mad. Roger kept asking her what was wrong. Alice did more than that—she sneaked into Elizabeth's room, found Judith's letters and read them, giving a detailed account to Roger afterward. When Roger merely turned away, Alice threw herself into a fit of rage which lasted nearly a whole day.

Judith's answer to Elizabeth was short: Miles would be camping twenty miles from the Chatworth estate on 16 February, just outside the village of Westermore. Sir Guy was willing to help Elizabeth in any way he could.

This letter Elizabeth slept with, carried about with her and finally hid behind a stone in the fireplace. She walked about on a cloud for a few days, then came down. Why should she think Miles would want her again? What could she do to make him want her?

"You are mine, Elizabeth," he'd said. "You were given to me."

A plan began to form in her mind. No, she couldn't, she thought. A giggle escaped her. She just really wouldn't have the nerve. What if she "gave" herself to Miles again?

As Elizabeth was in the solar conjuring delightful, naughty visions, Alice was in Elizabeth's room, slipping about and searching. When she found Judith's latest letter, she took it to Roger, but this time he didn't turn away. For the next few days there were three people in the Chatworth house who were making plans—all in direct opposition to each other's.

Chapter 15

"I MOST certainly will not!" Sir Guy said as he looked down at Elizabeth. His voice was low but it seemed louder than a shout.

"But Judith said you were willing to help me."

Sir Guy drew himself up to every inch of his extraordinary height. The scar across his face was a brilliant purplish red. *"Lady* Judith"—he emphasized the word—"has no idea you'd ask something so preposterous of me. How can you think of such a thing?" he said in a shaming voice.

Elizabeth turned away from him, gave a swift kick to the carpet on the ground. It had seemed such a good idea at the time: She'd get Sir Guy to deliver her to Miles, nude, rolled in a carpet. Perhaps the repeat of the scene would make him laugh and he'd forgive her. But Sir Guy refused to cooperate.

"Then what am I going to do?" she asked

heavily. "I know he won't see me if I ask him straightforward."

"Lady Alyx sent her daughter to Lord Raine and the child acted as an emissary."

"Oh no! I'll not let Miles get his hands on Nick. Miles would hire another nurse and add the boy to his collection. I'd never see Miles *or* Nick again." She leaned against a tree and tried to think. If she did arrange a meeting with Miles she doubted if he'd listen to her. Her only real chance was to make his eyes darken with passion and then he wouldn't be able to help himself. Perhaps she could talk to him, after they'd made love.

As she was thinking, she toyed with her long black cloak, a lovely thing of velvet lined with black mink. It covered her from neck to feet. A new light came into her eyes as she looked back up at Sir Guy. "Can you arrange to give me some time alone with Miles? Not in his tent but in the woods? And I mean really alone! No doubt he'll call for his guard, but I want no one to come."

"I don't like that idea," Sir Guy said stubbornly. "What if there were some real danger?"

"True," she said sarcastically, "I might wrestle him to the ground and take a knife to his throat."

Sir Guy lifted one eyebrow and ostentatiously shifted off the foot Elizabeth'd injured.

Elizabeth gave him a small smile. "Please, Guy, I haven't hurt a man in a long time. Miles is my husband and I love him and I want to try to make him love me again."

"I believe Lord Miles more than loves you—he's obsessed with you, but you've hurt his pride. No woman anywhere has ever given him any trouble."

"I'll not apologize for leaving Scotland with Roger. At that time it's what I had to do. Now, will you give me time alone with my husband?"

Sir Guy took his time before he nodded once. "I will no doubt come to regret this."

Elizabeth shot him a dazzling smile, her whole face lighting up. "I will make you godfather to our next child."

Sir Guy snorted. "In one hour Lord Miles will be standing here. I will give you an hour with him."

"Then you'll find us in an embarrassing situation," she said frankly. "I mean to seduce my husband. Give us at least three hours alone."

"You are no lady, Elizabeth Montgomery," he said, but there was a twinkle in his eye.

"Nor do I have any pride," she agreed. "Now go while I ready myself."

When she was alone, Elizabeth lost some of her bravado. This was perhaps her only chance to win her husband back and she prayed that everything would go well. With trembling hands, she began to unbutton her gown. She hoped she knew Miles well enough to know that he might be able to resist her logically, but could he resist her physically?

She hid her clothes under leaves and, nude, she wrapped the concealing cloak about her body. To the world she'd appear to be a lady of decorum. When she was ready, she sat down on a stump and began to wait.

When she first heard someone walking toward her, she stiffened, recognizing Miles's step, quick, light, purposeful. She rose to meet him.

At his first sight of her there was a look of welcome, of eagerness, but then his vision clouded and he looked at her coldly. "And have you misplaced your brother?" he asked.

"Miles, I have arranged this meeting in order to ask if we might live together as man and wife."

"All three of us?"

"Yes." She smiled. "The two of us with our son Nicholas."

"I see. And what, pray tell, will your brother do without the sister he has so often killed for?"

She stepped closer to him. "A great deal of time has passed since we last saw each other, and I'd hoped that by now you'd conquered some of your jealousy."

"I am not jealous!" he snapped. "You had a decision to make and you made it. Now I will have someone escort you back to your brother. Guards!"

A look of puzzlement crossed Miles's face when no men appeared at his call, but before he could say a word, Elizabeth opened her cloak, revealing her nude body. Miles, gaping, could only gasp.

Elizabeth let the cloak fall closed but held it open to reveal the length of her from her waist to her toes, rather like when she'd first met him and was draped in the fur pelts. Stealthily, like a huntress, she walked toward him, put her hand to the back of his neck.

Involuntarily, his hand went to touch the satin skin of her hip.

"Do I have to beg, Miles?" she whispered, her eyes on his lips. "I have been wrong in so many things. I have no more pride. I love you and I want to live with you. I want more children."

Slowly, Miles's lips moved closer to hers. He appeared to be using all his willpower to resist her. "Elizabeth," he murmured, his lips touching hers lightly.

Long-repressed and banked fires ignited between them. Miles's arms slid under the cloak, pulled her off the ground as he clutched her to him, his kiss deepening. His mouth moved over her face as if he meant to devour her. "I've missed you. Oh God, there were times when I thought I'd go insane."

"I'm sure I did," she answered, half laughing, half crying. "Why couldn't you realize I loved only you? I could allow no other man to touch me."

He kissed away her tears. "I hear John Bascum had four stitches taken in his head from where you struck him."

She kissed his mouth and stopped him from talking. Without either of their realizing it, they were starting toward the ground. Elizabeth's fingers were buried in the fastenings of Miles's clothes, while his hands roamed eagerly over her body.

"Unhand her!" came a deadly voice from above them.

It took both Elizabeth and Miles a moment to understand who was speaking.

Roger Chatworth held his sword on Miles.

Miles gave Elizabeth a hard look and began to stand. "She is yours," he said to Roger, his chest heaving.

"Damn you to hell, Roger!" Elizabeth shouted up at her brother, grabbing a handful of stones and throwing them at his head. "Just once, can't you stay out of my life? Put that sword away before someone gets hurt!"

"I will hurt a Montgomery if he—"

"You may try," Miles sneered, drawing his sword.

"No!" Elizabeth screamed, jumping up to stand between the two men, facing her brother. "Roger, let me make this clear. Miles is my husband and I am going to return to his home with him, that is if he'll have me after the fools you've made of both of us."

"Some husband he is," Roger sneered. "He doesn't come near you for months, hasn't even seen his own son. Is this what you want, Elizabeth? You'd give up the home I've provided for a man who cares nothing for you? How many women have you impregnated since Elizabeth, Montgomery?"

"More than you could in a lifetime," Miles replied calmly.

Elizabeth stepped closer to Miles as Roger

lunged. "If I had any sense I'd tell both of you to go to the devil."

"Let me rid you of him," Roger said, but when his sword tip touched Elizabeth's cloak, he halted. "Have you no shame? Have you greeted this man like . . . like this?"

"Roger, you are a pigheaded fool who understands only what is pounded into your head." With a swirl of velvet and mink she turned, stood on tiptoe and planted her mouth on Miles's. Miles was beginning to understand that this time Elizabeth was choosing him over her brother. He caught her to him in a rib-crushing embrace and kissed her with promises of tomorrow.

Roger, fuming, so angry he was trembling, was unaware of the man sneaking up behind him. Nor did he hear the swoosh of air as the club came down on the side of his head. Silently, he crumpled to the ground.

Miles and Elizabeth would have been oblivious to the crashing of a tree but something made Elizabeth's eyes flicker open. A club was coming down on Miles's head. She pushed him to the left just enough so that the club struck her and not him.

Miles did not at first realize what had made Elizabeth go so completely limp. With one hand supporting her, he turned, but too late to avoid the blow that felled him.

The three men, dirty, burly men, stood over the two men and a woman on the ground.

"Which one is Montgomery?" one man asked.

"How would I know!"

"So which do we take?"

"Both!" said the third one.

"And the doxy?" a man asked, using his club to part Elizabeth's cloak.

"Throw her in with them. The Chatworth woman said there might be a woman and to get rid of her, too. I'm plannin' to make her pay for each body. Now, get that man's clothes off while I tend to this one."

The third man cut a long strand of Elizabeth's blonde hair and tucked it into his pocket. "Come on, hurry up. The wagon won't wait all day."

When Elizabeth woke, the pounding, galloping pain in her head was so bad she wasn't sure she ever wanted to wake up. Even the ground under her seemed to be moving. As she started to sit up, she fell backward, banging her head not on the ground but on wood.

"Quiet, sweetheart," came Miles's voice from behind her.

She turned to meet Miles's intense stare. He wore nothing but his loincloth, his arms behind him at an unnatural angle, his ankles tied. Beside him, snoring, was Roger, also bound.

As Elizabeth's head cleared, she realized her own wrists and ankles were also bound. "Where are we?" she whispered, trying not to let her fear show.

Miles's voice was deep, strong, comforting.

"We're in the hold of a ship and I would imagine we're bound for France."

"But who? Why?" she stammered.

"Maybe your brother will know," Miles said flatly. "Right now we must free ourselves. I'll roll over to you and use my teeth to untie your hands, then you can free me."

Elizabeth nodded, willing herself to calmness. If Roger'd had anything to do with their capture, he wouldn't also be here, she told herself. When her hands were free, she gave a great sigh of relief, turned to Miles and instead of freeing his hands, she opened her cloak, pressed her bare body against his and kissed him. "Have you thought about me?" she whispered against his lips.

"Every moment." Eagerly he leaned forward to kiss her again.

Laughing, she pushed him away. "Shouldn't I untie you?"

"The parts of me that need freedom have it," he said as he moved his hips closer to hers.

Elizabeth buried her fingers in his shoulders and invaded his mouth with her own.

Only the loud, wakening groans of Roger made her pull away.

"If I didn't hate your brother before, I would now," Miles said with feeling as Elizabeth sat up, leaned over him, and began to untie the ropes on his wrists.

"What is this?" Roger demanded. He sat up, fell down again and finally managed to sit. "What have you done now, Montgomery?"

Miles did not answer the challenge but rubbed his wrists as Elizabeth worked on the ropes on her own ankles. As Miles began to untie his ankles, Roger exploded again.

"Do the two of you plan to free yourselves and leave me here? Elizabeth, how can you forget . . ."

"Do be quiet, Roger," Elizabeth said. "You've done more than enough harm already. Do you have any idea where this ship is taking us?"

"Ask your lover. I'm sure he's the one who planned this."

Miles didn't bother to answer Roger as he turned to Elizabeth. "I want to know whether I have your loyalty for the moment. If someone opens the hatch I'll jump him while you use the ropes to tie him. Can I depend on you?"

"Whether you believe it or not, you have always had my loyalty," Elizabeth said in a cold voice.

"Have you tried demanding our release?" Roger asked. "Offer them money."

"And will you empty your pockets for them?" Miles asked, glancing at the small strip of cloth that Roger wore.

No one said any more as the hatch began to open and a foot appeared on the ladder.

"Down!" Miles commanded and both Roger and Elizabeth feigned sleep as they sprawled on the wooden floor. Miles silently slipped to the far side of the ladder.

The sailor stuck his head down, seemed

satisfied with the two prisoners' silence and took another step. At the same moment he realized one prisoner was missing, Miles grabbed both the man's feet and sent him sprawling. There was no sound except a heavy thud, lost in the creaking and groaning of the ship.

Roger lost no time in springing into action as he lifted the sailor's head by his hair. "He'll be out for a while."

Miles was unbuttoning the man's clothes.

"And do you expect me to remain here while you take his clothes and escape?" Roger demanded. "I'll not leave myself at the mercy of a Montgomery."

"You will!" Elizabeth hissed. "Roger, I am sick of your distrust. *You* are the one who has caused most of the problems between the Montgomerys and Chatworths, and now if we're to get out of this, you must learn to cooperate. What can we do, Miles?"

Miles was watching her as he struggled into the too-small clothes. Sailors were often chosen because of their diminutive size since small men could maneuver more easily inside the confines of a ship. "I will return as soon as I've found out anything." With that he was up the ladder and out.

Elizabeth and Roger tied and gagged the unconscious sailor and left him in a corner.

"Will you always side with him?" Roger asked sulkily.

Elizabeth leaned back against the wall of the

ship. Her head hurt and her empty stomach was growing queasy from the motion. "I have a great deal to make up to my husband. Perhaps Miles was right and there was something I could have done the day you came to us in the crofter's hut. You've never been one to listen to reason, but perhaps I could have at least tried."

"You insult me! I have always been good to you."

"No! You've always taken advantage of what good you've done for me. Now listen to me. However we got into this mess, we must get out. You must cooperate."

"With a Montgomery?"

"With *two* Montgomerys!" she snapped.

For a few moments Roger was quiet. "Alice," he muttered. "She brought me the letter from Gavin Montgomery's wife. She knew where you were meeting your . . ."

"Husband," Elizabeth supplied. "Oh Roger!" she gasped. "Nicholas. He's with Alice, alone. We must get back to my son."

Roger put his hand on her arm. "The child has a guard and they have orders not to let Alice near the boy. They won't disobey me."

"But what will happen to him if we don't return?"

"No doubt the Montgomerys will take over his care."

Their eyes met and it was a moment before Roger realized what he'd said. He was very close to admitting that, just perhaps, he'd been wrong in his accusations of the Montgomerys. Maybe all Elizabeth's thousands of words had begun to sink in.

They turned, breath held, as the hatch door opened, and expelled it when Miles entered.

Elizabeth flew to him, clasped his neck, nearly knocking the bundles from his hands. "We think it was Alice who arranged everything. Oh my Miles, you weren't hurt?"

Miles looked at her suspiciously. "You blow quickly from hot to cold and back again. No, I had no trouble. I brought food and clothes." He tossed Roger a loaf of hard bread and handed a bundle of clothing to Elizabeth. After one glance at the bound and gagged sailor, silent, eyes wide open in fear, Miles sat down with Roger and Elizabeth.

Besides the bread, there was dried meat and a vile-tasting grog which Elizabeth gagged over.

"What did you see?" Roger asked.

Miles realized that Roger was swallowing a great deal of pride to ask such a question. "It's an old ship, falling apart, and it's run by a crew that's mostly drunk or dying. If they know we're prisoners, they're not interested."

"They sound like the type of men Alice would know," Elizabeth said in disgust. "Are we headed toward France like you thought?"

"Yes. I recognize the coastline. When it's dark we'll slip out, take one of the rowboats and row ashore. I don't want to risk a welcoming party when the ship docks." He looked to Roger and

Roger gave a nod of his head.

"And how do we get back to England?" Elizabeth asked, chewing.

"I have relatives about four days' ride from where we'll land. If we can get to them we should be safe enough."

"Of course we have no horses or food to last us the journey," Roger said, drinking deeply of the awful brew.

"Perhaps we can manage," Miles said quietly, taking the jug. There was a slight emphasis on the word "we."

"Yes, maybe we can," Roger answered just as quietly.

They ate in silence and when they'd finished, Roger and Elizabeth dressed in the sailors' clothes. The striped cotton shirt stretched taut across Elizabeth's breasts and she was pleased to see a flicker of interest in Miles's eyes. She'd already proved that though he might still be angry with her, he still desired her—and hadn't he said he'd thought of her "every moment"?

When it grew even darker in the smelly little room, Miles again slipped up the ladder and this time he was gone a frighteningly long time. He returned empty-handed.

"I stocked the rowboat with all the food I could find." He looked at Roger. "I must trust you to protect my back. Elizabeth will be between us."

Roger, like Miles, was too tall to stand in the hold. Miles could pass as a sailor in his ill-fitting clothes, a day's growth of black beard on his cheeks, his eyes wild and fierce, but Roger couldn't. Roger's heavier form had split the seams of the shirt and his aristocratic blondness could not be mistaken for that of a dirty seaman. And Elizabeth in the form-fitting clothes was hopeless. Her features were too delicate to ever look like a man's.

Under the watchful eyes of the bound sailor who was trying to disappear into the woodwork, they made their way up the ladder. Miles stayed several paces ahead, a small knife in his hand. It was the only weapon he'd returned with and he'd offered no explanation as to how he'd obtained it.

The cool night air made Elizabeth realize how hideous the hold had been and her head began to clear as a breeze rushed over her. Miles caught her arm, giving a slight impatient jerk, and she gave her attention back to the moment.

There were three men on deck—one at the helm, two sauntering about on opposite sides of the ship.

Miles ducked, to disappear in a tangle of enormous ropes, and instantly Roger and Elizabeth followed his example. Crouching until her legs ached, they inched along the ship wall, slowly, carefully so as to make no sound.

When Miles stopped, he waved an arm and Roger seemed to understand. He slipped over the side of the ship, and Elizabeth held her breath, expecting to hear a splash as Roger fell, but none came. The next moment Miles motioned her over, too. Without another thought, she threw a leg over the side of the ship and the rest of her followed. Roger caught her and silently lowered her to a seat in the rowboat.

Her heart was pounding as she watched Roger, Miles helping from above, begin to lower the little boat down the side of the ship. Muscles in Roger's arms strained as he took the weight, not letting it drop and hit the water loudly. Elizabeth made a move to help but Roger impatiently motioned her away. As she moved back to her seat, her foot caught on something. It was all she could do to stifle a scream as she saw a hand near her foot—the hand of a dead sailor.

Suddenly, the rowboat lurched and she heard Roger's intake of breath as he fought to control their plunge. For some reason Miles had abruptly released the ropes overhead. Roger managed to set the boat into the water with only a whisper. Pulling back, he looked up toward the ship.

Miles was nowhere to be seen and for a moment Elizabeth felt panic. How deep did Roger's hatred run? Could she fight Roger if he decided to leave Miles behind?

But Roger merely stood in the boat, looking up expectantly, his legs wide apart and braced against the rolling boat.

When Elizabeth was near tears of worry, Miles looked over the side, saw where Roger was and the next minute he tossed a body into Roger's arms. Roger seemed to be waiting for just this and he didn't fall when the body hit him. The next moment Miles was traveling down the rope with lightning speed and he was only half-in when Roger pushed off and began to row. Miles kicked the second dead sailor's body beside the other one, grabbed the second oars and started rowing.

Elizabeth couldn't say a word as she watched the two of them working together, the boat gliding away into the night.

Chapter 16

"LET'S GET rid of them," were the first words spoken after an hour of silence.

Miles nodded in agreement and kept rowing as Roger slipped the two bodies into the water.

Roger resumed rowing. "We'll have to have other clothes. Something plain that won't arouse suspicion."

"Suspicion of what?" Elizabeth asked. "Do you think the sailors will try to find us?"

Roger and Miles exchanged looks that made Elizabeth feel like an outsider.

"If we let it be known that we're of the Montgomerys or Chatworths," Roger began patiently, "we'd be held for ransom within minutes. Since we travel without a guard we must travel incognito."

"As musicians perhaps," Elizabeth added. "We should have Alyx with us."

The mention of Miles's new sister-in-law made Roger reminisce about the time Alyx saved his

241

life. The telling took until dawn, when the men finally reached shore.

"Keep your cloak about you and stay close to me," Miles ordered under his breath. "They'll be setting up a market soon and we'll see if we can find some clothes."

Even though light was just breaking, the town square was alive with people bringing in goods to sell. Roger, in his clothes with burst seams, his arrogant stance, caused many looks, as did Elizabeth, her hair dirty and tangled but her body covered in an expensive cape. But it was Miles who received the most looks—all from females.

A pretty young woman, surrounded by young men, looked up from her wares and met Miles's dark eyes.

Elizabeth stepped forward, hands made into claws. With a chuckle, Miles caught her arm. "How'd you like to have the lady's dress?"

"I'd like to have her hide nailed to my door."

Miles gave Elizabeth such a hot look that she felt her heart begin to beat faster. "Behave yourself and obey me," he said, walking toward the woman who was giving him such heated looks.

"And what can I do for you?" The woman fairly purred, her language a gutter French.

"Could I persuade you out of your clothes?" Miles half whispered, his fingers caressing a large cabbage as he spoke a perfect, classical French.

Elizabeth could have been part of the roadway for all the attention the woman paid her.

"Aye, you could," she whispered, her hand closing over Miles's. "And what would you like to offer in return?"

Miles drew back, his eyes alight, that half-smile of his that Elizabeth knew so well on his lips. "We'll barter a cloak, fur lined, for three suits of clothes and provisions."

The woman looked Elizabeth up and down. *"Her* cloak?" she spat.

By now two of the men had walked toward the group and from the look of them, they were the woman's brothers. Elizabeth, angry at Miles's flirting, even if it were for a good cause, looked up through her lashes at the men. "We have had a most unfortunate accident," she said in French, not quite as good as Miles's, but adequate. "We were hoping to trade this unworthy cloak for a few garments, although perhaps your sister's would be a bit small." At that she casually let the cloak fall to her hips, revealing a skin-tight shirt and pants even tighter. Miles angrily pulled the cloak back to her shoulders but not before the young men gasped in appreciation.

"Will there be a trade?" Miles said through clenched teeth, not looking at Elizabeth.

The brothers agreed readily, the sister having been pushed into the background.

A few minutes later, Elizabeth stepped into a doorway and changed clothes under the cover of her cloak. The dress she wore was plain homespun, loose, comfortable, concealing.

When Miles and Roger were also dressed

plainly but with tight hose displaying their muscular thighs, they filled packs with food and set off toward the south.

They were well out of town before Miles spoke to Elizabeth. "And did you learn that trick while at your brother's house? You seem to have recovered quickly from your fear of men."

"And what was I supposed to do? Stand by and let that slut maul you? No doubt you would have taken her against the wall if she'd asked that price."

"Perhaps," was all Miles said and lapsed into one of his infuriating silences.

"Why is it that you accuse me of all manner of bad doings? I have never done anything to deserve your mistrust. I stayed with you in Scotland and—"

"You ran away and nearly killed the MacGregor. You left with your brother," Miles said flatly.

"But I had to!" Elizabeth insisted.

Roger had been walking on the other side of Elizabeth, silent until now. "I would have killed you, Montgomery, if she hadn't gone with me. And I wouldn't have believed whatever she said about wanting to stay with you."

"Why are you telling me this?" Miles asked Roger after a pause.

"Because Elizabeth's ranted at me for a long time about how . . . wrong I've been. Perhaps there's some truth in her words."

They walked in silence for some time, no one

speaking his or her thoughts.

As the sun rose higher, they stopped and ate, drinking water from a roadside stream. Elizabeth caught Miles watching her several times and she wondered what he was thinking.

They passed many travelers on the road, rich merchants with donkeys laden with gold, many wandering peasants, musicians, blacksmiths and once a nobleman escorted by twenty armed knights. For an hour afterward Roger and Miles made derogatory remarks about the knights, ranging from their colors to their old-fashioned armor.

As the sun started its descent, the men looked about for a place to spend the night. Although they risked being arrested as poachers, Roger and Miles chose to stay in the king's forest, away from the campers along the roadside.

As they ate, Miles and Roger talked about training, mentioned a few people they both knew and generally acted as if they were old friends. Elizabeth walked away into the shadows and neither man even noticed. Several minutes later she was near tears as she leaned against a tree and listened to the night sounds.

When Miles's hand touched her shoulder, she jumped away.

"Is something wrong?" he asked.

"Wrong!" she hissed at him, her eyes filling with tears. "How could anything be wrong! You held me prisoner for months, made me fall in love with you, yet when I sacrificed everything to save your worthless life, you hated me. I have borne your child, I have conspired with your relatives and your own man to win you back, yet all I get from you is coolness. I've kissed you and you've responded but you've offered me nothing on your own. What must I do to make you understand that I didn't betray you? That I didn't choose my brother over you? You heard Roger say he would have killed you if I hadn't gone with him.'' She couldn't continue as the tears were choking her.

Miles leaned against a tree, several feet away from her. The moonlight silvered his hair and eyes. ''I thought only my brothers were subject to the old demon of pride. I thought Raine was a fool when he refused to forgive his wife for going to the king to beg for a pardon. I could have forgiven you a king but you chose one man over me, someone else's home over mine. And when I heard the stories of all the men you'd bedded I knew I could have killed you.''

When she started to protest, he put up his hand. ''Perhaps it's because I've dealt with so many unfaithful wives, women who've risen from my bed and put on their wedding clothes. Maybe that distorted my view of all women. And finally, you were my prisoner but you came to me so easily.''

''I fought you!'' she said hotly, insulted.

Miles merely smiled at her. ''Raine said I was jealous, and the irony of it was that I was jealous of the same man as he was. Raine believed his wife Alyx had a great affection for Roger Chatworth.''

"Roger, I'm sure, knew nothing of this."

"So I gathered when he told the story of Alyx saving his life. Alyx did it to save Raine because my brother is a hotheaded, stubborn man who never listens to reason."

"Raine!" Elizabeth sputtered. "Did he rage so that he tore his stitches? Did he have to be drugged to make him sleep?"

Miles gave her a quick smile, teeth flashing. "Raine wears out lances when he's angry. I have my own way."

He was silent for a long moment. "How is our son?" he asked quietly.

"He has high cheekbones like your brother Gavin. There is no doubt of the family resemblance."

"I never doubted it, not truly. Elizabeth . . . ?"

"Yes," she whispered.

"Why did you leave me? Why didn't you return to me within a week or so? I waited every day; I prayed for your return. Kit cried himself to sleep. So many mothers have left him."

Tears were rolling down Elizabeth's cheeks. "I was afraid of Roger. He wasn't sane. Brian had vowed to kill Roger and I was afraid that if I weren't there to stop him, Roger'd declare war on all the Montgomerys. I hoped to make him see the truth; I hoped to learn the truth about the hatred of the two families."

"And the men?" Miles said. "Pagnell told everyone of how you were delivered to me and every man who courted you made sure I heard all the details.''

Elizabeth put her hand up. ''You were not only the first man to make love to me, you were the first man to speak to me without a leer on his face, the first man to make me laugh, the first man to show me kindness. Even you have said I know nothing about men.''

''So you found out,'' Miles said bitterly.

''In a way, I did. I thought about it dispassionately and I knew that it would be better if I loved any man but a Montgomery. If I were married to someone else perhaps Roger would forget that I carried a Montgomery's child and maybe some of his hatred would leave him. So I decided to meet some men and see if maybe I loved you merely because you were the first.''

Miles was silent, his eyes burning into her.

''Some of the men made me laugh, some were kind, some made me feel beautiful, but none of them did all things. As the weeks went by, instead of fading, everything about you became clearer. I remembered your every gesture and I began comparing the men to you.''

''Even to the size of—''

''Damn you!'' Elizabeth cut him off. ''I did not bed any of the men and I have a feeling you know that, yet you want to hear me say it.''

''Why didn't you take them to your bed? Some of the men you met are very successful with women.''

''As you are?'' she spat at him. ''Here you stand demanding celibacy from me, yet what

248

about you? When I tell you there have been no other men will you allow me to come to your pure bed? This morning I had to drag you from a woman. How do you think I've felt while holding your son and knowing that at that moment you could be in bed with one or two—or more—women?''

"More?" he mocked, then lowered his voice seductively. ''There have been no women since you.''

Elizabeth didn't believe she'd heard correctly. ''No—'' she began, eyes wide.

''My brother Raine and I moved into one of his keeps and in a rage we dismissed every woman, even the laundresses. We trained all day, drank all night and cursed women constantly. Raine came to his senses first when his wife sent their daughter to him. Little Catherine made me miss my own children so I went back to Gavin's for Christmas and Judith—'' He ran his hand through his hair.

''I used to think Gavin was hard on his sweet little wife but I'd never been on the sharp side of her tongue. The woman never left me alone. She was merciless. She talked constantly about our son, sighed over the fact that her son would never know his cousin and she even hired a man to paint a picture of an angel with long blond hair holding a little boy inside my shield. Inside my shield, mind you! I told Gavin I was going to wring his wife's neck if he didn't do something but Gavin laughed so hard I never mentioned it again. When she received your letter about how you were willing to forgive me, Judith launched into me with renewed force.''

Miles closed his eyes a moment in memory. ''She enlisted Alyx's help and Alyx came up with a dozen songs about two lovers who were held apart by a stupid, vain man who just happened to look exactly like me. One evening at dinner Alyx led twenty-two musicians in a song that made everyone laugh so hard two men fell off their stools and broke ribs. Alyx was at her best.''

Elizabeth was so astonished at his story she could barely speak. ''And what did you do?''

He winced in memory. ''I very calmly bounded over the table and took Alyx's throat in my hands.''

''No!'' she gasped. ''Alyx is so tiny, so—''

''Both Raine and Gavin drew swords on me and as I stood there, about to kill this pretty little songbird, my brothers' swords at my neck, I realized I wasn't myself. The next day Judith arranged the meeting between us.'' His eyes twinkled. ''The meeting where you wanted Sir Guy to deliver you to me in a carpet.''

Elizabeth wouldn't look at him. She thought Sir Guy had been on her side, yet all along he'd been reporting—and laughing—to Miles. How the two of them must have slapped each other's backs at her wanting to seduce her own husband. What had happened to that prideful woman who'd once stood on a cliff edge and vowed never to submit to any man?

"Excuse me," she whispered as she swept past Miles on her way back to Roger.

Miles caught her in his arms, pulling her close to him.

When Elizabeth saw that he was smiling at her with such a *knowing* little grin, she brought her elbow down hard into his ribs and was rewarded with his whoosh of pain. "I hate you, Montgomery!" she yelled into his face. "You've made me beg and cry and taken all my pride." She tried to hit him again but he pinned her arms to her side and she couldn't move.

"No, Montgomery," he said, moving his lips near hers. "You love me. You love me so much you're willing to beggar yourself for me. I've made you cry in passion and I've made you cry tears of love."

"You've humiliated me."

"As you've done to me." He held her as she struggled against him. "Every woman has come to me easily but only you have made me work. Only with you have I been angry, jealous, possessive. You were given to me and you are mine, Elizabeth, and never again will you be allowed to forget it."

"I never did—" she began but he cut her off by kissing her. Once his lips touched hers, she was lost. She could no more argue with him than she could have run away.

His arms loosened their grip on her just long enough for her to slide her arms about his neck and pull him even closer.

"Never, *never* forget it again, Montgomery," he whispered by her ear. "You will belong to me always—in this century and in the next. Forever!"

Elizabeth barely heard him as she stood on tiptoe and raised her mouth to his.

She had no idea how much she had missed him physically. He was the only man on earth she could be with so trustingly, the only man she wasn't wary of. All the years of holding herself in reserve were showing themselves in her eagerness, her ferocity. She put her hands in his hair, feeling it curl about her fingers, and pulled his head closer.

A low, throaty laugh came from Miles. "A tree you said? Take the woman against a tree?" he said.

Miles knew what she wanted—not a sweet, gentle lovemaking but one of all the fury she felt. His hands began tearing at her clothes, one hand on the ties of her linen underwear, the other on his own trunk hose. Elizabeth kept kissing him, her mouth wrapped around his, tongues entangled.

When her back slammed into a tree, she merely blinked and applied her teeth to Miles's neck, tearing at his skin as if she meant to flay him.

Miles lifted her, put her legs about his waist, her skirt bunched between them. Neither of them cared for the niceties of removing their clothes. His hands on her bottom, he lifted her, set her down on his shaft with the force of a falling anchor.

Elizabeth gasped, buried her face in Miles's neck and held on for dear life as his strong arms lifted her up and down. Her head went back as she felt a scream building inside her. Sweat began to drip off Miles and he rubbed the salty stuff on her, plastering her hair to the both of them.

With one last, fierce thrust that sent Elizabeth into an ecstasy, Miles pulled her to him, shuddering, his hot body erupting again and again.

Elizabeth, her body tight, convulsing in waves of pleasure, felt quick tears in her eyes. Slowly she came back to earth, her legs feeling weak, aching from clasping Miles with every ounce of her strength.

He leaned away to look at her, caressed her wet hair, kissed her temple. "I love you," he said tenderly, then smiled roguishly. "And besides that you're the best . . ."

"I understand." She laughed. "Now are you going to let me down or are you going to kill me against this tree?"

With one more kiss, Miles set her feet on the ground and gave an ungentlemanly, prideful laugh when Elizabeth's legs collapsed under her and he had to hold her to keep her from falling.

"Braggart!" she hissed, clutching him, but she gave him a smile and kissed the hand holding her arm. "Am I really the best?" she asked as if it meant nothing to her. "You still find me attractive even after I've borne a child?"

"Tolerably so," Miles said seriously.

Elizabeth laughed, smoothed her skirts and tried to regain her composure as they walked back to where Roger waited.

Chapter 17

THE THREE of them walked together for two days and they were blissful ones for Elizabeth. There were nights of lovemaking and days of love. Miles gave her his complete attention. They held hands and talked softly or laughed uproariously at the silliest things. They made love beside a stream and later bathed in its icy water.

Roger watched them with an air of aloofness, and sometimes Elizabeth felt a pang of guilt for the pain she knew she was causing him. A few times he made remarks about Miles's unknightly behavior but Miles said that until he reached his relatives, he was a carefree peasant.

Their progress was slow and the four-day journey on horseback was stretching into several more days on foot.

On the fourth day, the trio left the roadside just before noon to rest and refresh themselves. Roger, after directing an unnoticed look of contempt toward his sister and Miles, walked away from them, deeper into the forest. When he'd first heard his sister had been taken prisoner, his pain had been great—but now he could see that he'd lost her much more completely than if she were a prisoner.

Reminiscing over his problems, he walked past the earth-torn edge of the little gully without paying the least attention. He was several feet past the obvious signs of a struggle before he recognized them. Turning back, he examined the earth.

He'd been walking along the edge of a steep-sided bank that fell away to a stream of rushing water and, clearly, on the edge were the signs of someone falling. Often, after a battle, Roger'd had to search for his men who were wounded and lost, and now his knight's instincts rose like the hairs on his neck. Immediately, he started down the side, skidding in his haste.

What he saw at the bottom was not what he expected. Sitting on a rotten piece of log, her feet hidden under a jumble of large rocks, was a pretty young woman, richly dressed in burgundy velvet trimmed about the neckline with large golden amethysts. Her dark eyes, almost too big for her face, looked up at Roger with pleasure.

"I knew you'd come," she said in English that was pleasantly and softly accented.

Roger blinked once in confusion but ignored her remark. "Did you fall? Are you hurt?"

She smiled at him, making her eyes turn liquid. She looked to be quite young, a child really, wearing a dress much too old for her. Dark hair peeped from under a pearl-embroidered hood. More pearls draped down the front of her dress.

"My foot is caught and I cannot move it."

Women! Roger thought, moving to examine the rocks that pinned her feet. "You must have heard me above. Why didn't you call out to me?"

"Because I knew you'd come for me."

Insane, Roger thought. The poor girl was possessed by spirits. "When I lift this rock I want you to move your foot. Do you understand me?" he said as if talking to an idiot.

She merely smiled in answer and when the rock was moved, she pulled her foot from under it.

Her right foot was pinned differently and Roger saw that if he moved one stone, another would fall and perhaps break her ankle. She was a little thing and he doubted her fragile bones could stand much.

"Do not be afraid to tell me," she whispered. "I'm not a stranger to pain."

Roger turned to look at her, at her big eyes looking at him with so much trust, and that trust both frightened him and made him feel powerful.

"What is your name?" he asked, studying and considering the rocks around her little foot.

"Christiana, my lord."

Roger's head came up sharply. His dirty peasant's clothes had not fooled her, so perhaps she wasn't stupid after all. "Chris then." He smiled. "May I borrow your eating dagger? I'll put together something to hold those rocks while I move these.'' He pointed.

She handed him the knife quickly and he bit his lips to keep from cautioning her about handing knives to strangers. The jewels on her dress were worth a fortune and the pearl necklace she wore was without equal.

He moved but a few feet from her to cut several tree branches. Removing his doublet, he pulled out his shirt and cut strips of cloth from the tail to use in building a platform to fit under the rocks.

''Why is no one searching for you?'' he asked as he worked.

''Perhaps they are; I don't know. I dreamed of you last night.''

He gave her a sharp look but said nothing. Girls everywhere seemed to be full of romantic ideas of being rescued. It was hard for a man to live up to.

''I dreamed,'' she continued, ''of this forest and this place. I saw you in my dream and I knew you'd come.''

''Perhaps the man in your dream was merely fair-skinned and resembled me,'' Roger said patronizingly.

''I saw many things. The scar by your eye—you received it from your brother when you were only a boy.''

Involuntarily, Roger's hand went to the curved scar by his left eye. He'd come close to losing his eye that day and very few people who knew how he got the scar were still alive. He doubted if even

Elizabeth knew.

Christiana merely smiled at his look of surprise. "I have waited all my life for you."

Roger shook his head to clear it. "That was a lucky guess," he said. "About the scar I mean. Now hold very still while I prop these rocks up." There was no need to tell her to be still as she'd hardly moved since he'd arrived.

The rocks were not small and Roger had to sweat some before he could move the largest one. And even as it rolled away, more came crashing down onto the weak, makeshift platform he'd created. With lightning speed he jumped onto Christiana, knocking her backward and rolling her away from the crushing boulders. Even as he moved her, he heard her intake of breath as the rocks scraped away some of her skin.

The sound of the rocks filled the air and Roger covered Christiana's body with his own, protecting her from dust and fragments. When it was safe, he started to pull away from her but she put her hands on the sides of his head and pulled his lips to hers.

For a long time Roger'd been concerned only with bringing his brother and sister back to him and he'd had no time for women. He'd had no idea his desires were so pent-up inside him. Once, years ago, he'd been almost carefree, laughing with pretty young girls, tumbling about with them in clandestine meetings, but his anger at the Montgomerys had changed all that.

At the first touch of the girl's lips, Roger's first

thought was: serious. She may look to be little more than a child, but she was a woman and her purpose was one of seriousness. She kissed him with such intensity that he drew back from her.

"Who are you?" he whispered.

"I love you and I have waited always to meet you."

Roger, lying on top of her, looked deeply into her dark eyes, eyes that seemed to be trying to pull his soul out of his body, and he was frightened. He moved off her. "We'd better get you back to your parents."

"I have no parents," she said, sitting up.

Roger looked away from her eyes that seemed to be accusing him of deserting her. Part of him wanted to run away from this strange woman and another part wanted to fight to the death to keep her near him.

"Let me see your ankle," he said at last.

Obediently, she turned and held out her foot to him.

He frowned when he saw it, cut and bruised, blood running freely. "Why didn't you show this to me?" he snapped. "Here"—he handed her back her knife—"cut off some of your underskirt. I can't afford to lose more of my shirt. It's the only one I have at the moment."

She smiled at that and began slicing away at a fine lawn petticoat. "Why are you here in France and dressed like that? Where are your men?"

"You tell me," he said nastily, taking the strips from her. "Perhaps tonight you'll dream the rest of my life."

As soon as he turned away toward the stream, he regretted his words, but damn! the woman gave him chills. He could still feel her kiss—an odd combination of a woman who wanted to jump into his bed and a witch who wanted his soul.

At that thought he smiled. He was getting fanciful. She was a young girl who needed his help, nothing more or less. The best thing he could do would be to dress her ankle and return her to her guardians.

When he returned to her with dampened cloths, he could see tears glistening on her lashes, and he was immediately contrite. "I'm sorry, Chris," he said as if he'd known her always. "Damn! Give me your ankle."

A small smile came through her tears and he couldn't help returning it, and she smiled broadly as she put her foot in his hand.

"Let me have your knife again and I'll cut away your hose," he said, after he'd gently removed her embroidered slipper.

Without a word, Christiana slowly raised her dress on one side to the top of her thigh and unfastened her hose. Her eyes on Roger, and his on her slim curvy leg, she inched the hose downward toward her bloody ankle. When she reached her calf she held up her leg. "You may remove the rest."

Roger suddenly felt sweat breaking out on his body and a flame of desire so hot shot through him that his veins seemed to be on fire. With shaking hands, he removed her stocking, one hand on fabric, the other on the back of her bare knee.

The sight of blood on her ankle soothed him somewhat and he began to calm. "You are toying with things you don't understand," he said tightly, wetting her ankle to get the torn stocking off.

"I do not play children's games," she said softly.

Roger tried to concentrate on the task before him as he carefully cleaned her ankle, then bound it. "Now we must return you," he said as if he were her father, but his left hand was still on her ankle and began to caress her leg as his hand moved upward. He replaced her dagger in the sheath at her side.

Her eyes locked with his. She didn't move away but seemed to welcome him.

Roger came to his senses abruptly. No matter how appealing this urchin was, she wasn't worth his life. Someone would be looking for her soon and if he, looking to be a peasant, were found making love to her, obviously a noblewoman, no one would ask questions before they put a sword through his heart. And besides, he wasn't sure he liked the idea of being intimate with this strange young woman. What if she were a witch and she did mean to take his soul?

"Why did you stop, my lord?" she whispered in a throaty voice.

Primly, he pulled her skirt down. "Because you're a child and I'm— Do you always offer yourself to strangers?"

She didn't respond to the question but the answer was in her eyes. "I have loved you always and will love you always. I am yours to command."

Roger felt himself getting angry. "Now see here, young woman! I don't know who you think I am nor who you are, but I think it's best that you get back to your people and I to mine. And I hope you pray to God—if you believe in Him—for forgiveness for your actions."

With that he bent, tossed her small body over his shoulder and began to climb the steep bank.

By the time he reached the top of the bank, both his anger and his passion had calmed. He was too old and too sensible to allow a romantic bit of a girl to bother him.

He stood her before him, holding her shoulders to steady her, and smiled. "Now where may I take you? Do you remember which way you came from?"

She looked confused for a moment. "Of course I remember the way. Why are you sending me away? Would you kiss me again? Would you kiss me as if you loved me in return?"

Roger held her at arms' length. "You are too forward and no, I will not kiss you again. You must tell me where you belong."

"I belong with you but—" She stopped as a blast from a stag's horn sounded. Her eyes changed to wild, frightened. "I must go. My husband calls. He must not find you. Here!"

Before he could speak, she'd taken her little dagger from her side and crudely cut the largest amethyst from the front of her dress. An ugly, irreparable hole was left in the expensive velvet.

"Take this," she offered urgently.

Roger's back stiffened. "I do not take tribute from women."

The horn sounded again and Christiana's fright increased. "I must go!" She stood on tiptoe, quickly kissed his tightened lips. "I have a beautiful body," she said, "and lovely soft hair. I will show you sometime."

When the horn sounded a third time, she gathered her skirts and began to run awkwardly, her ankle bending every few steps. She'd not gone far when she turned and tossed the amethyst toward him. He made no move to catch it. "Give it to the woman who travels with you. Is she your sister or your mother?"

The last words were called over her shoulder as she disappeared from his sight.

Roger stood still, rooted into place for a very long time, his eyes staring sightlessly toward the place where she'd disappeared. His head felt strange, light, as if he'd just been through some experience that wasn't real. Had the girl really existed or had he fallen asleep and dreamed her?

"Roger!" came Elizabeth's voice from behind him. "We've been looking for you for an hour. Are you ready to travel? There are a few hours before nightfall.''

Slowly, he turned toward her.

''Roger, are you all right?''

Miles had left his wife's side and was looking about the area. Sometimes men who'd been wounded had Roger's look—just before they fell down. Miles saw the amethyst on the ground, but before he could touch it, Roger swept it into his hand, fingers closing tightly around it.

''Yes, I'm ready to go,'' he said tersely. Before he left he gave one last look about the forest, his thumb rubbing the jewel in his hand. ''Her husband!'' he muttered angrily. ''So much for love.'' He thought about throwing the amethyst away, but he couldn't do it.

It was Miles who was truly aware of Roger's distant moodiness that night. Miles had snared a rabbit—illegally—and it was turning over a spit as the three of them sat around the fire. He didn't want to worry Elizabeth, telling her there was no danger—and indeed the life of the French peasant seemed carefree compared to life at her brother's house—but Miles was always on guard, always aware of potential danger. At night he slept lightly and he gained respect for Roger as he saw that the knight was also wary.

Elizabeth lay sleeping, her head in her husband's lap. Roger sat apart, turning something over and over in his hand. Miles was not a person to directly ask after something that wasn't his concern, but Roger felt the younger man's interest.

"Women!" Roger finally said with great disgust and pocketed the amethyst. But as he stretched out on the cold forest floor, his hand sought the jewel and held it all night.

The morning dawned bright and clear and Elizabeth, as usual, was extraordinarily happy. Another day and they'd reach the French Montgomerys. Then they could go back to England and their son and, like a fairy tale, live happily ever after.

"You seem especially happy." Miles smiled down at her. "I think you like this peasant life."

"For a while," she said smugly, "but don't get the idea I'll always wear rags. I'm an expensive woman." She rolled her eyes at him flirtatiously.

"You will have to earn your keep," he said arrogantly, looking her up and down.

"I do that well enough. I—"

She stopped as the clatter of many horses and many men forced them to the side of the road. It was obviously a rich group of men, their horses draped in silks, their armor painted and well tended. There were about a hundred men and baggage wagons, and in the middle was a young girl, her hands tied behind her back, her face bruised, but she held her head high.

Elizabeth shivered as she remembered all too well how it felt to be a captive, but this girl looked as if she'd been beaten.

"Chris," Roger whispered from beside her and it was a heartfelt sound.

Miles was watching Roger intently and when

266

Roger made a move forward, Miles caught his arm. "Not now," Miles said quietly.

Elizabeth turned back toward the passing procession. So many men for such a small girl, she thought sadly. Her head turned with a snap. "No!" she gasped up at Miles. "You can't possibly be considering rescuing the girl."

Miles looked back at the knights and didn't answer Elizabeth. When she spoke again he turned such hot eyes on her that she became silent.

The trio stood for some time after the knights went past. Elizabeth's mind kept screaming no, no, no! Miles couldn't risk his life for a woman he didn't know.

As they started walking again, Elizabeth began her plea as calmly and rationally as she could. "We'll be at your relatives' soon and they'll know who the girl is, who holds her prisoner—and why. Perhaps she killed a hundred people. Perhaps she deserves her punishment."

Both Miles and Roger looked straight ahead.

Elizabeth clutched Miles's arm. "I was held prisoner once and it hasn't worked out badly. Perhaps—"

"Be quiet, Elizabeth!" Miles commanded. "I can't think."

Elizabeth felt herself begin to shiver. How could he, weaponless, rescue a girl guarded by a hundred armored knights?

Miles turned to Roger. "Should we volunteer our services as wood gatherers? At least we'll gain entrance to their camp.''

Roger gave Miles a calculating look. ''This isn't your fight, Montgomery. The girl was beaten because of me and I'll get her out alone.''

Miles kept looking at Roger, his eyes blazing, and after a moment, Roger gave in.

After one curt nod, Roger looked away. ''I don't know who she is except that her name is Christiana. She gave me a jewel, cut it from her dress, and no doubt that's why she's been beaten. She has a husband and she is terrified of him.''

''A husband!'' Elizabeth gasped. ''Roger, please, both of you, listen to reason. You can't risk your lives for a married woman. How long have you known her? What does she mean to you?''

''I never saw her before yesterday,'' Roger half whispered. ''And she means nothing to me—or perhaps she does. But I cannot let her be beaten because of me.''

Elizabeth began to realize there was no sense in arguing further. She'd never seen Roger do something so foolhardy but she was sure Miles would risk his life for a scullery maid. She took a deep breath. ''Once, on the road, a peasant offered me a bouquet of flowers and she was allowed past the guard to give them to me.''

''You will remain behind,'' Miles said in dismissal.

Elizabeth didn't answer but set her jaw. The odds were better if three people attacked a hundred than if there were just two.

Chapter 18

THEY FOLLOWED the guard until nearly sunset when the men made camp, and quite easily Miles and Roger, forsaking their usual shoulders-back stance, slipped among the knights, their arms loaded with wood. In the shadows of the trees, Elizabeth watched. Her early offer of help seemed to be hollow, the words of a braggart. Now, watching all those men, it was as if she'd never left her brother's house. Even as she stood hidden, she glanced behind her to make sure none of the men was there, ready and waiting to touch her.

Both Miles and Roger had given her strict orders that under no circumstances was she to leave her hiding place. They'd made it clear that they had enough to do without worrying about her also. Roger'd given her the girl's amethyst and Miles'd told her how to get to his relatives—in case anything happened to either of them. Elizabeth'd felt a hint of panic at the pronouncement but she'd kept her fears to herself. The men wanted her to wait far away but she'd stubbornly insisted on a place where she could watch. They'd refused to tell her their plan and Elizabeth began to suspect they had no real plan at all. No doubt Miles intended to hold the men at swordpoint while Roger fled with the girl.

Watching, she saw a scuffling, awkward old man, who she couldn't quite believe was her proud brother, move slowly toward where the girl was tied. She sat, leaning against a tree, hands and feet bound, head lowered.

When Roger awkwardly dropped the entire load of wood on the girl's feet, Elizabeth held her breath. She didn't know how much contact Roger'd had with the girl and she looked too young to have much sense. Would she give Roger away?

There was a brief flicker across the girl's face—but that could have been from pain—and then her face calmed. Elizabeth almost smiled. The girl was certainly not stupid. There wasn't another movement or expression from her as Roger began to clear the fallen wood away. A knight, cursing Roger, kicked him in the leg, and as Roger rolled, kicked him again in the ribs. And even as Roger took the blows, Elizabeth saw the flash of a knife as he cut the bindings from the girl's feet under the cover of the wood.

But Elizabeth saw something Roger couldn't: Behind him an older man, richly dressed, hung with jewels, his garments interwoven with gold wire, had never taken his sunken little eyes off the bound girl. The dying sunlight caught just a bit of a flash of Roger's knife.

On the far side of the camp, Miles kicked a burning log out of the fire, setting some grasses on fire. He slipped away before he could receive punishment for his actions and several knights began to fight the fire.

But the diversion wasn't enough. The men guarding the girl didn't glance at the fire—and the old man continued to glare at her with hatred.

The dark seemed to be coming quickly but there was enough light for Elizabeth to see a shadowy Miles slip a sword from a scabbard.

He did plan to fight! she thought. He planned to create some commotion so Roger could get the girl away. If fire had failed, perhaps a little clashing steel would work.

Elizabeth rose from her safe ditch, made a quick prayer for forgiveness for sinning and began unbuttoning her coarse woolen gown all the way to her waist. Perhaps she could get the men's attention—and especially the attention of the old man.

Her entrance was quick and dramatic. She ran into the clearing, leaped the last few feet, so close to one of the fires that she almost straddled it. Hands on her thighs, legs spread, she bent forward, the open bodice gaping, and practically touched the old man's head with her breasts. Slowly, seductively, she began to sway her shoulders, back and forth, from side to side, one raised, the next one higher, always working back until she was leaning backwards over the fire. With one hand she pulled the cotton cap from her head and let her hair cascade down to her knees. It hung over the fire, turning almost red in the light and looking as if it were part of the flames.

When she straightened, her hands insolently on her hips, she gave a laugh—a loud, arrogant, challenging laugh—and she had everyone's attention. The old man looked at her with interest and at last his eyes weren't on the girl not two feet from Elizabeth.

Elizabeth had never danced before but she'd seen enough lascivious entertainments at her brother's house to know what could be done. One of the knights began to play a lute and another a drum. Elizabeth began to undulate slowly—not just her hips, but her entire body moving every inch from fingertips to toes. And she used her magnificent hair to advantage, swirling it about, slapping men across the face with it. When one knight came too close, Elizabeth swept downward, grabbed a rock and plowed her fist into the man's stomach.

Everyone laughed uproariously at the knight's pain and from then on it was more a chase than a dance. For Elizabeth it was a nightmare come true. She was back in her brother's house and his men were pursuing her. She forgot about the last months of freedom but regressed to a time when she had to survive.

On her toes, she whirled about a knight and

lifted his sword from his belt. With garments flying, hair tangling about her body, she dodged at the men trying to catch her. She didn't hurt any of them but she managed to draw blood now and again. Forcing herself to laugh and keep up the charade of dancing, she jumped atop a table set with food, kicking plates and goblets everywhere. When a knight's hand touched her ankle, she moved away, her heel "accidentally" coming down on his fingers. He went away with a cry of pain.

Elizabeth's nerves were at the breaking point as the men began to clap in rhythm. Bending, she turned her hair around and around in time to their applause. Hoping that by now Roger and Miles had had time to release their captive, she threw her skirts high, the men cheering at the sight of her legs, and leaped to the ground directly in front of the old man.

She landed in a low bow before him, head low, hair a curtain about her. Panting, sides heaving, she waited.

With great ceremony, the man rose and put one bony hand under Elizabeth's chin, lifting her face to meet his.

Out of the corner of her eye, Elizabeth could see that the girl was gone and now it would be only moments before someone noticed.

Elizabeth rose and, praying for more time, hoping to distract the men, shrugged her shoulders and let the top of her dress fall away to her waist.

There was a great hush among the people, almost all of whom were behind her. The old man's eyes greedily roamed over her exquisite, high, firm breasts. Then, with a smile showing blackened teeth, he removed his own heavy cloak and put it about Elizabeth's shoulders.

Holding onto the ties in a degrading manner, he began to pull Elizabeth into the darkness of the forest.

Concealed in her hand was a knife she'd taken from one of the knights. As the old man turned, he saw that the bound girl was gone, but before he could call out, Elizabeth moved forward, caught his earlobe between her teeth, pressed the knife to his ribs and growled, "Walk!"

They were enveloped in the darkness before the cry was given that the prisoner had escaped.

"Run!" Elizabeth commanded the old man, pushing on the knife.

Quickly, he turned and backhanded Elizabeth across the face.

But before he could move, Roger leaped from the trees, his big hands around the old man's throat. Perhaps it was the surprise or the excitement of Elizabeth's dance, but Roger barely touched him and the ugly old man fell dead at their feet.

Roger lost no time but caught Elizabeth's waist and shoved her up into a tree.

Knights swarmed across the ground under them, their drawn swords glinting in the moonlight. Roger put his arms around Elizabeth and held her close, her head buried in his shoulder. She was trembling over her entire body and even now, in the safety of her brother's arms, she could still feel the men's hands clutching at her.

"Miles," she whispered to Roger.

"Safe," was all Roger'd say as he pressed her even closer.

They waited for some time, through all the hue and cry of finding the old man dead. Finally, two knights carried the body back to the camp and the search for the girl seemed to be ended as the men saddled horses and began to ride out.

Roger held Elizabeth a while after the forest was quiet.

"Come," he commanded. "Montgomery waits for us."

Roger climbed down first, then caught Elizabeth, who still wore the old man's cloak. The velvet swirling about her, she ran after Roger through the cold, damp forest.

Elizabeth hadn't realized how worried she'd been about Miles's safety until she saw him again. He emerged from a stagnant pond, holding the hand of the girl. Both of them were wet, slimy, and the girl's teeth were chattering.

After one grateful look at Miles for his safety, Elizabeth removed the old man's cloak and put it around the girl's shoulders.

"It is his!" Christiana said, stepping away from the cloak as if it were evil.

Roger caught the cloak, tossed it back to

Elizabeth and removed his own doublet, wrapping the girl in it. She melted into Roger's arms as if she were part of his skin.

"We must go," Miles said, taking Elizabeth's hand. "They'll be back for her soon."

They traveled all night. Elizabeth knew she was past exhaustion but she kept going, sometimes stealing looks at the girl who'd caused this flight. Wearing Roger's doublet, which dwarfed her, she looked even younger and more fragile than she first appeared. She was never more than an inch or two from Roger's side even though sometimes branches hit her face. As for Roger, he didn't seem to want her any farther away.

Elizabeth hardly looked at Miles because his eyes blazed with anger and a few times he threatened to crush her hand in his. Once, she tried to talk to him and explain why she'd had to disobey his orders and enter the rescue, but Miles looked at her with eyes blackened with rage, and Elizabeth practically crawled back inside the concealing cloak.

Toward morning, Miles said, "We'll join the travelers on the road and we must get her some clothes."

Christiana still wore her bejeweled dress, the pearls about her neck. It somehow emphasized her fallen status—she still wore her riches but now her fine dress was torn, her hair matted, her cheek bruised and the slime from the pond was dried and still clinging to her.

When at last they stopped beside the road, near

a large group of travelers just waking, Elizabeth nearly fell in an exhausted heap. Miles caught her to him, pulled her across his lap. "If you ever do anything like that again, wife—" he began but stopped when he kissed her so hard her mouth was bruised.

Tears came to her eyes, tears of joy that he was safe. There'd been a time, when she saw Miles draw a sword, that she was sure she'd never see him alive again. "I would risk all for you," she whispered and fell asleep in his arms.

It seemed like only moments before Elizabeth was wakened again and they began walking just a short distance behind the other travelers. The girl, Christiana, now wore a coarse woolen dress with a large concealing hood.

At midday they stopped and the men left the women alone while they went to the travelers to negotiate for bread and cheese, using the hated cloak.

Elizabeth leaned against a tree, her body trying to relax, but Christiana's nearness prevented rest. She couldn't help resenting the girl who'd nearly caused their deaths.

"Will you hate me for long, Elizabeth?" Christiana asked softly.

Elizabeth gave her one startled look before turning away. "I do not . . . hate you."

"You are not accustomed to lying," the girl said.

Elizabeth turned on her. "My husband could have been killed rescuing you!" she said fiercely.

"As well as my brother! What hold do you have on Roger? Have you bewitched him?"

Christiana did not smile nor did she frown. Her big eyes blazed with intensity. "I have always dreamed of a man like Roger. I have always known he'd come for me. Last year my uncle gave me in marriage to a cruel man but still I knew Roger would come. Three nights ago I dreamed and I saw his face. He was traveling in coarse clothes and with a woman related to him. I knew that he'd finally come."

Elizabeth looked at the girl as if she were a witch.

Chris continued, "You curse me for putting the man you love in danger, but what would you risk to be with your man? Perhaps if I were braver I could have gone to the torture and death my husband planned for me, but instead I sat in camp tied to the tree and prayed with all my might for my Roger to come."

She looked away, down the road to where Miles and Roger were approaching, and an inner light appeared in her eyes. "God has given me Roger to repay me for what has happened to me before. Tonight I will lie with Roger and after that I am ready to forsake all life, if need be. I have risked his life, yours and your kind husband's for this one night with my beloved."

She put her hand over Elizabeth's and her eyes were pleading. "Forgive me if I have asked too much of all of you."

Elizabeth's anger evaporated. Her hand took

Christiana's. "Don't talk of death. Roger needs love perhaps more than you do. Stay beside him."

For the first time, Chris gave a bit of a smile and a single dimple showed in her left cheek. "Only force will take me away from him."

Elizabeth glanced upward, saw Roger standing over them, his face showing puzzlement. He's bewildered by all this, Elizabeth thought. Chris confuses him as much as she does us.

They rested only minutes, ate hurriedly and were again on their way.

That night, as Elizabeth snuggled in Miles's arms, she had her first chance to talk to him. "What do you think of this young woman you risked your life for?" she asked.

"I know she's dangerous," he answered. "She was married to the Duke of Lorillard. As a child I used to hear of his cruelty. He's been through seven or eight rich, highborn young women. They all seem to die within a few years of marriage."

"Is Chris highborn?"

Miles gave a snort. "She's descended from generations of kings."

"How do you know all this?"

"From my French relatives. They've had a few dealings with the Lorillard family. Elizabeth," he said solemnly, "I want you to keep these." He closed her hand over the long strand of pearls Christiana'd worn yesterday. "Tomorrow, late, we should reach the home of my relatives but in case we don't . . . No!" He put a finger to her lips to quiet her. "I want to tell you the truth so you can be prepared. The Lorillard family is powerful and we've taken the life of one member and now harbor another. They'll tear the countryside apart looking for us. If anything happens, take the pearls and go back to England to my brothers. They will take care of you."

"But what about your French relatives? Couldn't I go to them?"

"I'll tell you the story someday, but for now let's just say that the Lorillards know me. If I'm captured, the way to my people here will be blocked. Go home to my brothers. Will you swear that? No more attempts to rescue me, but get home to safety."

She refused to answer him.

"Elizabeth!"

"I swear I will go home to your brothers." She sighed.

"And what about the rest?"

"I will make no more promises!" she hissed at him, turning her face up to his to be kissed.

They made love slowly and deliberately, as if tomorrow would never come. Miles's words of warning made Elizabeth feel desperate, as if they had only a few hours together. Twice, tears came to her eyes, tears of frustration that they'd been so close to safety and one woman's lust had put them in danger.

Miles kissed away her tears and whispered that she was to live for the moment and she could save her anger and hatred until later when they had the leisure.

She fell asleep holding Miles as tightly as she could and during the night she moved on top of him. He woke, smiled, kissed the top of her head, pulled a wad of her hair out of his mouth, hugged her and went back to sleep.

Roger woke them before daybreak and after one look, Elizabeth was sure he'd never been asleep. Christiana appeared from the trees, her eyes alive, her lips full and reddened, whisker burn on her neck and the side of her face. As they began to walk, Elizabeth saw Roger constantly cast looks toward Chris—looks of awe and pleasure. By noon, he had his arm around the girl, pulling her close to him. And once, to Elizabeth's surprise, he caught Chris in his arms and kissed her passionately. Roger'd always been decorous, aware of his place in life, his knightly vows, and he never made public displays of affection.

Miles caught Elizabeth, pulled her away from the spot where she stood gaping at her brother.

It was an hour before sunset when men burst from the trees, swords drawn and pointed at the throats of the four travelers.

A man, old, ugly, stepped from behind the knights. "Well, Montgomery, we meet again. Take them!" he commanded.

Chapter 19

ELIZABETH SAT still on the horse for just a moment as she saw, through tears, the ancient Montgomery fortress. So many things had changed in the last few weeks that she wasn't sure either England or the massive stronghold would still be there.

One of the horses of the three big men behind her stamped impatiently, bringing Elizabeth to her senses. With a great cry, she used the ends of her reins as a whip and spurred the horse forward. For all that she'd never visited the Montgomery estates, she knew the plan of it well. In Scotland, Miles had told her about the place, even drawn a sketch in the dirt.

She headed for the heavily guarded back gate, the family entrance. As she came to the walls that surrounded the narrow entrance, she barely slowed her horse.

Immediately, guards, arrows aimed, challenged her.

"The wife of Miles Montgomery," one of the men behind Elizabeth bellowed upward.

Six arrows landed in the ground before Elizabeth's horse, and the tired animal reared, one hoof breaking two shafts. Elizabeth used all her strength to control the frightened animal.

Three armed knights now stood between her and the closed entrance.

"I am Elizabeth Montgomery and these men are with me," she said impatiently but with some respect. Not many places were guarded like this any more.

As if they were statues, the knights held their ground as more men dropped from the walls and aimed swordpoints at the men behind Elizabeth.

When twenty Montgomery knights were assembled, one guard spoke to her. "You alone may enter. Your men stay here."

"Yes, of course. Take me to Gavin. He can identify me."

The reins of Elizabeth's horse were taken from her and she was led into a clean, spacious courtyard before a large house. More buildings were tucked inside the high surrounding walls.

One of the guards entered the house and moments later a pretty woman appeared, her face smudged with flour, sesame seeds dotting her hair.

"Take me to your master," Elizabeth ordered the woman. "I have news that concerns him."

"Are you Elizabeth?" the small woman asked. "Do you have news of Miles? We were told you'd both been killed. Henry! Help her from her horse and bring the men with her inside and feed them.''

At that moment Bronwyn appeared in the doorway and behind her the little singer Elizabeth'd met years before, Alyx.

"Elizabeth!" Bronwyn cried, running forward.

Elizabeth nearly fell into her sister-in-law's arms. "I am so glad to see you! It's been such a long journey. Where's Stephen? We have to return and get Miles and Roger. They've been taken by a French duke and we have to ransom them or rescue them or—''

"Slow down,'' Bronwyn said. "Come inside and have something to eat and we'll make plans.''

"Henry!'' the woman behind Elizabeth commanded. "Fetch my stepfather and Sir Guy. Send them to me and prepare seven horses for a journey. Send a rider ahead immediately and have a ship prepared for travel to France. I want *no* delay. Is that understood?''

Elizabeth had stopped, gaping at the woman she'd first thought was a servant.

"May I present Lady Judith?'' Bronwyn said with some amusement.

Judith brushed her hand at a stray strand of hair and a flurry of golden sesame seeds fell away. "Do you know where Miles is held?''

"Yes, I've just come from there.''

"And ridden hard by the look of you,'' Bronwyn said.

"Hello, Alyx,'' Elizabeth said, extending her

hand to the quiet woman who had moved to stand beside Bronwyn.

Alyx nodded in greeting and smiled shyly. She'd never felt so insignificant before as she did now, surrounded by her magnificent sisters-in-law.

At that moment Sir Guy came running. The giant looked as if he'd lost weight. Behind him came Tam, his sturdy form fairly making the ground shake.

"You have word of my Lord Miles?" Sir Guy called, his eyes roaming over Elizabeth. "We were told you were dead."

"And who told you this?" Elizabeth asked, voice rising. "Did no one search for us?"

"Come inside," Judith said, her hand on Elizabeth's arm. "Tell us what has happened."

Minutes later Elizabeth sat at a big table, eating energetically of the vast quantity of food set before her, while telling her story. Around her were her three sisters-in-law, a man she didn't know—John Bassett, Judith's mother's husband—Sir Guy and Tam.

With her mouth full, she told hurriedly of how the three of them were tossed into the hold of a ship, how they'd escaped and traveled south until Roger decided to risk their lives for a bit of a girl who was someone else's wife.

Bronwyn interrupted with a barrage of hatred directed toward Roger Chatworth but Tam ordered her to be quiet. Surprisingly, Bronwyn obeyed the older man.

Elizabeth briefly told of their rescue of the young Christiana.

Judith asked many questions, both about Elizabeth's participation in the rescue and about Christiana. "I know of her," Judith said. "And I know of her husband and his family. The younger brother, not the duke, hates Miles."

"Why?" Elizabeth blurted.

"There was a young woman who—"

Elizabeth put up her hand. "Tell me no more. I think it's the younger man who holds Miles and Roger. The duke died in Roger's hands."

"He enjoys killing!" Bronwyn said.

Elizabeth didn't waste time defending her brother but continued with her story, telling of the old duke's sudden death. She stopped eating when she told of their capture by the dead duke's brother. Miles had been wounded when he pulled a knight from his horse, tossed Elizabeth into the saddle and slapped the horse's rump. She'd gone tearing down the weed-infested, rutted road, working hard at trying to get the dangling reins. When she did have control of the horse, she glanced backward to see half-a-dozen men chasing her. She whipped her horse forward and spent the next hours trying to escape them.

Elizabeth skipped over the next ten days of her story hurriedly. She used the pearls of Christiana's necklace to purchase her way back to England. Praying she wasn't hastening her own death, she hired three men off the road, men who'd once been soldiers, but their master had died and the successor wanted younger men.

The four of them traveled night and day, changing horses often, sleeping for only a couple of hours at a time.

When they reached the coast, Elizabeth had paid ten pearls for a ship and crew to take them back to England and she'd slept for the whole three days of sailing. They arrived in the south of England, purchased horses and a few supplies and took off again, never pausing until they reached the Montgomery estates.

"So," Elizabeth concluded, "I have come to get Miles's brothers. We must set out at once for France."

A knight entered, whispered something to Judith and left. "Lady Elizabeth," Judith said, "there are things you don't know. Soon after you, Miles and your brother were cast into the ship, Alice Chatworth"— Judith nearly choked on the name—"couldn't resist bragging about what she'd done. She sent a messenger and a letter telling us everything."

Alyx spoke for the first time, her voice soft but easily heard. "Raine, Stephen and Gavin left for France immediately while we"—she nodded toward Judith and Bronwyn—"came here to wait for news."

"Then the men are already in France?" Elizabeth asked, rising. "I must leave now. If I may have some men I'll find Miles's brothers and lead them to the place where Miles is held."

"Do you know the Duke of Lorillard's castle?

Do you know where his brother lives?'' Judith asked, leaning forward.

''No, but surely—'' Elizabeth began.

''We can't risk it. The duke was a 'friend' of my father.'' Judith sneered at this. ''I know where all four of the Lorillard estates are and I doubt if any other Montgomery does. Raine might, since he's fought in tournaments in France, but if the men have separated . . . no, it's decided.'' She stood.

''Like hell it is!'' roared the man at her side, John Bassett, as he rose to tower over her.

Judith merely blinked at his voice but remained calm. ''The horses are ready and we will ride soon. Bronwyn, do you have enough of those tartan skirts of yours? They'll be comfortable on the long journey.''

John grabbed her arm harshly. ''You'll not go risking your life again,'' he said. ''You nearly killed us all when you went after Gavin. This time, young lady, you'll remain here and let the men handle this.''

Judith's eyes turned as hot as molten gold. ''And where will you look for my husband?'' she seethed. ''Have you ever been to France? And if you by chance found him, where would you tell him to look for Miles? Use what sense you have, John! Leave the other women here but Elizabeth and I must go with you.''

Alyx looked at Bronwyn and then let out a yell of ''NO!'' that made dust trickle down from the ceiling.

Alyx's face turned a becoming shade of pink and she looked down at her hands. "I mean that Bronwyn and I would rather go with you. Perhaps we can help," she whispered.

"Bronwyn," Tam began while Sir Guy was looking down his nose in an intimidating way at Elizabeth. Instantly, the room erupted into argument. Alyx, having no man to tower over her, slipped away unnoticed, ran up the stairs to Bronwyn and Stephen's room and pulled several plaids from a trunk. Even upstairs she could hear the loud voices downstairs.

On impulse, she grabbed a bagpipe from the wall. Multicolored tartans over her shoulders, she set the pipes to wailing as she started downstairs. By the time she reached the Great Hall, where everyone stood looking up at her, they were silent.

She dropped the pipe from her mouth. "If you men ride without us," she said into the silence, "we will leave, alone, an hour later. Do you ride with us or before us?"

The men were quiet, jaws working, lips in tight lines.

"While we are wasting time," Alyx continued, "Miles is being held prisoner, or perhaps being tortured at this very moment. I suggest we ride—NOW!"

Judith walked forward, took Alyx's face in her hands, kissed both of her sister-in-law's cheeks. "We ride!" Judith declared, taking the plaids from Alyx's shoulders and tossing one to Elizabeth. "John, see to the supplies. Guy, go to my steward. We'll need gold for this journey. Tam, make sure we have arrows aplenty and check the strings on the bows. Bronwyn, make sure we have horses that can travel. Alyx, bring something to make music with. We may need it.''

Elizabeth began smiling at the first order. ''And me?'' she asked as everyone started off in different directions to obey Judith.

''Come with me,'' Judith said, starting up the stairs.

Halfway up the stairs, Judith paused, her eyes boring into Elizabeth's. ''Alice Chatworth contracted smallpox and although she lived, the unscarred side of her face was badly pocked.'' Judith paused. ''She took her own life by casting herself from the battlements of one of her estates.'' She looked away, then under her breath said, ''The same wall old Ela fell from.''

Elizabeth didn't understand the last statement but as she followed Judith up the stairs, she was glad Alice was dead. At least now she could be sure of her son's safety.

Elizabeth had heard talk of what a worker Judith Montgomery was but she soon decided Judith was a demon. She allowed no one any weakness—nor any rest.

They made the trip to the south of England in just two days, changing horses often. No one spoke but merely rode as hard and fast as possible. In many places the roads were so bad they were nonexistent, and they tore through newly plowed fields while farmers raised fists in anger. Twice Tam and Guy jumped from their horses, used battle axes to chop down fences. Behind them sheep grazed.

"The owner will take Judith to court," Elizabeth said, for the huge sheep pens were obviously owned by someone rich.

"This land belongs to Judith," Bronwyn called over her shoulder as she kicked her horse forward.

Alyx and Elizabeth exchanged looks of awe before they, too, set their horses at the usual spine-jarring pace.

When they reached the southern tip of England at dawn the third morning, a ferry waited to take them to the island where more of the Montgomerys lived.

"My clan is small compared to this famlly," Bronwyn said tiredly before she sat down in the wet bottom of the ferry, pulled her plaid over her head and fell asleep.

An hour later they were awakened and, as sleepwalkers, they mounted fresh horses and rode to the Montgomery estates. Even as tired as she was, Elizabeth felt the age and serenity of the fortress, the stones laid over two hundred years before by the knight known as the Black Lion.

Inside the gates, Judith touched Elizabeth's arm and nodded toward a child peeping out from a doorway. She was about a year and a half old, with dirty hair, torn clothes and the wary look of a hungry dog.

"One of Miles's children," Judith said, watching Elizabeth's face.

A surge of anger shot through Elizabeth. "She shall be mine when I return." With one last look, Elizabeth swept past the others and into the house.

They stayed at the old castle only long enough to eat, then were off on the ship that waited for them. All seven of them immediately curled up on deck and went to sleep.

Many hours later, when they were refreshed, the women began to discuss their plans.

"We will have to gain access to the castle," Judith said. "Alyx's music will open any door to us. Can either of you play or sing?"

Bronwyn swore she had a voice of lead; Judith admitted to being tone deaf. Elizabeth whispered, her throat dry, "I can dance."

"Good!" Judith declared. "Once we're inside—"

"You will do nothing," John Bassett said from behind her. "You will point out the new duke's estate to us and we will find your husbands and bring them to it. They will rescue Lord Miles." With that he turned on his heel and left them.

Judith gave her sisters-in-law a little smile. "Years ago I had a little trouble when I attempted to rescue Gavin. John has never forgiven me, and since he married my mother he feels responsible for me." She leaned forward. "We'll have to be more discreet in our planning."

Elizabeth leaned against the side of the ship and

suppressed a laugh. There Judith sat, so very pretty, so tiny, her hands in her lap, looking for all the world like a demure, helpless young lady. It was hard to believe her fierce spirit. Bronwyn stood by the rail, the sun flashing off the water and highlighting her strong-featured beauty. Elizabeth knew Bronwyn for the passionate, brave, loyal woman she was. And Alyx, so quiet and shy, looking as if she were afraid of all of them, yet Elizabeth had seen glimpses of her spirit through Alyx's magnificent voice.

And Elizabeth? Did she fit with these women? She wondered if she could stand up under Judith's scrutiny.

They purchased horses as soon as they stepped ashore in France and Judith led them southwest. For the last day Judith had been agreeing with everything the men told her. Once Bronwyn punched Elizabeth so that she looked up at John Bassett when he swelled out his chest as he lectured Judith. Tam also gave Bronwyn curt orders. Sir Guy spoke only once to Elizabeth.

Glancing up at him through her lashes, looking demure and angelic, she asked him how his toes were. The giant's scar whitened and he walked away. Bronwyn held her ribs as she nearly split her sides laughing. Judith, when told the story of Sir Guy's toes, gave Elizabeth a look of admiration and speculation.

Alyx merely tuned her lute and that act seemed to show whom she thought was going to win the power battle.

John Bassett rented rooms in an inn not far from the duke's estates, the one the locals said he was residing in at present. The three men had to leave the women alone as they went to search for the husbands. John looked as if he were going to cry when he met with stubborn silence as he begged Judith to swear to God that she would wait for the return of the men.

"Must I put a guard on you?" John asked, exasperated.

Judith merely looked at him.

"I've a good mind to take you with me, but we'll have to split up and it takes more than one mere man to control a hellion like you. There should be a special saint to guard husbands like Gavin."

"You're wasting time, John," Judith said patiently.

"She's right," Guy said, not looking at any of the women.

John caught Judith to him, kissed her forehead. "May the Lord protect you." With that, the three men left.

Judith leaned against the door and let out a deep sigh. "He means well. Now, shall we get to work?"

Elizabeth soon came to realize what a magnificent planner Judith was—and she knew how to use her gold. She hired a total of twenty-five people to spread word of the world's greatest singer and the universe's most exotic dancer. She planned for the excitement of expectation to be feverish by the time Alyx and Elizabeth appeared, for she wanted all eyes on them while she and Bronwyn slipped away.

In the early afternoon, Judith dressed in rags, blackened one front tooth with a nasty mixture of gum and soot and delivered fresh-baked bread to the duke's castle. She came back with wonderful news.

"Miles is alive," she said, scratching and discarding the filthy clothes. "The duke always seems to have prisoners and he always keeps them in the top of the tower. This tastes awful!" she said, scrubbing at her teeth. "It seems the whole Lorillard family are masters of torture and right now they're working on the girl.

"I'm sorry, Elizabeth," Judith added quickly. "From the gossip, I don't know if she's still alive or not, but the two men are."

"What about Miles's wound?" Elizabeth asked.

Judith put out her hands, palms up. "I couldn't ask directly and all I could find out was that the prisoners are always kept in the top of the tower."

"That should be easy," Bronwyn said. "We merely attach wings to our horses and fly to the top."

"There's a staircase," Judith said.

"Unguarded?" Bronwyn asked.

"The door to the rooms where the prisoners are kept is guarded but another stair branches up to the roof." Judith slipped a clean shift over her head. "There are windows in the rooms and if we could go down from the roof . . ."

Only Bronwyn was aware of the tight white lines forming at the corners of Judith's mouth. At times Judith seemed fearless, but she had an absolute terror of high places. Bronwyn touched Judith's arm. "You stay and dance to Alyx's music. Elizabeth and I will lower ourselves and . . ."

Judith put up her hand. "I could as likely dance as I could make the horses fly. Alyx would be singing, I'd never be able to keep the rhythm and I'd start looking at the tables and thinking of how many storage bins were needed for that much food. I'd probably forget to dance and start ordering the servants about."

All three women unsuccessfully tried to suppress giggles, both at Judith's accuracy and her forlorn expression.

Judith rolled her eyes at them. "I'm strong and I'm small and I can most easily go down a rope and slip inside a window."

No amount of talking could persuade Judith of any other course and soon they sat down to rest, each with her own thoughts of the dangers to come. Elizabeth never spoke of her fear of the men touching her and Judith's terror of high places wasn't mentioned again.

As dusk approached, Judith sank to her knees and began to pray and soon the other three women joined her.

Chapter 20

ALYX WAS the one who surprised the women the most. For the last few days she'd had the least to say, had followed her outspoken, beautiful sisters-in-law without a suggestion or complaint. But as soon as Alyx had a musical instrument in her hands and was told to perform, she far outstripped her sisters in flamboyance.

Judith and Bronwyn, dressed in filthy, concealing rags, blended into the procession that followed Alyx and Elizabeth. Elizabeth, strutting, already drawing attention to her well-endowed body, wore cheap cloth of garish, outlandish colors that would have attracted attention on their own.

As soon as Alyx entered the Great Hall of the old castle, she let out a note that made everyone pause. Bronwyn and Judith had never heard the full volume of Alyx's voice and they halted for a moment, listening with some awe.

"I'll give you a rhythm," Alyx whispered to

297

Elizabeth. "Follow it with your body."

Every eye was on Alyx and the beautiful woman beside her. Abruptly Alyx let her voice drop and once again the audience began to breathe, and with a mixture of laughter and applause, they began to move about. "Now!" Judith hissed at Bronwyn and the two women disappeared into a darkened hole in the wall.

With their very heavy skirts flung over their arms, they tore up the old stone stairs, up two flights, three flights, and as they neared the top, a noise made them flatten themselves against the wall. Listening with every pore, they waited for the guard to pass the opening.

Judith pointed to a crack of blackness on the left, away from the vigilant guard. They slipped into the opening with a whisper of sound. Rats squealed in protest and Bronwyn kicked one of the nasty things back down the stairs.

At the top of the stairs was an overhead door—a locked door.

"Damn!" Judith whispered. "We need a key."

But before she even spoke, Bronwyn went to the narrow trapdoor and began to run her hands along the edges. As she reached the far edge, she turned and gave Judith a triumphant smile, her teeth and eyes showing white in the darkness. Bronwyn threw an iron bolt and the door swung up easily. One loud squeak made them stop but they heard no sound of footsteps on the stairs. They squeezed through the opening and were on the roof.

For a moment they paused and breathed deeply of the clean night air. As Bronwyn turned to Judith, she saw the little woman was looking at the battlements with fear in her eyes.

"Let *me* go," Bronwyn said.

"No." Judith shook her head. "If something happened and I had to pull you up, I couldn't do it. But you can lift me."

Bronwyn nodded as she saw the sense in Judith's words. With no more sound, they removed their outer, coarse woolen skirts and began uncoiling heavy rope from the underside. Judith had paid four women to spend the afternoon sewing these skirts. Now the moonlight shone on their skirts of plaid, blue and green for Bronwyn, golds and browns for Judith.

As soon as Bronwyn's rope lay in a coiled heap, she went around the roof of the round tower to peer down from the crenelated battlements. "There are four windows," she informed Judith. "Which one holds Miles?"

"Let me think," Judith said, rope on her forearm. "That window is over the stairs, the opposite one facing the stairs, so the cell must be one of those two." She pointed to her right and left.

Neither of them had to mention that if Judith appeared in the wrong window it could mean her death.

"Come on, let's go," Judith said as if she were on her way to her own execution.

Bronwyn had used ropes all her life and, easily,

299

she knotted a sort of seat for Judith. The full tartan skirt was pulled between her legs and fastened into the wide leather belt. Her heart already racing, Judith stepped into the rope sling, part around her waist, some between her legs.

As she stood on the battlement, Bronwyn smiled at her. "Concentrate on your job and don't think about where you are."

Judith only nodded since fear had already closed her throat.

Bronwyn wrapped one end of the rope around a stone crenelation and used that to lower Judith slowly.

Judith repeated psalms to herself, swearing her trust in God, as she looked for toe holds. Three times pieces of wall crumbled away under her feet and each time her heart jumped to her throat as she paused, expecting any moment to have a guard above her cut the rope that held her life.

After long, slow moments, she reached the window and as her foot caught the stone sill, a hand grabbed her ankle.

"Quiet!" a voice commanded as Judith gave a sharp gasp of terror.

Strong hands caught her calves, then her hips, and pulled her inside the window. Judith, so very glad to once again be on firm ground, clutched the inside of the sill so hard she threatened to break her fingers.

"Aren't you the one that's terrified of high places?"

Judith turned to look into Roger Chatworth's

calm face. His shirt hung in rags on his strong body. "Where's Miles?" she said in a half-gasp, half-croak.

A sound from outside the cell made Roger grab her protectively.

"Talkin' to yourself, Chatworth?" The guard called out but didn't bother to walk toward the cell.

"No one better," Roger called back, holding Judith's trembling body.

"Who is above?" Roger said into her ear.

"Bronwyn."

Judith's answer was rewarded by an under-breath curse from Roger. She wanted to pull away from him but at the moment any comfort felt good. Roger drew her, still attached to the rope, to a far corner of the little room. "Miles is in the opposite cell," he whispered. "He's been wounded and I'm not sure he has the strength to climb your rope. The guard will sleep soon and we'll get out. I'll go first and then pull you up. But you cannot stay in this room alone. You must sit on the sill and if the guard looks in, you must jump off. Do you understand? As soon as I reach the top I'll pull you up," he repeated.

Judith let his words sink in. This was her family's enemy, had been the cause of Mary Montgomery's death. Perhaps he meant to kill Bronwyn and cut the rope holding her. "No . . ." she began.

"You have to trust me, Montgomery! Bronwyn can't pull you up and you couldn't possibly climb the rope. Damn women! Why didn't you send some men?''

That did it. Her eyes blazed. ''You ungrateful—''

He put his hand over her mouth. ''Good girl! Whatever I don't like about the Montgomerys, I like their women. Now let's waste no more time.'' With that, he led, half pulled, Judith to the window, picked her up and set her on the sill. ''Put your hands here''—he indicated the ledge of the sill—''and hold on. When I start to pull you up, use your hands and feet to keep from hitting the wall.'' He gave her a little shake since Judith was staring glassily at the ground far, far below her. ''Think about your husband's anger when he finds out you rescued a Chatworth before his brother.''

Judith almost smiled at that—almost. She did lift her head and visualized Gavin and imagined being in his safe arms. She swore she'd never again do anything so stupid as try to rescue a man again. Unless of course Gavin needed her. Or his brothers. Or one of her sisters-in-law. Or perhaps, too, her mother. And her children by all means. And—

The tug on the rope as Roger grabbed it above her head nearly sent her flying. ''Mind on your work, woman!'' he commanded.

She ducked his feet as he swung above her and, her senses once again alert, she tilted her head back and watched him climb the rope, hand over hand.

Bronwyn greeted Roger at the top with a knife aimed at his throat and held him there, suspended over the wall, hands supporting his body weight.

"What have you done with Judith?" Bronwyn growled.

"She waits below for me to pull her up and every minute you delay comes closer to costing her her life."

At that moment, several things happened. One, Judith, either in fear or necessity, swung away from the windowsill and the momentum almost made Roger lose his grip.

"Guards!" came a shout from below.

"The door!" Roger said, fighting to stay on the wall. "Lock the door!"

Bronwyn reacted at once, but by the time she reached the door, a guard was already through it. She didn't hesitate as she slipped her knife between his ribs. He fell atop the door and Bronwyn had to push him aside to shove the bolt home.

She ran back to where Roger was pulling on Judith's rope, and leaned between the crenelations to help. "What happened?" Bronwyn asked before Judith was even over the roof.

"Alyx and Elizabeth were tossed in the cell with Miles. I stayed and listened as long as I could but when the guard looked for Chatworth, he called out. What happened to him?"

Bronwyn assisted Judith onto the roof. "There," she nodded toward the dead man not far away.

"Who heard him call?" Roger demanded.

"I'm not sure anyone did," Judith said. "Hurry! We must get them out of this place."

"There isn't time. Where are your husbands?" Roger asked.

"Here in France but—" Judith began but stopped as Roger took the second rope from the roof floor and tied it to a battlement. "They're on the other side."

Roger ignored her. "There isn't time. The old man will be up here in minutes. We've got to get down and get some help."

"You coward," Bronwyn hissed. *You* escape. Judith and I will rescue our family."

Roger grabbed her arm harshly. "Shut up, you idiot! Do you forget that Elizabeth is my sister? I haven't time to argue but if we're all caught there'll be no one to lead a rescue. Now, can you get down that rope yourself?"

"Yes but—" Bronwyn began.

"Then do it!" He half tossed her over the wall, all the while securely holding her hand. "Go, Bronwyn!" he ordered, then gave her a quick smile. "Show us some of your Scots blood."

As soon as Bronwyn disappeared over the side, Roger grabbed Judith by the armpits and lifted her. "Good! You weigh no more than my armor." He half squatted. "Hang onto my back with all your strength."

Judith only nodded and obeyed, buried her face

in Roger's shoulder and closed her eyes. She didn't look when he lowered himself over the side. Sweat broke out on his neck and she was aware of how he was straining.

"Are you going to let an Englishman beat you?" Roger spat across the void to Bronwyn.

Judith opened one eye and looked with admiration at her sister-in-law. Bronwyn had the rope wrapped around one ankle, the opposite foot on top, her hands easing herself down. At Roger's words, she speeded up her travel.

Judith didn't even consider leaving Roger's safe, broad back merely because they stepped onto land. As if it were something he did every day, he peeled her hands then her legs away from his body.

Trembling, Judith watched as he ran to the bottom of Bronwyn's rope. She was still several feet from the ground. "Jump, Scot!" he ordered up at her.

There was a slight hesitation but Bronwyn obeyed, let go of the rope and landed heavily into Roger Chatworth's waiting arms. "You must weigh the same as my horse," he murmured while setting her down. "Is it too much to hope that you women have horses nearby?"

"Come, enemy," Bronwyn said, motioning with her arm.

Roger grabbed Judith's arm since she was standing still, looking straight up with horror to where she'd been. "Run!" he said and gave her a sharp slap on her rump. "Let's get my sister and

Chris out of this!"

Miles was standing in the middle of the room as if waiting for them, when the door was thrown open and Elizabeth and Alyx were pushed inside.

"To keep you company, Montgomery." The guard laughed. "Enjoy tonight because it'll probably be your last one alive."

Miles caught Elizabeth before she fell, then reached for Alyx.

Without a word, expertly, he sat down on the floor, arms about both women's shoulders, as Elizabeth began kissing his face enthusiastically.

"They were told you were dead," Elizabeth said between kisses. "Oh Miles, I didn't know if I'd ever see you again."

Miles, smiling slightly, his eyes alight, kissed each woman's forehead. "I can die peacefully now."

"How can you joke—?" Elizabeth began, but Miles kissed her lips and calmed her.

The three of them came alert as the single guard called out as he ran up the stairs toward the roof. A heavy thud followed the guard's disappearance.

In the silence, eyes looking upward, Miles said, "Bronwyn?"

Both women nodded.

Miles took a deep breath, sighed. "Tell me what you've done."

Alyx was quiet as Elizabeth told of their rescue plan, how Judith was going down the wall and into Miles's cell. Alyx was watching Miles, leaning against his strong shoulder, happy for his comfort, and she saw his eyes darken. Raine would wring my neck if I told him of such a plan, Alyx thought and hot tears came to her eyes.

"Alyx?" Miles said, interrupting Elizabeth's story. "We'll get out of here. Right now my brothers . . ."

She wiped her eyes with the back of her hand. "I know. I was just thinking that Raine will have my hide for doing this."

Miles's eyes twinkled. "Yes, he will."

"You're hurt!" Elizabeth suddenly announced, her hand running over a dirty bandage about his ribs. There wasn't much of his shirt left but what there was, Elizabeth had been exploring under.

She leaned away from him. Only moonlight came into the little room but even in that light, as she parted his shirt, she could see all the scars. Running her fingertips along one, she spoke, "You had no scars when I first met you and you've received all of them through me."

He kissed her palm. "I'll put a few scars on you—scars you get from bearing twenty of my children. Now I want both of you to rest because I imagine morning will bring . . . new events."

Elizabeth's main concern in life had been seeing Miles safe again and now that she leaned against him, knew he was strong and well, she was content. She closed her tired eyes and slept instantly.

Not so Alyx. She had not been traveling as long as Elizabeth and wasn't as tired. She closed her

307

eyes and was still but her mind raced.

After an hour, when the cell was barely growing light, Miles gently moved the women off him and went to stand before the window. With half-shuttered eyes, Alyx watched him, saw his awkward movements.

"Come join me, Alyx," he whispered, surprising her that he knew she was awake.

Alyx stepped over a sleeping Elizabeth and as she drew near Miles, he pulled her to him, his front to her back. "You've risked much to save me, Alyx, and I thank you."

She smiled, put her cheek against his wrist. "I'm the one who got us caught. The duke had seen me play in England somewhere, remembered me and also remembered that he'd heard I'd become a Montgomery. What do you think Bronwyn said when she saw Roger on the roof instead of you?" She turned in his arms. "You do think they got away, don't you? No guards were waiting for them at the bottom of the ropes, were they? Raine will come?"

With a smile he turned her back toward the window. "I *know* they got through. Look there, far to the west."

"I see nothing."

"In the haze, see the little sparkles?"

"Yes," she said excitedly. "What are they?"

"I could be wrong but I believe they're men in armor. And there, more to the north."

"More sparkles! Oh Miles." She turned, hugged his ribs tightly then suddenly let him go.

"You're hurt worse than you told Elizabeth," she said accusingly.

He tried to smile but there was pain in his eyes. "Will you tell her and give her more to worry about? She was brave dancing for all those strange men, wasn't she?" he said proudly.

"Yes," Alyx said, turning back around. Together they stood there as the day began to dawn, watching the little pinpoints of light as they grew nearer and nearer.

"Who are they?" Alyx asked. "I know there are Montgomerys in France but there must be hundreds of knights approaching. Who are the others?"

"I doubt if there are any others," he answered. "There are Montgomerys all over France, and in Spain and Italy. When I was a boy and first earned my spurs it bothered me that I could go nowhere that I didn't have an uncle or a few cousins breathing down my neck, but now I believe every one of my relatives to be beautiful."

"I have to agree with that."

"There!" he said, pointing straight ahead. "Did you see it?"

"No, I saw nothing."

He grinned happily. "It's what I've been waiting to see. There it is again!"

Briefly, for less than a second, Alyx saw a different flash.

"It's my Uncle Etienne's banner. We've always joked about the Montgomery banner he carries. It's nearly as big as a house, but Etienne says just the sight of those three gold leopards will send most people running—and he wants to give them time to leave."

"I saw it!" Alyx gasped. On the horizon had appeared three flashes of gold, one above the other. "The leopards," she breathed. "Who do you think—?" she began.

"Raine will be leading Uncle Etienne. Stephen is coming with the men from the north and Gavin will arrive from the south."

"How can you know that?"

"I know my brothers." He smiled. "Gavin will wait a few miles away for his brothers and all three armies will attack at once."

"Attack?" she said through her teeth.

"Don't worry." He ran his hand along her temple. "I don't believe even the Duke of Lorillard will try to stand against the combined forces of the Montgomerys. He'll be given a chance to surrender to us peacefully. And besides, his fight is about Christiana, not with the Montgomerys."

"Christiana. The girl Roger Chatworth rescued? What has happened to her?"

"I don't know but I'll find out," Miles said with such feeling that Alyx was silenced. She knew better than to try to argue with one of the Montgomery men about something he planned to do. Together they watched the approaching armies of knights and when Elizabeth awoke, Miles held her also.

Trying to cheer them, he made a bawdy jest

about Elizabeth's garish clothes.

"If Judith and Bronwyn liberated Roger Chatworth and the three of them went for help, which brother do you think they reached first?" Alyx asked.

Neither Miles nor Elizabeth had an answer for her.

"I pray it wasn't Raine," Alyx whispered. "I think Raine would strike first and listen second."

In silence, they watched their rescuers approach.

Chapter 21

RIDING NEXT to Raine and Etienne Montgomery was Roger Chatworth, his mouth set in a grim line, his right arm—his sword arm—bound tightly but still bleeding, and next to him was Bronwyn sporting what promised to be an extraordinary example of a black eye. Roger's arm was the result of Raine's first sighting of his enemy and Bronwyn's eye came about when she placed herself between Raine and Roger. Judith would have joined the fracas but John Bassett leaped from his horse, knocked her to the ground and pinned her there.

It took four men to hold Raine and keep him from tearing Chatworth apart but he did finally calm somewhat and allowed Judith and Bronwyn, who was nursing her swollen eye, to tell him what had happened. All the Montgomerys were remounted halfway through the story. When Judith told of Alyx being thrown in the cell with Miles, Raine once again leaped for Roger. Roger held him off with a sword held in his left hand while Raine's relatives calmed them both.

They were all quiet now as they approached the old Lorillard castle.

Gavin Montgomery sat in steely silence atop his horse, three hundred armed men behind him, and watched the approaching Montgomerys. Beside him sat Sir Guy, the giant's scarred face immobile. Guy didn't like to remember Gavin's explosion when he found out Judith had come to France with the men.

"She has no sense in these matters!" Gavin'd roared. "She thinks waging war is like cleaning a fish pond. Oh Lord," he prayed fervently, "if she is still alive when I find her, I will kill her. Let's ride!"

Stephen ordered his men to the eastern side of the castle while he and Tam rode toward where Gavin waited on the south.

"Women?" he bellowed long before he reached Gavin.

"None!" Gavin answered so loudly his horse lifted both forefeet off the ground.

In a cloud of dirt, Stephen and Tam turned west and headed for Raine. When Stephen saw Bronwyn, he nearly cried with relief, then frowned at her swollen eye. "What happened?" he shouted over the sound of the horses, not touching her but eating her with his eyes.

"Raine—" was all Bronwyn got out before

Stephen let go with a bellow of laughter. He looked fondly at Raine's big form held rigidly in the saddle.

Bronwyn didn't bother to look at her husband again but moved to the far side of Tam.

"Stephen," Judith called. "Is Gavin with them?" She pointed south.

Stephen nodded once and Judith, John behind her, was off like a shot of lightning toward the southern group of Montgomerys.

There was no fighting.

The new Duke of Lorillard, obviously just roused from his bed, his eyes red, his skin gray green from a night of excess, had not lived to his great age of fifty-eight by trying to fight the nearly one thousand angry men who now surrounded his house. Showing his faith in the honor of the name Montgomery, he walked into the armed knights and told Gavin that if he were given his freedom, the Montgomerys could have whatever, or whomever, they wanted from his castle without the loss of a single life.

Raine didn't want to accept the man's terms because the duke was surrendering not only his land but two of his sons as well. Raine believed that a man who'd do that should die.

Both Bronwyn and Judith pleaded for the easiest way to rescue the people from the tower.

In the end, it was Gavin, as the oldest, who made the decision. The duke and five of his guard were allowed to ride away after all the gates had been ordered opened.

Amid protests, the women were ordered to stay behind while the three brothers, Roger and a dozen cousins rode into the Duke's crumbling fortress.

Either the occupants didn't know—or didn't care—that they were under attack, or perhaps, as Stephen suggested, it was a common occurrence. They did not rouse themselves from their drunken stupors. Men and women sprawled about the floors and across benches.

Cautiously, swords drawn, the men stepped between the bodies and searched for the stairs Bronwyn and Judith had told them of.

At the top of the stairs the three brothers put their shoulders to a locked door that opened to the room containing the cells.

"Here!" Roger said, grabbing a key from the wall and unlocking the heavy wooden door.

They were greeted by Miles, looking calm and pleased with himself, an arm around each woman.

Alyx ran, leaped into Raine's arms where he held her very close, his eyes moist as he buried his face in her neck. "Every time you get near your sisters-in-law," he began, "you do something like this. From now on—"

With a laugh, Alyx kissed him to silence.

Elizabeth left Miles's arms and went to Roger, caressed his cheek, touched his bloody arm. "Thank you," she whispered. She turned to Gavin, their eyes meeting, and she nodded curtly to him. She couldn't forget the insults he'd paid her.

Gavin, with a grin that softened his sharp features, opened his arms to her. "Could you and I start again, Elizabeth?" he asked quietly.

Elizabeth went to him, hugged him and when Bronwyn and Judith arrived, more hugs and kisses were exchanged.

Miles's words broke the spell of happy reunion. With eyes locked with Roger's, he said, "Shall we go?"

At Roger's curt nod, Miles took a sword from the hand of a young cousin.

"Now's not the time for a fight," Stephen began but quieted at Miles's look.

"Chatworth has helped me. Now I go with him."

"With him?" Raine exploded. "Have you forgotten that he killed Mary?"

Miles didn't answer but left the room behind Roger.

"Raine," Alyx said in her softest voice. "Miles is wounded and so is Roger and I'm sure they're going after this woman Roger wants."

"Christiana!" Elizabeth said, coming out of her stunned state. She'd had no idea where her brother and husband were going. "Judith, Bronwyn." She turned.

Without hesitation, all four women started for the door.

Without a word, in unison, the men caught their wives about their waists, Raine catching both

Alyx and Elizabeth, and carried them to the cell where they promptly locked them inside. For just a moment the men blinked at both the variety and the virility of the curses coming from the women. Judith intoned from the Bible, Bronwyn in Gaelic, Elizabeth used a soldier's language. And Alyx! Alyx used her magnificent voice to shake the stones.

The men grinned triumphantly at each other, motioned to their young cousins to follow and left the room.

"I never thought I'd see the day I'd help a Chatworth," Raine muttered, but stopped when he heard the clash of steel.

Six guards, awake, alert, were guarding the room that held Christiana, and they attacked Roger and Miles on sight.

Miles's side wound opened instantly as he ran a sword through one guard, stepped over the fallen body and went for two more men. Roger's sword was knocked from his left hand, he tripped over the body of the man Miles'd killed, fell, grabbed the sword in his right hand, came up and killed the man looming over him. His arm wound tore open.

As another man came at Roger, he raised his wounded arm helplessly. But as the guard's sword neared Roger's belly, the guard fell forward, dead. Roger rolled away in time to see Raine pull his sword out of the dead man's back.

The three brothers welded together to protect Roger and Miles and quickly dispatched the

317

remaining guards. They wiped their swords on the nearby bed-hangings.

It was Raine who offered his hand to Roger and for a moment Chatworth only looked at it as he would an offer of friendliness from a deadly serpent. With eyes wide in speculation, Roger accepted the offer and allowed Raine to help him stand amidst the fallen bodies. Their eyes locked for just seconds before Roger went to the bed and pulled back the hangings.

In the center was Christiana, curled into a ball, wearing only a thin bit of wool, her body black and blue. Her eyes were swollen shut, her lips cracked.

Slowly, Roger knelt by the bed and touched her temple.

"Roger?" she whispered and tried to smile, which caused her lower lip to start bleeding.

With a look of fury on his face, Roger bent and lifted her.

Raine's hand came to rest on his shoulder. "We'll take her south to our family."

Roger only nodded and carried Chris out of the room.

Gavin assisted Miles in standing.

"Where are the women?" Miles asked.

His brothers were oddly silent and seemed to grow a little fearful.

"We, ah . . ." Stephen began.

Gavin's head came up. "I think I'll ride ahead. Here." He tossed a key to Miles. "Maybe you better look after the women."

"Yes," Stephen and Raine added hastily, all three stumbling over each other to get out of the room.

Miles looked at the key in his hand, realizing it was the key to the cell where he'd been locked. "You didn't!" he said but his brothers were gone.

For a moment he stood there and, at last, he began to laugh, laugh as he'd never laughed before. A few years ago he and his brothers had been living alone in their safe little world of mere battles and wars. Then, one by one, they'd married four beautiful, charming women and really learned what war was.

Just now he and his brothers had taken a castle and killed several men and they'd taken no notice of the danger, but when faced with four furious women locked in a cell, they turned cowards and ran.

Miles started for the door. Thank God he'd not been involved in locking the women up! He pitied his brothers when at last they saw their wives again.

Like hell he did! He thought of every time they'd treated him as their "little brother." Now they were going to pay for every trick they'd ever played on him.

He tossed the key up, caught it and, grinning, started toward the cell full of beautiful women. He just might lock himself *inside* for a few days.

What Happened to Everybody

CHRISTIANA RECOVERED completely, married Roger Chatworth and ten years later, after they'd almost given up hope, they had a daughter, who, to Roger's chagrin, married one of the Montgomerys from the south of England. The Chatworth name died out except, now and then, a child would be named Chatworth Montgomery.

Miles and Elizabeth either created or adopted a total of twenty-three children and one of their sons, Philip, was a great favorite of Henry VIII. Later, two of Miles's grandsons went to the new country of America and remained there.

Raine was hired by Henry VIII to train his young knights and Alyx became lady-in-waiting to Queen Catherine. The court was a happy place and the king listened to and put into action some of the reforms Raine wanted. Raine and Alyx had three daughters, the middle one inheriting Alyx's musical talent. There's a legend that some of our great singers of today are descended from Alyxandria Montgomery.

Bronwyn and Stephen had six children, five boys and a girl. Bronwyn's name became a legend in her clan and even today Clan MacArran children sing her praises. Bronwyn's daughter married Kirsty MacGregor's son. He took the name of MacArran and eventually became laird.

Lachlan MacGregor married one of Tam's daughters, became so enraptured with her that he turned clan business over to his men. Davy MacArran fought for power, won and became a MacGregor. But Lachlan's daughter, Davy's wife, wasn't the docile little thing everyone believed and in the end it was she who was actually the MacGregor.

Judith and Gavin held onto the Montgomery estates. They prospered and left the estate in such good shape financially that today it's one of the largest, richest private homes in the world. One of Judith's descendants runs the whole place. She's a small, pretty young woman with odd-colored eyes, unmarried because she's never met a man who's accomplished in his life half what she's done in hers. Next week she has an appointment to meet a thirty-year-old American, self-made millionaire, who says he's a descendant of a knight named Miles Montgomery.

I have great hopes for them.

Jude Deveraux
Santa Fe, New Mexico
June, 1982

The publishers hope that this Large
Print Book has brought you pleasurable
reading. Each title is designed to make
the text as easy to see as possible.
G. K. Hall Large Print Books are
available from your library and
your local bookstore. Or you can
receive information on upcoming
and current Large Print Books
and order directly from the
publisher. Just send your name
and address to:

G. K. Hall & Co.
70 Lincoln Street
Boston, Mass. 02111

or call, toll-free:

1-800-343-2806

A note on the text
Large print edition designed by
Bernadette Montalvo
Composed in 16 pt English Times
on an EditWriter 7700
by Cheryl Yodlin of G.K. Hall Corp.